"If it isn't the light of my dark days,"

Jonathan said.

"How are you feeling?" she asked.

"Better now that you're here. Hold my hand and I'll feel like dancing."

"Do you feel like eating some dinner?" she asked.

"If you come in and share it with me."

"I prefer to eat alone," she replied evenly. "Besides, I have to tend to the animals, so I won't be having dinner for a while."

"You can't mean that you'd prefer to spend your time with the cows rather than me."

"I can."

He had the look of a man who was sure he had the upper hand. "What if I told you I could take you away from all this?"

"I'd say take yourself away. I like it here."

"But I could give you everything you ever wanted."

His smile widened. Anne could see the challenge in his eyes.

Dear Reader,

When two people fall in love, the world is suddenly new and exciting, and it's that same excitement we bring to you in Silhouette Intimate Moments. These are stories with scope, with grandeur. These characters lead the lives we all dream of, and everything they do reflects the wonder of being in love.

Longer and more sensuous than most romances, Silhouette Intimate Moments novels take you away from everyday life and let you share the magic of love. Adventure, glamour, drama, even suspense— these are the passwords that let you into a world where love has a power beyond the ordinary, where the best authors in the field today create stories of love and commitment that will stay with you always.

In coming months look for novels by your favorite authors: Maura Seger, Parris Afton Bonds, Elizabeth Lowell and Erin St. Claire, to name just a few. And whenever you buy books, look for all the Silhouette Intimate Moments, love stories *for* today's women *by* today's women.

Leslie J. Wainger
Senior Editor
Silhouette Books

IMRL-7/85

Kathleen Korbel

A Stranger's Smile

Silhouette Intimate Moments

Published by Silhouette Books New York

America's Publisher of Contemporary Romance

SILHOUETTE BOOKS
300 East 42nd St., New York, N.Y. 10017

ISBN: 0-373-07163-9

First Silhouette Books printing October 1986

America's Publisher of Contemporary Romance

Printed in the U.S.A.

Books by Kathleen Korbel

Silhouette Desire
Playing the Game #286

Silhouette Intimate Moments
A Stranger's Smile #163

KATHLEEN KORBEL

blames her writing on an Irish heritage that gave her the desire, and a supportive husband who gave her the ultimatum, "Do something productive or knock it off." An R.N. from St. Louis, she also counts traveling and music as addictions and is working on yet another career in screen writing.

Chapter 1

Ya know, it's been a long time since I've had the chance to undress a handsome man." Anne pushed an errant strand of blond hair out of her eyes and returned to fumbling with buttons.

A masculine voice answered from behind her. "Don't you think you should wait till you get someplace warmer?"

"I will," she said, grimacing toward where Jim Thompson waited for her in the darkness. "I'm just checking him over to see whether he's worth taking home."

It was eight at night. Anne and Jim crouched together at the bottom of a steep ravine trying to assess the injuries of a man who'd been discovered there. They found themselves working in typically bad conditions. It was pitch-black and cold, the wind wet with promised snow. Bare-limbed trees set up a thrashing that drowned out the voices of the rest of the rescue party who waited above, and flashlights flickered back and forth like agitated spirits. The narrow gulley echoed with the turbulence of a gathering storm.

There was no ambulance or helicopter waiting to whisk Anne's patient away to the safety of a trauma center. He'd fallen on the wrong end of the Appalachians for that. Anne Jackson was a rural nurse; her helpers were farmers and storekeepers. Their transportation back down seven miles of negligible path to where they could reach a helicopter was horseback and travois.

Anne rubbed her hands against her pant legs to warm them up. The temperature was dropping so fast that her gloves offered little protection for numbing fingers. For a brief moment she even courted the idea of trying to finish the examination with her hands in her pockets. Then she picked up her flashlight and went back to work.

Her patient was a stranger, a tall man with darkly handsome features, probably a few years older than her. It was hard to tell much more from the brief glimpses she could manage with the flashlight. She could tell for certain that he wasn't from anywhere nearby. His outerwear was too expensive, his hiking boots spotless and too frivolous for daily use. Then there was the matter of what Anne discovered when she finally did get his jacket unbuttoned. She started to laugh. The man was wearing a custom-tailored, three-piece, pin-striped suit.

"Well, that does it," she announced with a grin as she showed Jim her discovery. "I'm going to have to take him home just so I can find out how he got here. It ought to be one hell of a story."

Jim chuckled with a shake of his head. "Who do you think he is?"

"I don't know," she said, her flashlight again sweeping the strong features and glinting against the warm-brown hair. "But I hope this isn't one of his favorite suits. I'm going to have to ruin it."

"You about ready to move him?" It was getting harder to hear Jim's voice above the wind. "I still need to have Silas and Ed send down the basket."

Anne straightened from where the injured man lay crumpled against a tree and jammed her hands back into her pockets. "Yeah, I think so. I'm going to need a little help splinting his leg first."

While Jim retrieved equipment, Anne took a moment to stretch out the kinks earned from an already long day of rounds. She felt as if there were sand in her eyes and wool in her mouth. And she was freezing. In the two years she'd lived back on the mountain she'd grown accustomed to people showing up unexpectedly at her door for help, but she'd never really gotten used to the long hours. She'd already been up since four that morning and was looking at at least another five hours before her patient was in the helicopter and she was back in bed.

Anne lifted her face to the harsh, swirling wind and took a breath of the biting air. The wild darkness made her shiver. On a night like this she could almost wish that she'd never given up the comforts of Boston.

Almost.

She took another look down at her patient with his expensive clothes and well-groomed good looks and recognized the familiar tug of antipathy. No, she decided with a scowl. On second thought, even the prospect of warm toes and a good brandy wasn't worth the thought of going back to Boston.

Ten minutes later it started to snow. They never made it to the helicopter. They never got farther than the two miles down to Anne's house, still high in the backwoods, still beyond the reach of conventional vehicles. Blinded by driving snow and wind, it had been almost more than Anne and Jim could manage to get the injured man to the horses. The rise from the gulley was steep and loose, good finger holds rare, and the footing treacherous enough to twice send Anne sliding almost to the bottom before finally reaching safe arms at the top. It took forty-five minutes to maneuver her patient that far.

By the time they deposited the man in Anne's spare bed-room, the snow was battering incessantly at the windows, and covered the ground in a thick, white blanket. A fire was stoked in the living room, and in the bright red-and-white kitchen three men huddled over cups of steaming coffee. Anne spent two hours in the bedroom before she had the chance to get hers.

She took her stethoscope from her ears for the final time to hear the clock strike midnight. The wind had eased to a dull whine, and the conversation in the kitchen had degen-erated to sporadic monosyllables. The air was close with the heat of the fire and the smell of drying wool.

Anne admitted the first feeling of relief. It looked as though her patient would be all right. Even though he was still unconscious, his vital signs were finally as stable as a rock. His injuries appeared to be manageable now that his temperature had reached a safe range. And he was begin-ning to show signs of coming to, which meant that she might just get some sleep herself. Now all she had to do was get the rest of the rescue party out of her kitchen and on home.

Anne wondered again just who her patient was. She could almost have mistaken him for a rancher of some kind if she didn't know better. Even with the pallor and bruising from his injuries, he was deeply tanned, his angular face rugged and windburned. His hands were work roughened and strong, the fingers almost gracefully long, and there wasn't an ounce of city bred fat to be found on his long frame. Probably six foot one or two, he was tightly muscled, with the almost hungry, lean look of a backwoods man.

But this man was not from any backwoods. From years of all-too-unhappy experience, Anne recognized all the hallmarks of social privilege. Above and beyond the beau-tiful suit she'd had to cut off, he showed evidence of a lot of high-priced pampering. Someone from a top salon in New York had recently had his hands in that thick chestnut hair, and a manicurist had been at those nails. The cologne he wore was exclusive, and the down outer layer that had helped save him was L. L. Bean's best.

All of which meant that the outdoor labor he performed hadn't been herding cattle or felling trees. More likely mountaineering in Switzerland or skiing the Dolomites. Anne could easily visualize him in the rigging of his sail-boat as he sped up the Atlantic coast in the America's Cup race, trading dares with the other contestants. The perfect fantasy man. A brunette version of her ex-husband, Tom.

She scowled irritably, suddenly sorry that her handsome patient wasn't a farmer or miner from nearby. She had a feeling that she knew just what kind of person he'd turn out to be, and that she'd end up hating him for it—a painful re-minder of what she'd escaped by running home to the mountain.

As if aware that he was being scrutinized, Anne's patient began to stir. She took hold of his restless hands and leaned toward him.

"C'mon," she coaxed gently, "talk to me, mister. I want to know who you are. Open your eyes and talk to me."

He responded, though his words were jumbled and mean-ingless. Only the name Charlie stood out clearly. When he began to speak in French, she answered until she realized that she was responding to a very smooth proposition.

"Not tonight," she said, smiling wryly, wondering just what memory she'd tapped. "I have the feeling you're going to have a headache."

When he did come to, he did it with a start. His eyes snapped open and he bolted upright.

"Take it easy," Anne said soothingly, pushing him back down. She stopped suddenly, the rest of her words lost within the unexpected jolt of contact. She was stunned, thrown off center by the clear lake-blue of his eyes. Bot-tomless, sunlit blue. When those eyes opened, features that had been handsome became mesmerizing, magnetic. There was power there, a vitality that compelled. This was a man people watched and listened to and followed. A shudder of recognition rocked through her for a man she'd never met.

Anne realized that she was staring, unable to control the surge of lightning his touch suddenly sent through her. She caught herself just short of bolting from the room.

"You're fine," she said, struggling to keep her voice level and professional even as the ground fell away. "You had a little accident."

He stared at her, his eyes unfocused and frightened. Anne found herself wanting to touch his face, to gently guide him back to lucidity. She didn't.

"It's okay," she said, smiling, trying to keep his attention focused. "My name's Anne. Can you tell me yours?"

"I ..." It seemed to surprise him that he didn't have the strength to express himself. His eyes wandered again. "What ... happened?"

"You fell, but you're okay. How do you feel?"

"I hurt ... everywhere."

"I know. You were pretty banged up. You're okay, though." It was a good idea to keep repeating pertinent facts. People who had suffered concussions tended to have short, disjointed memories. Besides, Anne couldn't seem to think of anything else to say. "Can you tell me your name?"

"Was anyone else ... ?" He moved to ease some discomfort and discovered an even greater one. His face tightened with the surprise of it.

"No one else was hurt. You were alone." She was losing him again, his eyes blurring with confusion and pain. Again she fought the urge to reach out to him. She had never in her life reacted like this to a man—not even Tom—and it unnerved her.

His eyes drifted closed again, and Anne straightened, still shaken by her reaction. Now that his eyes were shut he seemed no more than another good-looking man, slightly worse for wear, who had the misfortune of reminding Anne of the people she'd once courted as her right.

She stood abruptly. The thought of her life in Boston hadn't really bothered her in a long time. The last thing she needed on this dark, snowy night was to find herself rehashing a painful past. Yet that seemed to be what she was about to do. Anne took one last look at her sleeping patient, her eyes unconsciously accusing, and turned to leave.

She met Jim heading in from the kitchen.

"He okay?" At five foot ten, he stood a few inches taller than Anne, his rust ponytail haloed in the hall light.

Anne took a minute to hang her stethoscope on the door before answering. "As far as I can tell. He's stitched and splinted and warm as toast. It would sure be nice to have some diagnostic equipment up here to make sure, though."

He grinned. "It'll make a difference when the clinic's open."

"I know," she said on a sigh, automatically checking the cracked face of her watch. "But we couldn't have even gotten him that far tonight. There has to be a better way."

"We'll get you a heliport for Christmas."

Anne finally grinned back and linked arms with her friend. "Don't make promises you have no intentions of keeping. C'mon, let's see if you guys can get home."

"Don't hold your breath. Silas is planning to camp out on your couch until we find out just who your mystery guest is."

She scowled playfully. "One of these days it's going to dawn on him that I'm not ten years old anymore."

Jim guided her back down the short hallway with a laugh. "Like I said, don't hold your breath."

When Anne walked into the kitchen the other two men stood to greet her. Wearily waving them back down, she disengaged herself from Jim and headed for the stove.

"There isn't any more we can do tonight," she said simply. "Better get on home while you can."

There wasn't an immediate answer to her offer. She filled a mug and brought it back to the big oak table. The oldest of the men who sat there scrutinized her as she eased herself into the chair across from him. She was already beginning to stiffen from the evening's exertions, but it wouldn't do at all to let him know. Taking a good sip of the hot brew, she fought the urge to confront the challenge in those watery blue eyes and be done with it. That was not the way to handle Silas, though. He defused more easily with patience and control.

"He should be okay," she said evenly, eyes back to her coffee. "I'll just keep an eye on him for a while to be sure."

"He sure was lucky Ef found him," Silas offered laconically, his own gaze retrieved. "One night like tonight woulda killed him for sure."

"He's just lucky that the fall didn't do it first. Six inches one way or the other and we wouldn't have needed to bother going after him until spring."

"I imagine his family'd be up here before that," Silas said, his eyes still as carefully averted as Anne's. "He sure ain't from around here."

Anne couldn't help but laugh. "I'll drink to that. Nobody around here's dumb enough to walk off a mountain."

"Not in a suit, anyway." Jim said with a grin. That elicited a round of chuckles and bemused head shaking.

"I don't suppose you found a name in those fancy duds?" Anne asked.

Silas laughed with a short, wry bark. "Not likely, seein' as how it was Ef that found him first."

"Yeah, I did notice that he disappeared awfully fast," she said and nodded with a rueful grin, thinking more of how the mug in her hands felt almost unbearably hot. She'd taken a good part of the slides up and down the ravine on her now-tender palms. Without thinking, she blew on the chafed skin to ease the stinging.

Jim reached out and pulled her hand over for inspection. "That looks awful," he scolded. "You'd better see to taking care of yourself."

"It doesn't really bother me." She shrugged, smiling at his concern even as she railed at his bad timing. She might never get Silas home now. "All in a day's work."

Silas frowned down at her in his patriarchal way. "Not a lady's work to go traipsin' down a mountain like that in the middle of the night."

"I told you, Silas," she chided, unable to prevent a playful grin from crinkling her gray eyes. "I'm not a lady. I'm a nurse."

He scowled, the deep creases on his weather-beaten face growing with disapproval. Anne had a good deal of trouble refraining from another grin. Silas had considered her as one of his own children since her mother had died years ago. He'd been with her on that day. He'd always been there when Anne had needed him, his gentle strength a fulcrum against which the rest of the world could balance. And he always treated her as if she were still the small girl who used to beg him for piggyback rides and make thrones from his huge, handcrafted chairs.

With what little energy she had left, Anne lurched to her feet, coffee still in hand, and turned to the silent third of the trio. John Edward had watched the preceding exchange with quiet amusement. He looked up at Anne with carefully passive eyes.

"John," she said, "I'll just go in and see if your things are dry for the trip back. Would you like to bring the horses out?"

"Sure thing, Annie."

When he stood, so did Jim and Silas. Silas took up a position next to Anne, still none too pleased.

"You can't take care of that man by yourself," he protested, as much from moral as practical considerations. Anne confronted the tall, scarecrowlike old man who all but dwarfed her.

"I can take care of him and ten others like him," she said gently. "The real work's been done. All I have to do now is baby-sit. You don't need brains or brawn for that so I'm the perfect candidate." She hurried on with the clincher before Silas had the chanced to protest. "Silas, I don't want Sarah to worry about you. You know her. This very minute she's standing by the front door watching the snow, and she won't move till you get home."

Jim and John had already edged toward the front door. Anne followed without again challenging Silas eye-to-eye and helped pick drying coats and hats from the quilt rack in front of the couch. Silas kept his silence as a matter of principle, but he began to dress along with the others.

John had just shut the door behind him when Jim poked into his jacket for gloves and came up with a surprised look on his face.

"Oh, Annie, I almost forgot. I have something for you."

Anne looked over to see him pulling a long envelope from his pocket.

"This came for you this afternoon, and when John stopped by for me, I figured I'd bring it along. Special delivery letter."

He waited for Anne to take the envelope, but she hesitated, having already seen the return address. For the second time in an hour, Anne felt her foundation slipping away, this time for an entirely different reason. Anger knifed through her stomach and brought bile to her throat.

The corner of the envelope bore the ostentatious logo of a distinguished Boston law firm. The best legal minds in Massachusetts, especially if you had corporate piracy in mind. Anne should have known. It was the law firm that Tom and her brother Brad had always used.

She'd told them to leave her alone. That she'd come home to Cedar Ridge to get as far away from him as she could, to save what was left of her sanity. She'd never wanted to hear from Tom or Brad again. It seemed that they couldn't leave well enough alone.

She accepted the letter from Jim and immediately folded it into her pocket. Silas, standing next to her, watched in growing astonishment. He'd never had a special delivery letter in his life, and considered them second only to divine revelation in importance. He simply could not understand her cavalier disregard for this one.

"Annie," he objected as tactfully as he knew how. "It must be important if they went to all the trouble of sendin' it special delivery."

She smiled, trying to keep her tone light. "Silas, it's from Brad. He sends birthday cards special delivery. But just in case it is bad news, I'm not about to read it until I've had a good night's sleep. Maybe I'll open it tomorrow after I've had my coffee." Maybe never.

Anne knew that Jim would understand. Silas did not. Wide-eyed and silent, he glared at her even after Jim had passed him his big coat. Anne was saved from another lecture by John's timely reappearance. Silas merely shrugged, as if he'd once again given up on comprehending her, and followed John back out into the night. Anne watched his angular frame bend into the white wind and wished again that she could tell the old man how much she loved him.

Jim paused beside Anne before stepping out the door. "Are you all right?" he asked quietly, motioning vaguely in the direction of the envelope.

She grinned ruefully. "Sure. It just galls me that I can still react like that to them after all this time."

His brown eyes softened with empathy. "Cassie'd say you have every right. Put that thing away until the morning and get some sleep. You won't be much good to you or your patient if you don't. The Thompson kitchens will take care of dinner tomorrow."

"Thanks, Jim." She smiled at her friend. "Give those babies a kiss for me."

He shook his head slowly, admiration in his eyes. "You know something? You're quite a lady."

"Go on and get out of here," she ordered with mock severity as she pushed him toward the door. "You keep talking like that, and I'm going to ask for a raise."

Anne stood at the window for a few long moments watching the men disappear into the darkness. Then, turning away, she pulled the crumpled envelope from her pocket and deliberately dropped it into the trash.

It took Anne another hour before she had time to relax and dry her hair in front of the great crackling fire in the living room. The lights were out in the cabin, with only the molten glow of the fire washing over the rough wooden walls. Anne eased herself down to sit cross-legged on the giant hooked rug in front of the couch, her old hairbrush in hand, another cup of coffee beside her. She'd finally taken the time to peel off her soggy clothes and slip into the comfortable warmth of her flannel nightgown and robe. The salve she'd spread on her hands was beginning to ease the tenderness even as her other joints set up a chorus of protest.

She knew that she should have been in the extra bedroom waiting for her patient to wake up. Somehow she couldn't bring herself to do it just yet. Before she walked headfirst into a new problem, she needed the time to sit and unwind from the demands the day had already put on her.

She hoped that she could relax without slipping into a coma. When she'd climbed up earlier to the loft where she slept to change clothes, her big old four-poster had almost beckoned to her. If she chanced going up there again, that old bed might just reach out and catch her.

Anne smiled wryly and leaned a little to the side, catching the braid of her hair on one hand and slowly unknotting it. When her hair fell free, cascading over her shoulders, she took the brush to it and shivered at the heady sensation. The straw-gold curtain shimmered richly in the firelight, lush and full. It had always been Anne's outstanding feature, a treasure that had transformed her patrician features into a singular beauty. Tom had always loved to touch it, running his hands through it as if it were a magical gold. He had encouraged her to wear it up, sleekly styled so that it complimented the cool gray of her eyes and classic lines of her face.

She had to admit that she'd always turned heads when she'd walked into a room of the social and political elite. She was the essence of sophistication, one of the ten best-dressed boss's daughters on the Eastern Seaboard. Now when she had finally gained the self-esteem to match the picture she'd once presented, it seemed that she was much better suited to braids: easy to take care of and practical. The way her life had become.

Anne sighed and straightened, her hair swinging behind her to brush at the small of her back. The coffee was the last of the pot Silas had brewed, and it tasted bitter and hot, helping to wake her from the comfort of warm clothes and a fireplace. Maybe enough for her to stay awake through a book. She hated it when she found herself rehashing the follies of her life, and she resented emotions that had never been properly put in their place at the conclusion of relationships. The well-groomed stranger in her bedroom and a special delivery letter were quite successfully dredging up regrets that she thought she'd given up long ago.

For some reason, she thought of Jim and how he reflected the changes in her own life. Once she would have considered him an anachronism, the kind of man one heard about in *National Geographic* or *Mother Earth News*. Who could imagine, after all, an ad exec from Chicago who pulled in seventy-five to a hundred thousand a year giving it all up for a life like the Waltons'? But Jim Thompson had done just that.

Tom would have savagely dissected Jim's manhood with the precision of a surgeon. Sipping at his vodka martini, he would have wondered how any man could survive the ignominy of running away from the real world to hide in, of all places, the Appalachians. His laughter would have been cruel and unforgiving.

Even her father would have been bitterly disappointed if she'd brought Jim home from college instead of Tom. Tom had had what her father had called an inborn knack for big business. Anne, in a rare moment of insight during her first year of marriage, had correctly labeled it the jugular instinct, an instinct that Jim simply didn't have.

Her reflections were interrupted by the first sounds of a man struggling for consciousness. As quickly as her aching limbs would let her, she got to her feet and headed for the bedroom.

Only a small night-light was on by the bed. Within its soft pool of light she saw her patient moving a bit, as if caught in a bad dream. His brow, swathed in a bandage, puckered momentarily before his whole face took on a frown. He looked as if he were trying to remember something. His hands lifted aimlessly from the bed, seeking the air and then dropping again. The pain even touched his subconscious, and he made little moans as he moved.

Anne reclaimed her seat and resumed trying to talk her stranger back to consciousness, this time with more caution and not a small amount of trepidation. It didn't take him as long this time. Within a minute or two, his eyes opened and focused on her.

Anne decided that it was definitely too late for her to still be up. Her reaction was even stronger this time. She had to restrain herself from looking away from him, afraid all of a sudden that with just his eyes he would pierce the innermost corners of her soul. Again she felt herself go rigid in response to the heat he stirred in her.

The minute his eyes locked into hers she felt that jolt, as if the chair wouldn't hold her. His eyes were clear now, not so fogged with confusion. Anne saw in them the winter sky above the pines. Alive, kinetic.

Her smile was unconsciously stiff. "How are you feeling?"

He let his gaze wander over the shadowy room for a minute and then return to rest on Anne's face. "Pretty bad. What happened?"

"You must have been hiking in the park and gotten lost. We found you just beyond it, in a ravine." She didn't think to mention the suit.

"The park?"

She nodded. "Great Smoky Mountain National Park. Do you remember being there?"

It took him a moment to answer. "I ... I guess so. Is this ... a ... hospital?"

"Oh, Lord, no." She grinned, genuinely amused. "I'm a rural nurse. You're at my house on the backside of Bennett's Mountain. We couldn't get you any farther than this. It's snowing outside."

"Snowing." He rolled the sound of the word around as if considering a new phenomenon. "I wouldn't have ... gone back ... in the snow."

Anne was enough of a mind to appreciate the distinction he made. He would go in his best suit, but not if it were snowing. Real city logic.

"I'm sure you wouldn't have," she said, nodding. "It didn't start until after you fell. Can we notify anyone?"

He nodded slowly to himself as if his actions had been justified. When he winced with the discomfort of the action, Anne found herself leaning toward him, almost sensing his pain.

"What's your ... name?"

"Anne," she said quietly, suddenly wanting to hold him, to rock him to an easy sleep, and just as suddenly realizing how ridiculous the idea was. "What's yours?"

His face softened into a smile, but the light was fading in his eyes. Anne bent closer as if to follow the flight of his attention.

"You're ..."

"A nurse," she repeated.

"Beautiful." She could hardly hear his voice, but he managed a more wry smile before letting his eyes close. "I feel so ... tired."

"Best thing for you," she agreed, realizing with a start that she'd again taken hold of his hand. "Can you tell me your name first?"

She was too late. Surprised, she watched him as he slept. He looked like a tousled little boy, making her want to reach over and brush the dark hair back from where it tumbled over his forehead. It occurred to her then that his voice matched his eyes, clear and quiet.

She sat where she was for a moment, willing the fire to die in her, listening to the silence around her as she marveled at the spark that attracted her to a stranger. Spark! Hell, it was more like bonfire. She spent all of her time wishing for the Jims of the world and still became caught in the allure of another Tom.

Maybe she'd be wrong. Maybe when he woke up in the morning he would still be as quiet and genuine as he was tonight. She found that she wanted that very much.

No matter what, she thought as she looked down at him, the mysterious electricity once again dimmed, she was going to get him back out of her house as fast as she could and get on with her life. Blue eyes or not, she was a big enough girl to be able to keep her professional distance. And that would be that.

Chapter 2

So, you weren't a dream after all."

Anne's eyes shot open. For a moment, she couldn't remember where she was. The sight of her patient brought her abruptly back to reality. She'd ended up crawling into an overstuffed chair in the corner of the guest room sometime the night before, and had evidently not made it back to her own bed. Every muscle in her let her know what a smart idea that had been.

Wondering what time it was, she took a minute to rub at the sleep in her eyes before attempting to launch herself from the soft cushions. She was not looking forward to testing her morning-after muscles. Pain was not her favorite wake-up call.

When she finally did lurch up, there was no choice but to quickly admit to a temporary setback. She mouthed a surprised little "Ooh," and sank right back down. Her patient watched every move in silence.

Anne couldn't help but notice that his eyes were even more uncannily bright in the daylight. Only a surrounding ring of darker blue seemed to delineate the iris at all. This morning they were more alert, more in control. And even more mesmerizing.

"I'll be up in a minute," she said grinning sheepishly, her eyes only briefly meeting his as she tried to quell the sudden staccato of her heart. It was too early for this. "I'm a little stiff this morning from a bit of surprise mountain climbing last night. How are you feeling?"

"Like I tried to share a small seat with a truck," he said, his voice very quiet as if its proper use would cause discomfort. He was smiling, though. "I started to feel better the minute I woke up and saw you.... You were here last night?"

"You remember?" Foolishly, Anne felt dread, waiting for his pleasant demeanor to change, waiting to be disillusioned.

He shook his head slightly. "Your face, not much more."

She nodded to herself as she once again tried to launch herself from the chair. Every joint protested vigorously, and her knees were tender from where they'd made contact with every rock on the slope, but everything was in working order. She made it over to stand by the bed without too much difficulty.

"You were found last night at the bottom of a nearby ravine."

"And you sat up all night with me?" He snapped off a perfect, flashing smile that sent Anne's stomach plummeting. She recognized the look with sick fatalism. Barracuda teeth, she called it. Tom had a similar look. She saw the control grow on the stranger's face, the facade take shape before her eyes, and she knew without a doubt that her instincts had been right. She was going to hate this man, regardless of his magnetism.

She had wanted so much for him to be different.

"I wasn't sure how badly you were hurt," she answered, realizing with some regret that her voice had automatically taken on the smooth, icy tones she'd cultivated on the cocktail party circuit. Suddenly Boston wasn't nearly as far away as she would have liked.

"How badly am I hurt?"

"Well, I know for sure that you broke your leg, you have a dandy cut on your forehead and you're scraped up just about everyplace else." As she talked Anne took out her medical equipment and began to check the injuries she'd listed. It occurred to her that he must have had a similar conversation sometime in the past. The night before she'd discovered a number of scars that wrapped around his left side. Fine lines now from very good plastic surgery, they represented a once-severe injury. "Where else do you hurt?"

"Besides everywhere?"

"Besides everywhere."

"My back, down low. And my chest, right about here." He motioned to an area of bad abrasions.

She nodded, gently palpating the point midway across the right side of his chest. "You probably cracked a couple of ribs when you landed. You wound up wedged against a tree. I'd imagine that your backache's from a muscle strain, judging by where you say it hurts."

"Aren't you going to feel it to make sure?"

Again she froze. Why couldn't he keep that suggestive gleam out of his eyes, or come up with a half-human response? Just the tone of his voice was so much like Tom's that Anne found herself bracing for the hurt and humiliation that had to follow. It was all she could do to remain still.

"No," she told him, straightening, "I'm going to make breakfast. Do you feel like some soup and toast, or would you rather just rest awhile?"

"I'd rather get to know you better."

Her smile was rigid. "That wasn't one of the choices."

He wasn't in the least fazed. "In that case, I'll rest up so that I can have the strength later—when it is."

She ignored that. "As soon as we can get you down the mountain we'll transport you to a hospital. Right now it's a

little difficult to travel. We had our first snowfall of the
season while we were picking you off the mountain, and I'm
afraid it was a beaut. Until we can get you to civilization, is
there anyone who should be notified?''

His expression remained nonchalant, but Anne could see
that he was tiring. "Oh, I'm sure there is, but don't bother.
I don't think I'm going to feel like putting up with them for
a few days.''

"You're on the wrong side of the mountain for visitors,"
she said. "Phone lines are down from the snow, and nobody can get up here unless it's on horseback."

He looked astounded, eyeing the room about him as if
expecting to see kerosene lamps and chamber pots.

"The peace and quiet can be deafening," she said, turning for the door. A parting thought kept her there for a moment. "If you need anything, yell. My name's Anne. I'm
afraid that since we didn't find any identification on you, I
don't know yours."

"My wallet? My briefcase?"

"If you had them when you fell, you didn't by the time we
got to you."

"What do you mean?" he demanded, his voice imperi-
ous and condescending. "I have some important papers in
that briefcase. Somebody'd damn well better find it."

"Actually," she retorted dryly, "I have it. And I'm split-
ting the credit cards in your wallet with my cohorts. We're
going on a shopping spree in town tomorrow."

He wasn't amused. A cold disdain lit his eyes. "I doubt
that any of the hicks in that two-horse town would know
what to do with a credit card if they had one."

That did it. If only he could have kept his mouth shut,
Anne would have gladly drowned in the tides of his eyes.
She could have at least dreamed that there were still, in fact,
some decent people in the society she'd left behind. This guy
was making her more and more glad that she'd gotten out
when she did.

"And may I say for all the hicks who had the questionable sense to pull you up a ravine in a snowstorm," she said, trying very hard to keep her voice even, "you're welcome."

For a moment he glared at her as if at a not-too-bright salesperson. Then, with a suddenness that left Anne confused, he sighed, and the emotion drained from his face as if the effort were too great. "I'm sorry, Anne. I seem to have forgotten my manners. Jonathan Bradshaw Harris. And I think I'll get a nap now and try to eat something later."

Anne walked out quickly to prevent staring open-mouthed at him. He wouldn't have noticed. His eyes were closed by the time she reached the hallway.

Anne had been mistaken. Her patient wasn't going anywhere. There was a good foot and a half of snow on the ground. She saw it the minute she stepped into the kitchen and looked out the windows. The wind had eased during the night so that the snow wasn't blowing hard, but it still fell heavily and steadily, making visibility limited. The hills looked like vague watercolors painted in shades of gray, the firs by the barn spearing black and sudden into the light morning sky. If the snow kept up, they wouldn't be able to get Mr. Harris down the mountain for days, and after Anne's initial conversation with him, that prospect didn't appeal to her at all.

Dressing quickly in an old flannel shirt and jeans and shoving a heavy knit cap on her head, she threw on her jacket and headed out to tend the animals.

Her big bay gelding, Andy, greeted her by stamping impatiently against the side of his stall. He wasn't a fan of the cold weather, especially when she had to saddle him up on frigid winter mornings to make rounds. He never balked from her touch, but let her know nonetheless exactly how he felt. Anne smiled at his call and protest, knowing that he would be far friendlier when he realized that this day was to be spent lounging in the protection of the barn.

Pulling on the heavy door, she shut out the white morning and enveloped herself in the warmer, damp smells of hay and animals and leather. Her father had often said that she should have been born in his grandmother's time when the farm had been a working one. She had always loved taking care of the animals, and had spent some of her most contented moments grooming the horses or milking the cow.

Today, though, her private demons wouldn't leave her alone long enough to enjoy the peace the physical work usually afforded. The chores she did were by now so rote that she ended up with even more time to think and remember.

Maybe if she'd only gotten the letter from Brad, or just had the unexpected visit by a handsome stranger in wolf's clothing she could handle everything with more composure. But one arriving right on top of the other had proven too much. Suddenly the old pain gnawed at her like fresh fire.

For the past two years, Anne had done everything in her power to wipe out the events that had driven her back to the mountains. She'd severed her ties with the city and reestablished relationships made during the years her family had used the cabin as a summer home away from the pressures of her father's position. Leaving the power and wealth behind her, she'd resurrected the simple customs of the generations of Jacksons who had lived on the land before her. She had carefully structured her life to include only the present and those selected memories that could no longer hurt her.

She'd become so involved with life on the mountain that if it weren't for the few keepsakes she'd brought with her from Boston, she could have almost thought that there had never been a life there at all. The wealth and the crowded existence of the socially elite might not have ever existed. She could have almost thought that there had never been a business.

She frowned, hating even the sound of the word that had so shaped her life.

Business.

Jackson Corporations Limited had not been just a business, but a living thing. Her father had created it with equal parts dream, ambition and obsession. JCL had in turn bestowed her family with more status than even status-hungry Boston had demanded and given power beyond even educated imaginations. It had transformed old family names into a dynasty, a dynasty that should by rights be handed over to the oldest child. Or, in the case of Peter Jackson, who held fast to the belief that women had no place in the crucibles of power, to the oldest son.

What had been unfortunate was the fact that the oldest son, the only son, was an unworthy heir. Bradley Jackson had been blessed with none of the natural leadership, organization and charisma that had served his father so well. A weak, resentful child, he had never earned his father's respect or trust. After waiting longer than Brad had thought reasonable for the authority he equated with his birthright, and which his father, for fear of his business refused to give, he resorted to the natural talents he did have. He schemed with a willing brother-in-law to rob his father of the very empire he had created.

In the end Brad and Tom won. Peter Jackson died, a man broken in spirit, and Anne, caught between father and husband, lost everything in a fight she wanted no part of. She had come home to bury her father and stayed, too distraught by what had been done to ever consider going back.

Anne stopped a minute, the memories beginning to suffocate her. Her eyes rose, drawn to a small yellow glint in the barn's soft gloom. It was still there, above her head on a nail she'd driven into the stall post, the small plain gold band she'd hung up two years ago, the symbol of why she'd vowed never to leave the mountain again.

Unbidden, the picture of Tom taunted her. Handsome, electric, intelligent, overachiever Tom McCarthy had thrown her away in his lust for the power he saw in her father. She looked at the ring and knew that it had been Jonathan Harris, with his electric blue eyes and power-modulated voice, who had blown this particular ill wind back into her life. He was so much like Tom that it was like being forced to face her ex-husband again here where she'd finally left him and where she still sought to exorcise the memory of that last meeting.

It had been November, a clear bright day when the mountain had been brilliant with autumn. Anne had brought her father home to the cabin when the fight for control of the company had become too vicious. He'd looked sickly and so suddenly old. She'd thought that maybe the isolation would help.

Then Tom had appeared, tall and blond, well-groomed and controlled. She'd known why he'd come and instinctively tried to hide from it. She remembered it now coldly, as if it were part of a bad movie she'd seen instead of the final dissolution of a marriage she'd so long cherished.

He came up behind her, his sleek cap of blond hair glowing like a halo in the afternoon light. It was then that he finally admitted to her what he and Brad were doing, as if she hadn't already known. They were about to take final control of the company away from the man who'd given his life to it.

He reached down to touch her hair as it hung freely down her back.

"Anne, come home." His tone was smooth, well modulated, prepared. She heard no pain or grief to make the words sound honest.

She steeled herself against this. For as much as she hated him, she still, even after what he'd become, loved him desperately.

"What for, Tom?" she asked, her eyes away on the peaceful hills. "What is there to come home to?"

"Come home to me, Anne." It didn't seem to occur to him to mention love or need. "I'll take care of you."

Was that why she'd married him? Had she needed someone to take care of her?

"Like you took care of my father? He trusted you, Tom. He couldn't have given you more opportunity in that company if you'd been his real son."

"Don't be stupid, Anne. I'm giving you another chance. All that old man ever gave you was the money to mingle with the right crowd."

She'd turned on him then, the anger rising. "He is my father. And he's never in his life deliberately hurt me. You, on the other hand, seem to have made a career of it. I think you'd better go."

He'd allowed an eyebrow to arch, as he gave one parting shot. "You father and I are the same person," he said with some satisfaction. "If we weren't, you'd never have married me. You're dependent on men like us, my love."

He had turned back to the road before she finally said it, sealing their future. "You'll hear from my lawyer on Monday."

It had been the last time she'd cried.

Anne was collecting the eggs when she heard the muffled sounds of hoofbeats. More than one horse was approaching the cabin. She picked up her basket and walked over to give a much more amiable Andy a parting pat on the nose before opening the door.

The snow hadn't stopped while she had been inside. She had to lean heavily on the door to get it open, and the tracks she'd made two hours earlier were almost obliterated. She was beginning to despair of ever getting Jonathan Harris down the mountain.

"Annie, there you are."

Silas strode quickly over from the porch, followed closely by Jim.

Anne grinned at the look on Silas's face. "What are you doing back up here so soon?" she asked. Silas took the basket and pail from her just as he always did.

"Sheriff's busy," Jim offered with a slow grin, "and since we were coming up this way anyway, we told him we'd check up on your patient for him."

"I'm not harboring a notorious criminal, am I?" she asked mischievously in Silas's direction.

"Don't know." The old man shrugged, opening the door for her. "Never did come up with any identification."

"His name's Jonathan Something-or-other Harris," she said obligingly as she pulled off her jacket and gloves to hang before the fire. The men followed her lead, stamping the snow from their boots on the throw rug by the door.

"He awake?" Silas asked.

"He was. Coffee, anyone?" She didn't wait for an answer but headed out to the kitchen and the coffeepot. She wanted some even if they didn't.

"Can we talk to him?"

"Sure, if he's awake," she said with a nod. "He doesn't have much stamina right now, but you can find him in the guest room if you want to grill him."

"Silas," Anne asked quietly a moment later, "is there any way we can get him down the mountain?"

"Is he hurt bad?" he said frowning.

"Not really," she admitted, pulling out some coffee cake she'd baked a few days earlier. "I'm afraid there's a personality conflict. He's beginning to remind me of Tom, and I don't want to end up pitching him back over a cliff in a couple of days."

Silas nodded, suppressing a half grin. "Can he go on horseback?"

"No."

"Then we can't. Snow's already too deep for a wagon, and the radio's callin' for another foot or so before it stops."

"Another foot?" she immediately protested, turning on him. He was pouring coffee into mugs for her and shaking his head in disbelief.

"Annie," he admonished, "you've got the fanciest stereo in the county up here. Why don't you at least listen to the weather once in a while? You wouldn't keep gettin' surprised like that.''

It was no use trying to explain her little quirk to Silas. She'd tried once and ended up sounding paranoid even to herself. But at first even hearing the sound of a professional radio announcer had brought her too close to the city. After a while she had truly begun to prefer the comfort of silence over the repetitious babble of a radio—even the best one in the county.

"We won't even be able to get him down on horseback for much longer," he continued, evidently not expecting an answer. "That's why we came now, so we could get a name and notify kin."

Anne almost made the mistake of letting Silas know how his news affected her. She nearly screamed. But he was looking at her closely, his eyes suspiciously noncommittal, and Anne realized that he was only inches from staying for the next few days. That would have been even worse than just having Mr. Harris on her hands. She smiled without a word and handed him a cup of coffee.

After Silas went off to join the one-man posse in the bedroom Anne realized that she needed a dish towel. The extras were in the hall closet across from the guest room where Silas and Jim were interrogating her patient. She stood alone in the kitchen for a minute listening to the sounds of conversation that came from the down the hall, the compulsion pulling at her. Like an itch, she thought absently, that needs to be scratched.

It didn't take her more than a minute to give in to temptation.

By the time she reached the hallway she knew Silas had heard Mr. Harris's opinion on the notification of relatives. He was asking if there were any reason Mr. Harris didn't want his family called. To someone like Silas that was as unthinkable as it was suspicious. Anne had to repress a grin. Jim would appreciate her reaction, but neither Silas nor Jonathan Harris would.

The impulse died when Jonathan answered Silas's question. Suddenly Anne felt as if she'd missed something.

It wasn't so much what he said, which was something about avoiding company hassles, but how he said it that baffled her. Smiling ruefully, he spoke with the same quiet respect most of the people in the area expressed when talking to the old man. No condescension, none of the smug patronization Tom or Brad had always shown for someone from the mountains.

Anne was impressed. If nothing else, he was certainly a crafty animal. She imagined that whatever it was he did, that he did it very well. And if he wanted something in that rarefied atmosphere in which he traveled, he usually got it.

At that moment Jonathan caught her staring at him. Without missing a beat he flashed a knowing grin at her that knocked into her like a kick. Those damn white, perfect teeth. Why didn't they seem to bother anybody else as much as they did her?

When her first reaction died, something else dawned on Anne. Jonathan was giving her a message. In his eyes she saw the admission that he was a different person than the men he faced. His initial reaction to being caught up here outside his universe would never do, and he proposed to change his attitude when he dealt with these people. She also had the very unsettling feeling that he considered her as much an outsider as him, which made her fair game.

She felt totally confused. Jonathan Harris seemed to be going out of his way to keep her off balance. He caught her this time with her mouth open.

"Don't worry about me," he was saying to Jim and Silas even as his eyes held Anne's. "I'll behave. My nurse trusts me even less than you do. She won't let me get away with anything."

Silas and Jim turned to see her standing across from the doorway. Anne allowed herself a slow, controlled smile just for Mr. Harris.

"He's right, Silas. I'll probably end up bringing in the shotgun from the barn. Just in case Mr. Harris tries to steal the chickens."

Jim couldn't quite control the corners of his mouth. Anne decided that if he thought it was so funny, he could stay up here instead of her. She'd much rather run a general store than tap-dance with Mr. Harris for a week. Come to think of it, she thought as she swung the towel over her shoulder, maybe she should let Silas stay up here. Then she could just ride off and not have to worry about Jonathan at all.

By the time Jim and Silas finished the interrogation Anne had the table set and fresh bread out. Silas appeared in the kitchen doorway, a suspicious frown clouding his features. Anne knew that it had everything to do with the fact that Jonathan was playing the mysterious stranger. Knowing Silas, she was sure that he would ride straight down to the station to have the sheriff run Jonathan's name for wants and warrants. She couldn't help the grin this time as she invited him to sit for another cup of coffee.

"We'll try and have somebody up here every day to check on you, Annie," Jim offered as he sat. "And I'm sure I can get the boys at the phone company busy on your lines."

Anne sat across from him. "If you're worried about my virtue, Jim, don't. Even the best mashers I've known would have trouble making time on a broken leg. I can move a lot faster than he can."

Silas didn't take to her levity. "It won't hurt any to accept the help, Annie." He frowned his admonition. "You don't know who that man is. For all we know, that fancy name of his ain't even real."

"That just shows he has a classy imagination." She grinned. "If he's a burglar, he must be a good one. That was a five-hundred-dollar suit we cut off him. As for his true identity, get ahold of Ef Tate. I'll bet he's sporting a brand new Gucci wallet that has all of Mr. Harris's ID."

"We tried him already," Jim said grinning dryly as he finished his coffee in a gulp. "He's the soul of innocence. I'm afraid Mr. Harris isn't going to see his wallet again."

"Another cup?" Anne asked automatically.

"No, thanks, Annie," he apologized. "I think we'd better get going."

She smiled, knowing that Silas had undoubtedly been pressing to at least get as far as the nearest working phone to check out Mr. Jonathan Harris. In the perverse humor she was in, she hoped something would show up, just to see not only Silas's reaction, but Jonathan's.

Taking his cue from Jim, Silas quickly finished his coffee and followed him to his feet, the old chairs scraping noisily on the red tile floor.

Jim turned to Anne as they walked into the living room. "I could probably arrange for someone to stay up here with you if you want."

Anne shook her head. "Only if they can cook and clean windows."

"Annie," Silas admonished.

Anne waved aside the objection and stood by the front door as the men donned their coats. "I promise I'll be fine," she assured them with a gentle smile. "Unless he's a great healer or a lot more determined than he looks, Mr. Harris won't be out of bed for at least a few days. He'll be no trouble or inconvenience. Besides, if the snow doesn't stop, I don't want to have to end up feeding all kinds of people. Two's more than enough."

Anne's word sparked a reaction from Jim. "I forgot. That dinner I promised is out on the mare."

"Let me get my coat," Anne offered, reaching for her down jacket. "No sense you having to traipse in and out when I have to go out and see you off anyway."

A few minutes later, Jim handed her five large plastic containers that all but filled her arms.

"Jim," she accused, surveying them. "This isn't dinner. It's a week's rations for Fort Benning."

He answered after he'd mounted the large dappled mare he used for deliveries to the homes on the mountain. "You know Cassie. Product of an Italian mother. She just wanted to make sure you'd be okay if we didn't get up here for a few days."

"I think this should probably take me through Labor Day," she said, smiling. "Thanks."

"Is there anything else you need?" Silas persisted.

Anne shook her head. "If you can figure out a way for it to stop snowing so that I can be free of Mr. Harris's stellar company, all my troubles will be solved, and I promise I'll be a happy woman again."

She waited as long as it took for her riders to disappear into the snowy fog before turning to go back inside. Out of habit, she checked the indoor-outdoor thermometer by the door as she stamped her boots. Fourteen wet, blowing degrees. She certainly hoped Mr. Harris realized how lucky he was not to be lying out under a couple of feet of snow tonight.

There wasn't any sound from his room as she passed, so she assumed he was asleep again. She wasn't surprised. Besides the fact that his injuries had sapped his strength, he was probably bored to death already. She wondered if he had ever eaten from a vegetarian menu, as he would if he had an appetite tonight. Cassie was one of the best vegetarian cooks Anne knew. Opening the refrigerator door with three fingers, Anne piled the containers inside, unaware that the anticipatory grin on her features was almost malicious in its glee. If he were indeed like Tom, he'd choke. Anne wouldn't wait for dinner.

Once the food was put away, Anne made a beeline back through the living room to work on the fire, her mind consumed with the truth of the words she'd said to Silas. If only she could get her unwelcome houseguest back to wherever he came from, she could get back to the soothing peace of her routine. Then her life would be what she'd waited two years for it to become.

As Anne bent to gather more wood from the stack by the door, she bumped into the trash can. It briefly occurred to her that it was getting full and needed to be emptied. Especially with that fancy envelope from Boston in it.

Then she turned to stoke the fire, all thoughts of her past once again deliberately shoved aside.

Chapter 3

By six o'clock the next evening the snow had topped thirty inches and still fell steadily. Anne sat in a wing-back chair by the front window looking morosely outside. She'd finally turned on the radio as Silas had suggested, only to hear that the state was under hazardous weather warnings. Most secondary roads had been closed, especially at higher elevations. The airport was shut down and every piece of snow-removal equipment had been on the major highways since early morning. And more snow was to come.

That explained why no one had ventured up to see her that day. She was glad they hadn't, really. There was probably more than enough for them to do everywhere else. The meteorologist came on the air again to give an updated report that sounded depressingly like all the others. His voice frazzled and apologetic, he assured the public that weather of this severity in this area was a freak of nature. More like one of the plagues of Egypt, Anne amended for him, able to picture him repeatedly loosening his tie and running his hands through his hair as the snow continued to pile up without his permission.

She could have told him why the state was suffering the first October blizzard in memory. It had everything to do with the fact that she had Mr. Harris as her surprise house-guest. She was snowed in with him because, with the exception of Tom or Brad, Jonathan Harris was the last person on earth with whom she wanted to be stuck in an isolated cabin.

It's Murphy's Law, she thought. When she'd worked in the emergency room, it had moved from the eleventh to her first commandment, neatly displacing all the others. If anything could possibly go wrong it would, and at the worst possible moment. Here she sat, once again living proof of that axiom.

It wasn't that Jonathan didn't need her help. He most certainly did. The concussion he'd suffered would have had him on breathing support for at least the first twelve hours. He'd slept away the vast majority of the day, not able to keep any kind of solid food down until lunch. He wouldn't be going anywhere for a while on that leg, and she'd have to guess that at least three of his ribs were broken. All that added to low back strain and exposure made him a pretty sorry sight.

It was just that she felt he had the personality of a snake. Peppering his speech with cute little clichés culled from the *Cruising Corporate Head's Guide to New York*, Jonathan seemed to believe that given enough time, any woman would melt for his hundred-watt smile and religiously unoriginal turn of phrase. And that soon that same woman would ask for no more than to serve his every whim. Anne expected to see the venom appear when it finally got through to him that she would want no part of it. Just like it had happened some three years ago with Tom.

What truly galled Anne was the fact that beneath all that gloss and party-game atmosphere, she sensed another person entirely, someone she could like and respect. Maybe it was just a newfound optimism, but she thought she might have seen a little of his true self the first night when his eyes had been so very vulnerable. She wanted to think that the word games were just a protection, maybe a habit.

Face it, she thought dourly as she watched the snow steadily pile up outside her bay window, you don't want to think that you could be attracted to that kind of personality again. You don't want Tom to have been right about needing that kind of man.

There was no question that she found Jonathan handsome. She'd caught herself peeking in at him much more than was necessary and had to admit that even with the ravages of his fall, he still stood right up there in the unforgettable-looks category. But she'd known and worked with a host of handsome men before. On more than one occasion she'd found herself in stressful and emotionally charged situations with them and had handled it with levelheaded common sense every time. It bothered her very much that she was in danger of losing that precious objectivity with the one man she most needed it for.

So engrossed was she by the increasingly depressing cant of her thoughts that it took her a moment to hear her patient's voice. When she did, she scowled, wishing that she could tape his mouth shut. She imagined that he considered himself original by calling her Florence Nightingale. Heaving a sigh of capitulation, she uncurled her feet from beneath her and got up to answer the call.

"Ah," he said, smiling as she walked through the door, "if it isn't the light of my dark days."

"How are you feeling?" she asked, pulling the chair over again and sitting down. She took note of the fact that only a small amount of blood had seeped through the bandage on his head, and that the inevitable bruising had begun under his eyes. She also noticed for the first time how small crow's feet creased the corners of his eyes when he smiled, somewhat easing the ruggedness of his features.

"Better now that you're here." He grinned, showing her all his teeth and ruining that impression of familiarity. "Hold my hand and I'll feel like dancing."

She ignored him, pulling the cover back from his feet to check his injured leg for color and pulse. It, too, was swollen and bruised, but the circulation was unimpaired.

"Does your leg hurt?" She examined the wrappings, but they hadn't slipped or kinked and didn't really need the check.

"Only when I laugh."

"Does your foot feel tingly and cold at all?"

"No more than the rest of me."

Anne replaced the covers and straightened up, wondering how she could get around rewrapping his head.

"Aren't you going to check my chest?" he demanded, reaching for the sheet.

Her smile was a bit chilly. "Not unless you stop breathing and turn blue. Do you feel like eating some dinner?"

"What's on the menu?"

"Lentil and cheese casserole, cucumber salad, nut bread and peaches."

"Of course." He nodded with mock severity. "It all fits. The communal period, right?"

"Pardon?"

He motioned vaguely with one hand to signify her environment. "The communal period. Vegetarianism, *Foxfire Manuals* and homesteading. Are you preparing for the end of the world?"

"No. Just dinner." She got to her feet.

"I'll eat on one condition," he decided, reaching for her hand. She deftly avoided it with a move she'd perfected at Mass General. He pulled what was meant to be a handsome frown of disappointment. "You come in and share dinner with me."

"I prefer to eat alone," she replied evenly. "Besides, I have to tend the animals, so I won't be eating for a while anyway."

"You can't mean that you'd prefer to spend your time with the cows rather than me."

She offered a dry smile. "I can."

His eyes narrowed as if he were gauging her, his smile almost sly. The look of a man who was sure he had the upper hand. "What if I told you that I could take you away from all this if you wanted?"

"I'd say take yourself away. I like it here."

His smiled widened. Anne could see the challenge in his eyes. What she did not see was warmth. "I could give you everything you ever wanted."

Anne actually had to close her eyes when she heard that, the sense of déjà vu too painful. "I'll give you everything you'll ever want, Anne. Everything," Tom had promised. In the end, he had taken it instead.

She took a slow breath to quell the urge to scream and opened her eyes again. "This may come as an unpleasant surprise to you, Mr. Harris," she said quietly, "but I had everything I wanted before you fell down my cliff. And after you're gone, I'll have it again."

This time when Jonathan smiled, Anne could actually see the challenge die and be replaced by what she could have sworn was sincerity. She found herself staring.

"Please," he said, his voice sounding earnest. "I really hate to eat alone. And I'd like to have the chance to know more about my benefactor. If I ease up a little, will you stay?"

Anne had the irrational impulse to applaud the performance she was witnessing. Somehow, she couldn't. She gave him another chance to surprise her.

"It'll take me an hour or so before I can get to dinner."

"That's okay," he said, the veneer already solidly back in place. "It'll be worth the wait."

When Anne did get back with dinner, she found that he'd fallen asleep again, his face peaceful and quiet. That angered her anew. It annoyed her that the mind inhabiting that handsome, rugged face could spoil the image by constantly bartering on the sincerity and honesty suggested there. She hadn't seen a chin so square and strong since Gary Cooper; the cheeks were solid as granite ledges, as if etched by wind and water. Even his nose perfectly suited his face, straight enough to have been drawn. It was just that none of his features fit the personality. It was like watching a movie with the sound track out of sync.

He stopped her as her hand touched the door, about to leave him to his sleep.

"You're not going to back out of our dinner date at the last minute, are you?"

Anne turned to see his eyes open and gently mocking. Their light seared her enough to make her answer abrupt. "I thought you were asleep."

"As good an excuse as any," he said with a shrug. "But I don't let beautiful women shirk their commitments, especially to me. Is that the vegetarian delight I smell? It awakens gustatory anticipation."

Anne got out a small folding table as she thought how, even on his back, Jonathan Harris remained able to command control of a situation. It also occurred to her how typical it was of his kind—not the ability to do it, the need. There had never been any problems in her own marriage until she realized that she no longer wanted to delegate every decision in her life to Tom.

She set everything out on the table and then reached into the closet for more pillows to prop up Mr. Harris for dinner. He was reaching over very carefully to nibble at the salad while he waited, allowing that he was, indeed, hungry. Again Anne wondered how hungry he'd be after tasting something as alien as cheese and lentil casserole.

She walked around to the head of the bed to help him get to a sitting position to eat.

"No thanks," he told her agreeably. "I'm going to sit in that old chair you slept in."

She balked a minute. "I'm not really sure you're ready for it."

"Nevertheless," he said with a smile, "that's where I'm going to eat. With your help or not."

"Were you this stubborn the other time you were hurt?"

Jonathan stared at her, the humor dying in his eyes. Anne wasn't quite sure what she saw there instead, but it made her uneasy.

Finally, he offered a short nod. "Yes. Now, how 'bout a hand?"

Anne acquiesced with a shrug. After getting the chair situated next to the bed, she bent to pull him up into sitting position.

"This will be uncomfortable," she warned, still not sure it was a good idea, "so I'll take it slowly. Let me know if you need to stop."

"I know the routine," he snapped a little sharply. "Let's get going."

Anne moved as quickly and efficiently as possible until he was sitting on the side of the bed. Even as easy as the movement had been, she saw Jonathan's jaw clench with pain and perspiration break out on his forehead.

"C'mon," he gasped, seeing her hesitate. "The chair."

She stooped again to get him to his feet. Her arms around his chest, she felt the iron-hard tension of his muscles and the power of the arms that encircled her for support. Jonathan had been successfully seated in the chair a good few minutes before Anne could get her pulse to slow down.

Then she caught the tension in his suddenly pale face, and remembered that he'd neither asked for nor received anything for pain since he'd arrived. There was no question but that he was in pain.

"Are you okay?" she asked quickly, her fingers trapping the bounding pulse at his wrist. "Maybe you should lie back down."

"Don't you move me an inch," he chided with a grin that was a shade tighter than he'd wanted. "I can see four of you, and they all have the most beautiful frown of concern. I'm flattered."

"Do you need anything for the pain? I don't have much, but..."

"What pain?" He was quickly regaining control. "That's hunger you see. All I need is some of that lentil and cheese casserole you promised."

"Are you sure?" She couldn't understand him. There was no reason for him to play John Wayne. That wasn't the way his kind of man handled a situation like this. They were more apt to become demanding and loud. Yet she could see, only because she was used to looking for it, that he was still fighting against the pain and dizziness the exertion had brought on. He controlled it with a fierce concentration that amazed her. He wouldn't accept her help.

Guided by instincts her profession had long ago taught her, Anne turned for the door, leaving him the privacy he seemed to need.

"Coffee or tea for dinner?" she asked, not bothering to look around.

"Coffee's fine."

She took a little extra time in the kitchen, hoping it would be enough. Harris had spent the whole afternoon running true to form, when suddenly he had thrown her a complete curve. There it was again, that anomaly, the small bit of information that didn't fit. Realizing that if she weren't careful she could easily grow to respect Jonathan Harris, Anne found herself hoping yet again that he wasn't only what he would appear to be.

The high, shrill whistle of her grandmother's teakettle broke Anne's reverie. She reached for it, turning off the flame. Steam had filmed the window over the stove, disguising the faint white of the snow. The roof creaked a little beneath the ponderous weight, and Anne could hear the low, sad moan of the wind as it probed the windows and doors. The sounds of the cabin in the snowstorm gave her comfort, the feel of a familiar place crowded with happy memories. The house on Beacon Hill had never evoked that kind of feeling and never would. Anne assembled the things for the tray and thought yet again how thankful she was that she had this little cabin to wear around her like a warm cloak to protect her from the madness of life. She also wondered if Jonathan Harris had a place like this where he was safe.

Jonathan's attitude during dinner angered and unsettled her even more. When she first reentered the room, he was totally at ease and in control, as if the moment of weakness had never happened. Everything was a target for his caustic tongue, from the snow to her choice of attire. She did notice, however, that he made short order of the food before him. Anne only wished that her own appetite could hold up to his sense of humor.

"You're not from around here," he said suddenly as he refilled his plate from the table. Anne couldn't help but stare at him. Her Boston accent had certainly softened since she'd been in the mountains, but no fool could have possibly missed it.

"Your powers of observation, Mr. Harris—"

"Jonathan," he interrupted with a stern wave of the fork. She ignored him. "—are overwhelming."

"Thank you." He smiled with satisfaction. "Why did you leave Boston?"

"I became tired of living there."

An eyebrow rose. Anne recognized the reaction. How could anyone give up all that, et cetera, et cetera. Maybe that was why he so delighted in baiting her. Perhaps he felt the same disdain—the sense of smug superiority that bred condescension and intolerance—that Tom had when he'd discovered that Anne wasn't returning from the mountain to the real world. Anne decided not to enlighten Mr. Harris further on the subject. He chose not to take the hint.

"Beacon Hill?"

Her startled reaction gave her away.

"I thought so," he said, nodding and returning to his food. "Most people don't have the money to run away from home in such style. What happened? Was your grandfather a robber baron, and you couldn't stand the shame of it anymore?''

"No," she answered pointedly, her eyes flashing at his attitude of smug superiority, "I got tired of swimming in the same waters as the barracudas."

Anne stood to leave, unable to remain for any more and not even bothering to take her half-finished dinner with her. She didn't even get to the door before he called out.

"Anne, I'm sorry. Don't leave." That strange note of sincerity had once again found its way into his voice. Anne stopped with her hand on the door, trying her best to understand why she hadn't already walked out, or better yet, heaved the casserole into his lap.

"I promise to behave." He spoke up again. "I guess I haven't."

She didn't answer, struggling with her indecision and angered by it.

"Anne," he said quietly, "I was out of line. Don't go."

She faced him then, even more irritated and confused by the contradictions in his words and actions, and wondered what capitulation would cost her. The strength of his eyes ate at her resistance.

"This isn't New York," she said with very careful control. "If you insist on playing New York word games, no one will talk to you. Especially me."

The bravado in his smile dimmed a little. "Ah, but you're such a worthy opponent."

"Worthy perhaps, but not interested. Unless some kind of truce is called, I'll be more inhospitable than a cold north wind to a bare backside. Your choice, Mr. Harris."

"You'll sit back down?"

After a small hesitation, she nodded.

"Good. I'll try to stay on neutral subjects." He motioned her to her chair and resumed his dinner. "I already have a question."

Anne looked up warily as she sat down. He immediately grinned at her reticence.

"It's only about your reading material," he defended himself, hand raised.

"You want to read something?"

He nodded, still grinning, his face disarmingly boyish. "I'm sure I will. You don't offer much up here in the way of diversion."

"You're right," she countered evenly, going back to her dinner. "The ballet left last week, our museum collection's out on loan and baseball season doesn't start for another five months."

"Touché." He bowed stiffly, his eyes almost as clear as the first time Anne had seen them. "That wasn't my point, though. Right now, I'm more interested in a far more existential question having to do with the choice of reading material available at this library. It's really...unique."

He motioned to the floor-to-ceiling bookcases that lined the wall opposite his bed and held her collection of paperbacks, old nursing manuals, magazines and a variety of keepsakes she'd never had the heart to remove from what had for years been her room. Anne's eyes were immediately drawn to the top shelf where her old dolls sat in a tumbled and comfortable row. The largest of them were her Raggedy Ann and Andy dolls her mother had made the year before she had died. They were perched on either end and watched the room with timeless eyes and sewn mouths.

"I don't throw anything away," Anne said. "It all ends up here at one time or another. The good books are in the living room."

"Then I'll have to get in there soon if this is any indication." His eyes roved among the hundreds of titles. "I must say that I'm astounded by it."

Again she followed his gaze. "Why?"

"Oh," he began, his hand up for elaboration, "the disparity. The contradictions." He pointed. "The *Foxfire Manuals*, and *Mother Earth News*, those fit. *Nursing*, *Guide to Medicinal Plants*, even Kahlil Gibran. Those all go with the vegetarian stew and braids. Very communal." His hand moved again, discovering more. "The classics . . . I imagine there are more in the living room. . . ."

She nodded automatically.

"Those are marginal; a bit frivolous. But *Time*, *Wall Street Journal*, William F. Buckley? No self-respecting homesteader would be caught dead with those. And *Tax Shelters*? Richard Nixon's autobiography? Unheard of. Simply unheard of. Are you an imposter, *madame*?"

His tone was so easy and light, without a trace of condescension, that Anne knew he meant no offense. She found herself grinning.

"You're a victim of preconceived ideas," she accused, pointing her fork at him. "Where does it say that a modern homesteader isn't allowed to read *Time*? Just because one is isolated doesn't mean she wants to be caught unprepared." She was reminded of Silas's admonition on that very subject and couldn't help but grin again. "And who says I'm not allowed to read anything I want? I happen to belong to three book clubs and subscribe to magazines that also make the community circuit."

He shook his head with a mischievous grin. "You should be putting money into the crops and time on the chores. Sunup to sundown."

"I'm a nurse," she countered, "not Grandma Walton. I raise enough to feed myself and do enough chores to keep from tripping over hungry animals."

"What about the *Tax Shelters*?" He demanded. "The last time I heard, nursing didn't exactly rank among the most lucrative professions."

"It doesn't even rank that low," she assured him. "The book was my father's. That, Nixon and the subscription to the *Wall Street Journal*. He also had the finest paperback collection of murder mysteries in seven states."

She didn't realize that as she scanned the titles, she lost her smile.

"Past tense?"

She nodded. "He died about two years ago. You can tell what a pack rat I am if I can't even throw out a book on tax shelters." The truth was that she hadn't managed to work up the nerve to go through any of her father's things. Silas had carried most of them up to the attic for her but the books had been left here.

"You brought them here from Boston?"

She turned back to him, trying to loose the past's hold on her. "No. We used to come here during the summer. It was the only way father could escape the business. I took the house over and worked it again after he died."

She didn't notice that at her words Jonathan's eyes snapped open. "Well, that explains the Nancy Drew mysteries, I guess." He was watching her, as if expecting to find something in her face. After a moment he let his eyes wander over the room and then settle back on Anne, the color fading oddly as he squinted in examination.

Anne had gone back to her dinner. She nodded with a smile. "I kept every one. I figured that I'd give them to my little girl to read someday."

"If you'll pardon my asking, how did you come to spend summers here? It's a little off the beaten track, you know."

"My father was born here." Anne looked up and found a sudden frost in his eyes. It confused her. "This house has been in my family for about seven generations. My grandfather was the first to leave it during the Depression. When you're up and about, you'll see the quilts that are hung on the living-room wall. The oldest belonged to my great-great-great-great-great grandmother Sarah from before the War of 1812."

"The house looks pretty sturdy for being so old." Jonathan met Anne's eyes and spoke with quiet interest, but it was as if the life in his voice were dying. Anne could hardly manage an answer.

"The, uh, living-room walls are all that's left of the original stucture, and those have been refinished. The second story, kitchen and bedrooms are all new. And, of course, there's the modern plumbing. This homesteader does admit to enjoying her conveniences now and then."

"I can well imagine." His smile sprang on her like a trap. She saw his eyes sweep the room hungrily before landing with wolfish glee on her startled face. "Especially since you were the baby girl of one of the scions of Boston industry." He wagged his finger at her in an almost accusatory manner. "I've finally placed you," he announced triumphantly, the last of his easy-going manner disappearing in a chilling flash. "Pete Jackson's daughter, heiress to two separate fortunes, toast of Boston social society, patroness of the arts, marital catch of the decade . . . you were caught, weren't you? And you made quite a name for yourself by making a career of sorts well below your allotted station in life. Not exactly what daddy would have wanted you to do, was it?"

Anne didn't even bother to wait for him to finish before getting to her feet. Barely able to keep her silence, she began to gather together the dishes, the line of her jaw rigid with the struggle for control. It was all she could do to keep from hurling something at him. Not for the questions, which she had expected sooner or later, but for the attitude. With deadly, unerring aim, he had used his voice and eyes like lethal knives to humiliate her. She had spent the last two years recovering from that kind of pain, and she trembled with the familiar feel of it.

Jonathan didn't seem the least distressed by her reaction, evidently still too pleased with his coup to care.

"Not willing to answer the charges?" he finally asked.

She stopped briefly and turned on him, her eyes like steel. "Are you always this predatory, or do I just bring out the best in you?"

"An opportunity I simply couldn't pass up." His teeth gleamed almost maliciously now. "I thought you'd at least fill me in on how you arrived at this most interesting crossroads in life. It is, after all, a long way from Debutante of the Year."

"It's where I choose to be. That's the only information you're entitled to."

He shrugged nonchalantly. "I'm a bit disappointed. I at least expected some of that world famous breeding to peek through. A well-placed sneer, a haughty stamp of the foot."

"I'm sure it would make you feel right at home. These days, though, I find that I prefer a much more direct method of communication." She paused a moment, her eyes delivering the full promise of her next words. "A twelve-gauge shotgun, for instance."

And then she walked from the room.

The dishes were washed with great vigor and staccato rhythm that evening. Color flaring high in her cheeks, Anne seethed over the conversation she'd been roped into. She was furious with Harris for lulling her into a false sense of security only to spring his verbal trap with all the cheap theatrics found in a bad movie.

What was worse, she couldn't understand how she'd let him get away with it. She knew better. It was, after all, a carbon copy of the trick Tom had perfected on her with such destructive precision, especially toward the end. When she'd tried to fight his takeover of the business, he had taken to dissecting her in public with brutal delight. The feeling, she realized, was as painful and infuriating as it had always been. Mr. Harris was successfully resurrecting an ambivalence that Anne hadn't had to deal with in a long time, and she hated him for it.

She knew she should go and get Jonathan back into bed, but the thought of having to be that close to him kept her in the kitchen even as it unaccountably attacked her pulse rate again. Damn, it just wasn't fair.

By the time she did get in, however, he was so worn out that it was all he could do to carry out his part of the maneuver. Anne covered him up and wiped the perspiration from his drawn face, her mind consumed all the while with the picture of Tom as he'd told her what kind of man she needed.

"I'm going to head upstairs now, Mr. Harris," she finally said, putting her equipment back on the closet shelf.
He hadn't made any comments when she'd changed the
dressing around his head. "If you need anything for pain
you'd better let me know now."

"I don't get a little bell to ring?"

She didn't realize how deathly tired her own voice
sounded when she answered. "Not unless you brought along
your own butler to answer it. I'm going to bed now."

"I'll let you go on one condition." This time he didn't
even make an attempt at her hand. "You might as well call
me Jonathan."

"It doesn't make any difference to me," she said with a
shrug, not bothering to face him.

"Then Jonathan it is." She wondered if he'd meant that
to sound hearty. He sounded almost as disinterested as she.
"I mean, it's only fair since I don't know which last name
to call you by if you insist on remaining formal."

She faced him then, stonelike. "I told you already that
you were right. My name is Jackson."

"No. I mean your name now."

"Jackson," she repeated and left.

Chapter 4

Wednesday was traditionally Anne's baking day. Whenever she wasn't out on rounds, she spent the better part of the day baking loaves of grain, sourdough and vegetable breads, coffee cakes for breakfast and any number of muffins and rolls. Many of the proceeds were passed out among her needier neighbors, but Anne was glad that she worked hard enough to keep off the calories from what she kept and ate each week. It was a weakness she'd given in to early and often, deciding that honey and cinnamon were certainly a healthier addiction than tobacco or alcohol.

She finished tending the animals early, trudging heavily through snow that still fell and flew in fits and starts. Then, after retrieving last night's teacup from the little Hepplewhite table by the couch and patting distractedly at the cushions, she gathered breakfast together for her patient.

When Anne knocked on the bedroom door, she was invited in with a monosyllable. She thought it just as well. She wanted to get through this and on to her baking. If Jonathan were uncommunicative, she wouldn't have to waste valuable time and energy on his games.

"I thought you might like to get around a little today," she suggested without making eye contact. She kept her mind on the day ahead as she set out the food. If only she could make it through this quickly. Damn Jonathan Harris. He'd cost her sleep and peace of mind, and still the sight of morning sunlight striking the hard planes of his face threatened to steal her breath.

"You won't walk me out the front door and shut it behind me?" he asked without emotion.

"Not unless you sorely tempt me." She busied herself moving the easy chair over to the window where he could see outside. "The only thing you have to remember when you get up is to not put any weight on your injured leg. You can put your arm around my shoulder to steady yourself until you can use crutches."

"And when will that be?"

Anne positioned herself by the bed. "When your broken ribs let you." She helped him pull himself up to a sitting position and swing his feet over the side again. She worked in silence, wanting to avoid watching his face. She didn't want to see the struggle that he waged to move this far, the stoic concentration reflected in the steel-tight muscles of his jaw. It would only make her want to reach out to him again. After last night, she knew how impossible that would be.

She gave him a few moments to gather his strength before going on.

"The game plan's the same as yesterday. Put your arm around my shoulder, and when I straighten, get to your feet."

She bent at the knees, the correct physiological position, and prepared to help him stand. Jonathan slid his arm around her neck as before. Then he stopped. Anne was forced to finally make eye contact, discovering a controlled half smile that held no humor.

"Quite the professional," he taunted quietly. "I have to admit that I miss the beatific smile you bestowed on me the first night I was here. I'm afraid you've changed."

The look Anne gave him in response left him in no doubt as to whose fault she considered that to be. "Haven't we all?" was all she said.

She should have looked away again. Better yet, she should have straightened back up and walked away. Her chance for escape passed even as she glared at Jonathan, the challenge in both of them inexplicably dying.

With the devastating speed and shock of lightning, Anne suddenly found herself trapped, unable to move, unable to defend herself from the pain of contact. It was as if for that brief moment she and Jonathan were fused, united. Only his touch and the contact of their eyes held them, but it was enough to set Anne to trembling.

There was a physical reaction, she couldn't deny that. Her skin suddenly felt as if it had bumped against dry ice: burning and freezing, curling her toes and crawling along her scalp like a premonition. Her knees lost their rigidity, and she had to lock them straight to keep them from buckling altogether. Her lungs couldn't hold enough oxygen, and her heart found an entirely new rhythm. It was without a doubt a physical reaction, but if it had only been that she could have handled it, no matter how powerful.

What threatened to overwhelm her was what she found in Jonathan's eyes. Without warning, and for only the barest of moments, the veneer disintegrated over those fathomless pools of blue, and Anne became certain that she would fall in and become lost.

Like currents that shifted at different depths of the sea, Jonathan's eyes bared emotions that both bewildered and compelled Anne. She saw a vulnerability, a feeling of open space and invitation there. Beyond that, pain existed someplace she wasn't allowed to pry, a bare wound that still festered. She could see memories that she wouldn't be allowed to touch and the vacillation of a man who wasn't as completely in control as this one pretended.

But what left her more shaken than even those places in him she suddenly wanted to explore was the discovery of a deepest, primal place that stunned her. She briefly caught a flash of anger—almost hatred—that was directed exclusively at her. This was not the cool disdain of a man who simply thought her beneath his consideration, but an active, seething cauldron of hot animosity.

Just as quickly as it appeared, it was gone. Before Anne had the chance to react to the revelation in those potent eyes, the veneer was back up, the smooth patina of civilization concealing the anger. Once again Jonathan watched her with the cold, hard eyes of tolerant amusement.

Anne took a breath, struggling to regain her own composure. The last thing she could afford to do with this man was to lose control. If she did, he'd leave her in pieces scattered in the snow.

"Straighten when I do," she said very quietly, her face a careful mask.

Jonathan challenged her with a smile of smug superiority. "Are you really that cool?"

Anne faced him deliberately as she fought for the upper hand. "I really am."

Anne wasn't sure whether Jonathan's body shook from exertion or the perilously close confrontation. She knew that she was trembling too, and that made her angry. The weight of his rock-hard body against her as she helped him to his feet sent a jolt through her that threatened her heart rate again. She didn't have to look up to feel the electricity of his eyes on her. Her skin tingled with the power of it.

Of all the times for her to react like this to a man. It made her want to do rash things like confront his anger and hostility to defuse the glare he leveled at her. If he'd been anyone else in the world, she would have wanted very much to make love to him.

But he wasn't anyone else. The facade was too familiar, and she'd seen the inconsistencies that lay beneath. There was too much lightning in him, too much frost. After all the time Anne had spent constructing her fragile peace of mind, she didn't need this man to come along and shatter it with his volatile eyes and callused hands.

She'd intended to let Jonathan try walking out to the front room. She ended up only being able to make it twice around the bedroom before steering Jonathan toward the easy chair.

If she hadn't been so caught up in her own confusion as she lowered him into it, he would never have surprised her. He had both arms around her neck to ease his descent. Anne bent her knees to let him down and then leaned forward to scoot him comfortably back into the chair. At that moment, he pulled her over.

Badly off balance, she fell against him, her reaction a startled cry. He moved more quickly than she'd given him credit for, lacing his fingers into her hair and pulling her face to his for a kiss. She couldn't avoid the deliciously salty taste of his lips.

Anne's first instinct was to succumb, to match the bruising power of his mouth with her own. The heat that had been building in her exploded like a nova with the contact of his lips. His taunting caress lit fires she'd thought were dead long ago. She felt his breath catch in surprise and knew that he was as aroused as she. Their meeting could have been cataclysmic, but if there was one thing Anne prided herself on, it was control.

Jerking upright, she glared coldly at the triumph in Jonathan's eyes. "Don't expect outrage or hysterics," she suggested with frozen restraint, the taste of humiliation beginning to rise again with the look in his eyes. It was all she could do to keep from wiping at her mouth. "I don't play those games."

"You want me," he accused with great satisfaction.

Her eyes never wavered, never surrendered. "About as much as I want the flu. Listen, I don't know what it is about me that sets you off, but I won't stand for it."

"What sets me off," he countered with cold displeasure, "are spoiled little rich girls who think they're the light of the world because they packed away the designer dresses for a season. Lady, you're a phony."

"And you," she snapped back, "are a conceited, self-centered bastard who'd better enjoy his privacy. Because if you keep this up, that's what you're going to get."

Without another word she turned on her heel and walked out.

The pattern of baking day had become a comfortable ritual since Anne's first return to her mountain home. Today, she observed the custom as if it were a rite of cleansing. Concentrating on the immediate tasks at hand, Anne worked very hard to block out the escalating friction in her very small cabin.

First organizing her ingredients across the long butcher-block counter, she pulled the sourdough starter from the icebox and set the oven. Once that was done, she donned her official baking apron, an old blue gingham that had been in the house as long as she could remember. The apron was a formality, really. By the end of the day her face, hair and hands would be liberally dusted with flour, and there would be white smudges on either side of the seat of her pants where she would unconsciously wipe her hands. She pinned her braids around her head to keep them out of the way and set to work.

Anne mixed the yeast breads first and let them rise while she mixed and baked the vegetable breads. As the yeast breads cooked, she would begin to mix the rolls and coffee cakes. It didn't occur to her that the noise of her movements was a little louder today, or that when she kneaded the dough for her breads it looked as if she were punishing it. She did notice that it only took about half an hour for her to begin to feel better. The cathartic effect of baking day had been documented well enough two years earlier.

Anne had just pulled her first two loaves of bread from the oven and set them on the counter to cool when she heard a knock at the front door. She looked up, startled from her preoccupation, and found herself staring across the cabin to the door as if it would offer explanation. Then she remembered that Jim had promised to stop by. Maybe he'd also found out something about the not-so-mysterious Jonathan Harris.

"Coming!" she yelled as the knock sounded again. Shedding bread and oven mitts, she headed in for the living room.

"You sure have a lot of company," Jonathan offered as Anne walked by the hallway.

"That's because they don't trust you," she couldn't help but retort. His answering chuckle unaccountably surprised her.

When Anne opened the front door, she was taken completely by surprise. It wasn't Jim who stood before her, but Jim's wife Cassie, donned in fur-lined parka and snowshoes. Almost as tall as Anne, she was in her mid-twenties and looked for all the world like the proverbial Indian princess. Her skin was a beautiful olive color, her eyes as black as her hair. And every one of her ancestors hailed from central Europe.

"Cassie, are you crazy?" Anne demanded.

"Just frozen." Her friend grinned. "Let me in before my nose falls off."

Anne made way for Cassie to enter and closed the door behind her, all the while shaking her head.

"It's five miles to your place," she protested again. "You shouldn't have walked up here."

Cassie grinned, shedding parka and boots. "I'd rather be here than housebound with three kids. The silence was soul saving; the cold I wasn't as fond of. If I'd wanted that, I would have stayed in Chicago. Got any tea?"

"Sure I do. C'mon in."

Anne brewed up some tea and sliced into the warm zucchini bread. Then popping two more loaves into the oven, she sat down to join Cassie.

Cassie accepted her tea and sat in one of the cane-back chairs Silas had made for Anne's father. "From what Jim says about your patient, I thought you might need a chaperone." Cassie had never been known for beating around the bush.

Anne's answering scowl was more thunderous than she realized. "More like a referee."

Cassie's eyebrows lifted. "Sure didn't take him long to get on your bad side. What did he do? Make some passes?"

Anne shrugged uncomfortably. "Any number of them. All indiscriminate and well rehearsed." Until the last one. She felt the heat rise again in her cheeks.

"I see you were impressed."

"I lived with a man like that for three years, which was plenty long enough to learn the style intimately."

Cassie nodded. "What I want to know is if we're going to find that poor man down a cliff again."

Anne had to laugh, her indignation easing a little under Cassie's easy humor. "No," she admitted as she pulled the kettle off the stove and poured the steaming water into earthenware mugs. "My parents raised me to be a Christian. The worst I'd do is hang him by his feet from the loft. I'd only do that if he really provoked me."

"It got close, huh?"

Anne looked up to see the empathy in those dancing eyes. Cassie took a long sip from her mug and set it back down. "Well, I'm gonna have to go in and properly chastise him before I leave. Besides, I want to see if he's really as handsome as I hear."

"More so," Anne had to admit, her eyes on the honey she was dolloping into her tea. "But please don't say that to him. I'm the one who'd suffer."

Anne was grateful that Cassie had come. She had the knack to defuse Anne's housebound anger and restore her perspective. As always, Anne asked about Cassie's three children. She enjoyed that topic of conversation much more, having always used Cassie's brood as a substitute for the children she'd never have now she was divorced. Cassie was the kind of person who made everyone want to be a mother. Anne fed on her glow when she recounted in graphic detail the antics and tribulations of motherhood.

Anne hadn't realized how long they had been talking. When the timer went off she jumped, surprised by it. She hadn't prepared anything to follow the loaves that were in now. She hopped up, she grabbing the oven mitts. Cassie followed her to her feet and started rummaging through drawers.

"What are you looking for?" Anne asked over her shoulder, the air from the wall oven hot on her cheek.

"Apron. I want to help. I haven't been able to bake bread in ages."

Anne pulled out the last loaf and shoved the door closed. "There's probably an extra one in the hall closet."

Cassie was already on her way out. "That makes sense...."

Anne busied herself with the next batch of bread and didn't discover for a good few minutes just how long Cassie was taking to return. She looked over in the direction of the hall and heard voices. Cassie was in checking out Jonathan Harris for herself. Anne grinned as she leaned back and forth, kneading the bread dough with a bit less enthusiasm. Cassie was fearless and forthright, cursed with an insatiable curiosity and blessed with the courage to salve it. There were more than a few times that Anne envied her that.

Cassie didn't reappear for a good twenty minutes or so. When Anne saw her, she had a privately amused look on her face.

"Is he really so much like your ex?" she asked, dropping Anne's apron over her head and tying it in the back.

"Every inch of him, down to the cute green alligator he probably has on his pajamas back in New York."

"He doesn't wear any."

"Cassie!"

"It happened to come up in the conversation," Cassie defended herself without bothering to look over as she started measuring out flour into a bowl. Anne decided not to ask just how it had come up. "And he's not really from New York. He was born in Wyoming. But you're right. He is awfully handsome."

"He is that," Anne conceded as she worked her own bowl. "It's too bad he has to open his mouth and spoil it."

"He sure seems fascinated by you," Cassie countered casually.

"That's because there's nothing else up here to keep him occupied," Anne retorted dryly, her quiet answer contrasting with the color that flared along the ridges of her cheeks again. It made her angry that she was flattered by what Cassie had said. After what had happened that morning, she should have no room for that kind of reaction. It was just that he was a handsome man, and small vanities like that were hard to leave behind.

Cassie nodded, as if to herself. "Could be, could be."

Anne looked over to the secret smile in Cassie's eyes and straightened from her work. "What's that supposed to mean?"

Cassie shrugged. "Oh, nothing. You know me, always reading more into something than really exists."

"Out with it."

The smile broadened. Cassie still didn't bother to look up. "Oh, I don't know. He strikes me as...all bark. Kind of like the fourth-grade boy who hits the girl he likes the most."

"You've been on this mountain too long."

Cassie grinned and went on mixing. The two of them worked in a companionable silence for a time, both enjoying the quiet comfort of the Jackson kitchen. The timer buzzed, and Anne moved to the oven to pull out the latest batch of bread. She hummed tunelessly under her breath as she brushed stray hair from her forehead with the back of her arm and left another smudge of white there.

When they finally broke for lunch, Cassie insisted that they set up the table in the guest room and visit with Jonathan. Anne knew that it would be easier to survive a meal with Cassie present, but still couldn't manage to get in there soon enough to help her set up. Cassie didn't seem to mind in the least.

When Anne finally brought in the food, Jonathan was smiling and politely polished, commenting generally on the wonderful aromas that filled the house and the decaying state of the weather. He was nothing if not the perfect gentleman, which made Anne furious. She knew that he was pulling out all of his best manners for Cassie, and she couldn't understand why. Maybe the problem wasn't just Jonathan after all, but Jonathan and herself.

Anne answered when she had to with studied politeness as she helped ready for lunch, but she never quite faced Jonathan. It didn't seem to matter since Cassie was happy handling the majority of the conversation anyway.

By the time he was ready to eat, Jonathan had been sitting up in the chair for quite a while. Anne could see that he was beginning to wear thin, but it seemed that he refused to let it get in his way.

"This keeps getting better and better," he announced. "If I would have known there was so much to see outside New York, I would have left a long time ago."

Anne ignored him. She was sure that Cassie would have laughed at her reaction had Jonathan not been in the room. "Quiche?" she asked instead.

His answering smile, as he held out his plate to be served, reminded Anne of the wolf as he spotted Red Riding Hood's grandmother. If only it had happened five years ago, Anne would have found it all amusing and tolerated the leering with good-natured amusement. The wounds were still too new, though, and Jonathan seemed too much like Tom to let them heal. He'd managed to break right through the armor of isolation she'd so carefully built and instinctively attacked her most vulnerable spots.

Anne realized suddenly that Cassie and Jonathan had been talking, and that she'd been staring directly at Jonathan with undisguised anger. He couldn't have missed it, and yet he was blithely conversing with Cassie as if Anne weren't even in the room. She quickly lowered her eyes to her plate, embarrassed by her own bad manners. She'd have to try to be more civil.

"Where do you live in New York?" Cassie was saying, ignoring Anne's sudden lapse in courtesy.

"Upper Sixties, near Central Park," Jonathan answered.

Cassie nodded. "Nice. We have some friends there. Do you work nearby?"

Anne looked up in time to see a delighted, knowing smile light Jonathan's eyes as he waved his fork in Cassie's direction. "I really work in Philadelphia. I commute."

Cassie grinned right back. "We'll find out sooner or later."

"Well then, let it be a surprise. I love surprises."

"Will it be?"

"A surprise?" He shrugged. "I guess not really unless you're back in New York. But allow me my little game anyway." He took a drink of coffee and smiled ruefully. "The truth of the matter is that I don't want to be bothered with any of it right now. I'd like to consider this as my vacation in the mountains. When people know who you are, they expect certain things from you. This way there's no pressure."

Cassie persisted, quite undaunted. "Won't somebody miss you?"

"I imagine so."

"But you don't want to notify them."

"I don't think so." He went back to eating, the same irreverent smile still playing across his face. Cassie laughed and went back to her own meal. Anne stared at them both and stopped eating hers.

"You're giving up awfully fast, Cassie."

Cassie took the accusation with aplomb. "It's all in the timing, Annie."

"Yes, but you don't have to stay here with him. He could be the vicious criminal Silas thinks he is. I'm not sure I'd want to talk to him then." She caught herself wanting to grin. "Maybe we shouldn't even call him Jonathan."

"You could find something to talk about," Cassie responded as if Jonathan weren't there. "We've already discussed his sleeping attire and Wyoming. Neither of those has anything to do with his criminal career."

"You don't know that."

"She wants to know if my name's real," Jonathan said. "Tell your spies that, yes, my name is real. I don't have the energy to invent a name like that. I use all my energy just being vicious."

"I've never met a criminal with a middle name of Bradshaw," Cassie obliged as she picked lurking anchovies from her salad. "Most of them are something like Bubba or Billy."

"Bradshaw is my grandmother's maiden name." He reached over to steal the anchovies Cassie was piling at the side of her plate. "That's Emily Baldwin Bradshaw. Baldwin was her mother's maiden name... should I go on?"

"I don't think so." Anne shook her head. "That wouldn't leave us anything to talk about tomorrow."

Jonathan looked up from the fish he was popping into his mouth. "We could talk about you."

Even though Anne saw that his eyes were gentle in their teasing, she stiffened. "No, we won't."

Cassie stopped in the middle of dishing up seconds. "Her grandmother's name was Ellen Josephine McLaughlin. She was born over on the next ridge."

Anne shot Cassie a warning glance, afraid that the conversation would get around to Boston after all, and that

Jonathan would attack like he had before. She had begun to relax for the first time since Jonathan had woken up, and she didn't want to jeopardize it.

Cassie chose to ignore her. "Anne was born here in the cabin, but she was raised in Boston. Somewhere near the bay."

"Boston's one of my favorite cities," Jonathan offered.

"I hate it," Anne retorted evenly, returning to her food.

His eyebrows raised. Cassie grinned, enjoying the sparks.

"Well, you've been to New York, haven't you?" he coaxed.

"I hate New York."

Cassie laughed over at Jonathan. "And you call this a vacation?"

"Don't worry," he retorted, "I'll get to her. I can be very persuasive."

Anne looked up, trying to keep her voice light. His eyes carried no further than this conversation, but she couldn't help but think of the aggression in them earlier. "Well, she isn't very impressed," she said. "She's spent better meals in the barn."

Cassie saluted with a fork. "Touché."

"I'm an injured man," Jonathan defended himself. "I should at least be recognized for making the effort."

Cassie turned for Anne's reaction. Anne shrugged easily, permitting a smile she didn't feel. "I guess I feel pretty generous today. I'll give you points for remaining an enigma in the face of Cassie's persistence."

He grinned brightly. "I'll take that as a compliment."

"Was that so difficult?" Cassie asked as she helped dry dishes after lunch.

"Was what so difficult?"

"Talking to Jonathan."

Anne flashed her a sour look. "It's so important?"

"I'm not the one stuck in the same cabin with him," Cassie shrugged. "I can go home."

"And I can put him out into the snow. No jury in their right mind would convict me."

"Ease up, Annie. You were being entirely sociable in there after the first few minutes. Why the sudden change of attitude?"

Anne thought of his kiss and the unwanted fire it had ignited. And then she thought of Jonathan's eyes when he'd done it. She finished putting away the cups before answering. "Because I'll lay odds that the minute you walk out of here, he reverts to form."

"I think you're making all this up to protect your sense of self-righteous indignation."

"And I think he's putting on a show for you. The charming, witty, much-maligned rich boy from New York. I get the picture."

Cassie shrugged her resignation. "Okay, be that way. I was just trying to help. Since you won't accept it, I might as well go on home."

Anne took a look at the clock and nodded in agreement. It would be about dark by the time Cassie got home. Anne had to admit that she would sorely miss the enjoyment of her unpredictable company.

"Well, at least take some bread with you," she offered, reaching to pull some out.

"Caramel rolls, maybe," Cassie said, nodding. She hung her towel over the white pig's head that protruded from the wall by the sink and turned to Anne. "But there's something else I want more."

Anne looked over to see that Cassie had something important she wanted to say. "Well, spit it out."

Cassie grinned broadly. "The whole darn mountain wants to know what's in that letter."

Anne found herself staring suspiciously at Cassie. "What letter?"

Now it was Cassie's turn to stare. "Come on, Annie. The special delivery letter. Except for Mr. Harris, it's the most interesting thing to happen up here in months."

"Your sense of priority is beginning to atrophy," Anne said dryly. "In Boston the snow would have at least made honorable mention."

Cassie was not to be put off. "The letter, Annie."

Anne tried to shrug offhandedly as she walked Cassie over to her coat. "It was nothing. A bit of business about my mother's trust."

Cassie might have been satisfied with the explanation if she hadn't pulled her coat off the hall tree and sent the whole thing crashing onto its side.

"Oh, I'm sorry..."

Anne bent with her to pick up the various articles of clothes now scattered over the floor. "Don't worry about it, Cass. Next time I'm over for lunch, I'll dump out your silver drawer."

"Annie..."

Anne turned to see Cassie stand up beside the waste basket, unopened legal envelope in hand. "I knew I should have dumped that thing out," she muttered to herself.

"You didn't even open it."

Anne shrugged with forced nonchalance. "I make it a point not to correspond with people I don't like."

Cassie walked over and took Anne's hand, placing the envelope firmly in her grasp. "You can't ignore it, honey. It might be important. Just read it through once. While I'm in saying goodbye to Jonathan." She smiled with friendly warning. "Or, I'll read it myself." She waited until Anne had ripped open the envelope before heading for the guest room.

When Cassie returned to a few minutes later, it was to find Anne standing before the fireplace, letter in hand, her eyes staring and empty. Cassie's heart lurched. Something terrible had happened.

Chapter 5

"Annie? Annie, what's the matter?"

Anne couldn't bring herself to answer. She could only stare at and past Cassie as if she weren't there, shaking her head slowly. Cassie led her to the sofa and sat her down.

"I have to get to Boston," Anne finally managed to say, turning to her friend. "I have to go now before he closes."

"Closes what? Honey, what's in that letter?"

Anne took a breath to steady herself against the panic that threatened to choke her. "Cassie, he lost it. He's lost Cedar Ridge."

"What do you mean he lost it? Who lost it?"

"Brad. He put up the deed to Cedar Ridge to finance a futures deal . . . and he . . . he lost it." Her hands were at her mouth as if to stifle the enormous, overwhelming fear. It was too much to comprehend.

All she had asked was to be left alone. She hadn't wanted their money or their power or their madness. All she had wanted for the first time in her life was some peace. She had asked them for no more than the only home she had ever known and enough of her mother's estate to survive. No more. Now they'd taken even that from her.

"Anne, how could he do that?"

Again Anne shook her head, still trying to understand what her husband and brother had done to her. "Oh God, Cassie, I have to get up there and save it. I have to get to Boston."

"Annie, you can't. Nobody's going anywhere in this weather. I'm not even sure I can get a telegram out yet."

Anne stood, giving motion to the anger that was beginning to curl in her stomach, an anger that threatened to drown even the fear. She walked to the window, watching the snow as it drifted lazily across the yard. The sky was heavy with it, the wind picking up a little. The storm wasn't over, and she was trapped by it, impotent to stop her brother from selling her home out from under her to a resort developer. The snow, so benign and soft and white, whose quiet beauty she'd always loved, was stifling her and she wanted to scream. She wanted her hands, literally or figuratively, around her brother's neck. Better yet, Tom's. After all this time, she knew well enough who had orchestrated this deal.

"He can't really do it, can he?" Cassie asked. "It belongs to you both."

"It belongs to him. My father left me very little. Father was of the school that felt that money matters were better left to the men. That way Brad and Tom could take care of me." Anne turned from the window to find that Cassie had followed her over, anxiety creasing her forehead.

"You could contest it," her friend offered. "Maybe buy it outright. You have your mother's inheritance."

Anne shook her head, crowded again by the real fear that she would lose her cabin, her home. "That money is sunk in the clinic. I don't have enough to buy Cedar Ridge back." She found herself staring into the colors of the fire. The wood smoke lent a warmth to the air, a familiar comfort. The fireplace had been built by her father with stones from the mountain.

When Anne spoke again her voice was so quiet that Cassie could hardly hear it. "Cassie, what am I going to do?"

It was dark by the time Cassie finally left to go home. She tried to stay longer, insisting that Anne needed her there, but Anne was adamant. She didn't want Jim and the kids worrying about Cassie trying to get home, especially when more snow was threatening. Even though Cassie could see right through her and Anne knew it, she gave it one of the game-trooper routines as she saddled up Andy for Cassie's ride home.

"I'll be back up in the morning," Cassie promised.

"No you won't," Anne retorted evenly. "You have babies to take care of. Just set Andy loose tomorrow. He'll come home."

"Annie, you can't face this alone."

Anne's answering smile was genuine. "I won't, Cass. You can help most by keeping an eye out for the first flight to Boston. And by sending a telegram as soon as you can, telling them that I'm on my way."

"Do you want me to get ahold of your lawyer?"

For a moment, Anne blanked. "I don't have a lawyer."

Cassie stared at her. "You're kidding."

"No. I found out too late that the family friend I used for my divorce was a better friend of Tom's."

"You must know somebody."

"I'll find someone."

Cassie threw up her hands in frustration and turned to mount Andy. After knowing Anne for as long as she had, she knew better than to pursue the matter. Anne would, indeed, find someone. Cassie just hoped that whoever he was would be smart enough to save Anne's home. Cassie had a bad feeling about the whole thing.

Anne didn't go back inside for quite a while after Cassie had gone. The hard work she was able to do in the barn helped keep the terror at bay. Every time she paused, the words of her brother's terse letter returned to taunt her until she thought that the only thing left that would save her sanity would be for her to take a long hike into the woods for a good scream.

She had no idea how she would ever get any sleep until she made it to Boston. She wasn't even sure that she could stand to spend any time in the house. There were too many memories there for it to be comfortable tonight.

Surely it was a mistake or Brad's idea of a bad joke. She'd wake up tomorrow to find Jim at the door with another letter that said to disregard the previous one. Even Brad couldn't be cruel enough to pull her feet out from under her like that. Even Brad couldn't sell the land where he and seven other generations of Jacksons before him were born. It wasn't just home; it was a legacy.

Anne stopped a moment and leaned on the pitchfork she'd been using. Brad certainly would be stupid enough to let Tom do it all. And once done, Brad wouldn't give it a second thought. He had never been comfortable on the mountain, claiming that there were the spirits of too many ancestors wandering the place who probably didn't like him any more than his father did. He would never even know that the cabin was gone. Anne stared blankly ahead and fought back tears for the first time in two years.

"Have you been avoiding me again?" Jonathan demanded from his room as she walked past. She gritted her teeth, not at all sure she would be able to remain civil. She could tell that he had already discarded the gentlemanly demeanor he'd proffered to Cassie, and she was really afraid that his nasty personality would drive her beyond control this time.

"Do you need something?" she asked, going on through to the kitchen.

"A bit of beautiful company would be nice."

Anne reached the kitchen with its aroma of baking bread and suddenly wished that Cassie hadn't gone home. It was going to be difficult to even be in this room tonight where the memory of Anne's mother still lived in the warm aromas and frayed comfort of the furniture. The teakettle her grandmother had used sat on the stove, and the old kitchen witch that had hung in the sink window for as long as Anne could remember still kept the room safe. Even the old Depression dishes and glassware and the red gingham curtains that matched the tablecloth, familiar sights that had comforted her when she was first alone, now tore unbearably at her. How could she get through the night surrounded by what she would lose? How could she sleep with the memories whirling madly in her mind?

For the first time since she'd moved to the mountains Anne seriously considered getting drunk. She still had her father's old stock of liquor, so supply was no problem. Jonathan wouldn't care. Except for his leg, he was doing pretty well. Maybe if she were drunk, she could stand the additional strain of his company.

"Annie, you're ignoring me again."

She stalked to the door of his room. "The name," she said slowly, suddenly losing her temper, "is Anne. A-N-N-E. Now, what is it that you need?"

He feigned a hurt look. "What happened to noblesse oblige? We were doing so well when Cassie was here. I thought you were beginning to like me. She did."

"Cassie's a generous person."

"And I'm a tough one. You'll find that I don't intimidate easily." His smile was hard.

"More's the pity."

With her words the look in his eyes melted into the more familiar smugness. "I'll find a way, Anne Jackson. You're attracted to me. I consider your coolness a challenge. And I love challenges."

She refrained from comment. "Do you want dinner?"

"I want you." Again it seemed that his eyes didn't agree.

"That wasn't a choice."

His smile broadened. "It will be."

He ate alone. Finding that she needed most of her energy to cope with the news she'd received, Anne served dinner and cleaned up in near silence.

For Jonathan's part, even the momentary lapses he'd allowed into a gentler personality disappeared. He spent all his time true to form, goading and challenging, as if pushing Anne to react to his outrageous behavior. At any other time Anne wouldn't have given him the satisfaction. Tonight, it didn't seem to make any difference.

At nine, she found herself standing in the living room with nothing left to do to keep her occupied. The animals were bedded down, the house was sparkling clean for a change, enough baking had been done to last a month and Jonathan was quietly reading in his room. Anne sat alone with nothing to do but think about the letter.

She remained rooted in one spot searching desperately for something to do to keep her busy. It had to be involved enough that she'd have to pay attention to what she was doing. The needlepoint that sat on the sofa wasn't enough, and any of the books that lined the walls on either side of the fireplace were too much. She walked back into the kitchen and brewed some coffee, although she wasn't thirsty, and pulled out some cookies she didn't feel like eating.

"I was heating up some coffee and thought you might like some." She stood in the doorway of Jonathan's room with tray in hand. He looked up from his book, even more startled than Anne by her actions.

"What's this?" he asked. "A second chance?"

"Just coffee," she replied evenly.

"Will you sit with me?"

"For a moment." She heard herself say it and still couldn't believe it. His eyes were like aquamarines tonight, like faceted gems that flashed surface sarcasm and hid the deeper levels. She almost thought that if she moved a little she could find something else there. Well, at least sparring with him would keep her mind from Brad's idiocy.

"What shall we talk about," he asked, "your grandparents or mine?"

"Yours."

She set down the tray and stood to evaluate the condition of her patient. He'd been sitting up since morning and now looked stretched. "Would you like to get back to bed first?"

"I do that and I may not get around to the coffee."

She sat across from him in the straight-backed chair. "How are you feeling?"

He smiled, his eyes inexplicably softening. She didn't know why he seemed to be making an effort to be nice, but she was grateful. "Pretty good. When do I get to scale the living room?"

"In a couple days if you're still feeling like it. By tomorrow I imagine you can be up and around your room more."

"Child's play."

She had to laugh. "Only with a pair of sound legs and a full set of working ribs."

"I've made it with less."

She raised an eyebrow, believing him. "In that case, let's take a turn around the block now."

He met her gaze with a challenge of his own. "All right. I've been wanting to see what the living room looks like anyway."

Anne blinked. "You're serious."

His answer was given with a wry grin. "Best way I know of getting back on my feet is getting back on my feet."

The procedure for helping Jonathan to his feet was the same; the walk was not really that far. And the spark between them just as potent when they got close. Anne felt the tension ignite in her like a stifling pressure, threatening her breath and attacking her pulse.

Jonathan stood unsteadily and leaned against her, his chest heaving. Anne closed her eyes for a moment against the urge to hold him. To find those places she could share and cherish. For these fleeting moments of contact, she felt as if she had tapped a primal energy source, and that at the core of that energy lay the secret to Jonathan Harris. For those brief seconds, Anne found herself wishing that that core was made up of the blue of his eyes rather than the venom of his words.

"How long ago did you have that injury?" she asked as they made their way toward the door, Jonathan's arm tightly around her shoulders. Her arm circled his waist, and her hand spanned the scars.

"A long time ago."

"Fall off another cliff?" She couldn't believe how well he was doing. The lines of his face were etched with a fierce concentration that awed her. He never took his eyes from the far wall of the living room.

"Something like that."

"Why do you push yourself so hard?" The question came out before Anne realized: but she had to know. What drove him? What fires fueled that will?

For a moment he took his gaze from his objective and turned to her. Anne could almost see the flames deep in that blue, and a flash of vulnerability that tore at her.

"Twice in my life I was helpless to keep people I cared for safe from being hurt," he said turning back to the wall. "The second time it happened, I vowed never to be helpless again." They walked farther, his posture rigid. "Never."

They had made it back to the room before Anne spoke again.

"I think you can use the crutches tomorrow."

He nodded. "You didn't ask any questions about what I told you."

Anne gently swung him into bed, bending to support his injured leg as he brought it up. He looked so strained, so very tired for the effort he'd made.

"You aren't ready to tell me about it yet," she answered, sinking wearily into the chair.

Jonathan looked over in surprise. Anne knew she'd read him right when she saw the confusion. The vulnerability made a brief return to his eyes.

"Will you tell me what had you so upset earlier when your friend Cassie was here?"

Anne avoided his direct gaze, her hand picking at the lint on her jeans. "Oh, I, uh...find myself helpless to save something I care about."

When she finally lifted her eyes to him, they were rueful, the pain carefully hidden. It didn't seem to matter. Anne had the feeling that Jonathan found it anyway.

"Can I help?"

She shrugged uncomfortably, wondering where the enmity had gone. In the time it had taken to help Jonathan walk through the rooms of her house, they seemed to have gained an unexpected bond. The bond of unspoken understanding and respect.

"I don't know. I'm waiting for the phone to come back up, and for Cassie to get a telegram out."

His eyes were the gentlest she'd seen them. "Do you want to tell me about it?"

She shook her head, confused tears threatening. "No. Not now. I think both of us need a good night's sleep."

For a moment Jonathan's eyes melted, the blue a sweet, warm light in response to her pain. Then, before Anne could react to the change, a wall went up, a brittle, cynical edge that forced her away again. Once more Jonathan hid away where it was safe. He rolled over on his back and addressed the ceiling.

"Would you like another kiss?"

Anne stared, not as surprised as she should have been. It occurred to her how lonely his battles must be for him. "One per patient is my limit."

He turned to her with a slick smile. "Does that mean we're progressing to bigger and better things?"

Anne stood up suddenly and glared down at him. "I'm progressing to bed. Upstairs. Alone." She couldn't account for the unexpectedly shrill pitch of her voice. "If I hear one more ridiculous proposition out of you, you'll progress outside. In the snow. Alone!"

By the time she got up to the loft, she was wondering what had so abruptly set her off like that. She hadn't really been that taken aback by Jonathan's sudden mood swing. He'd done it before, and chances were, he'd do it again, even if he had begun to trust her with a glimpse behind his facade.

Anne looked back down toward where the guest room door was, as if to better divine an answer to a question that bothered her more than she wanted to admit. Without warning she was struck by the image of Jonathan's eyes as he'd talked about helplessness. The moment when they'd been so vulnerable, when Anne had wanted to reach out and ease the struggle there. Her mouth opened silently, her chest rising a little faster.

She had been so close to him at that moment, so close to whatever the real Jonathan Harris was, that it had frightened her. She didn't want to be close to him or any man; but especially to him. And yet she had begun to succumb to that translucent fire of his eyes, the electricity of his touch. When he'd turned on her again, betraying the moment of fragile contact with barbs tipped in malice, she had protected herself by biting at him like a shrew.

The same way he seemed to respond to her.

Anne stood where she was for a while longer, unable to go on. Something Cassie had said nagged at her about the little boy who hit the girl he liked the most. Oh Lord, she thought with sick dread, what if Cassie were right? What if Jonathan were as drawn to her as she was to him and reacted with the same defense mechanism? Anne thought of the abrupt personality changes, the jibes and directed attacks, and felt worse. It made more sense than she liked.

Please God, she prayed, not now. I can't handle this. I can't even handle the fact that I'm becoming more and more drawn to this man. His quiet strength and hidden pain, the brief flashes of empathy that give so much promise all compel me. A matched set of ambivalences is more than any person can handle in a small cabin in the snow. How can I be expected to deal with it now when my life is on the line?

Thanks all the same, but if you have a new love interest in mind for me, it'll have to be some other time or place. Or person. I can't afford this one.

Yet even as she consciously turned away from the thought of Jonathan, Anne couldn't avoid the fact that her heart still hammered oddly in her chest, or that she could feel his powerful arms around her as vividly as if he were actually there with her.

She knew it was futile, but she went about getting ready for bed, brushing her long hair, slipping into a long flannel nightgown and climbing in under her big down comforter before turning off the small light by her bed. Downstairs, the fire in the fireplace was slowly dying, its soft red light licking up the chimney opposite the loft. The house was quiet, the wind gently brushing through the pines outside. Somewhere an owl called, a low, mournful sound of night. It was chilly enough that the comforter felt like the embrace of familiar arms. A wonderful night to fall asleep. Only Anne couldn't.

She lay still in the pleasant warmth of her bed, trying her best to relax, and knowing that she wouldn't. She stared at the flickering shadow patterns on the ceiling without relief, the demons chasing her in the dark of midnight. First Jonathan's, and then the ones her brother and husband had unleashed.

As the night passed with agonizing slowness, the loss of her home drove everything else before it with a vengeance. Fears and ideas and plans raced madly in her head, each a desperate attempt to deal with the unbearable reality of what had happened. The irrational became plausible in the dark and the impossible possible.

It would be simple. She would confront Brad and force his hand, contest the will and buy the land back. She would walk up to Tom and laugh in his face when he told her it was all only a ploy to win her back. She'd laugh at both of them when they told her she'd never get the land back again. She could be in control. She'd worked two long years to repair the damage done to her self-esteem, and except for one incredibly handsome stranger with piercing eyes and Tom's mannerisms, she'd managed to maintain a respectable amount of independence.

All she had to do to save her home was get far enough away from Jonathan to escape his turbulent magnetism. She needed to travel to Boston where she could find some breathing room and hire a reputable, firebrand lawyer who wasn't already in her husband's pocket.

For hours she tossed and turned, her brain feverish with plans of confrontation, her body exhausted from the strain of the past three days. If only she had someone to talk to, someone she could call up and burden with the dread that refused to ease. If only there were a friend in Boston who could recommend the proper channels to take to save Cedar Ridge.

Again, she thought of the fact that she had left no friends in Boston. She'd left no friends anywhere in her former life. The relationships she'd formed when in nurses' training had died of neglect when she'd become taken up with the world her marriage to Tom had created, the world she'd been born to and groomed for her entire life.

The people she'd known in her hospital days had been the most similar to the ones she knew here on the mountain. They were a rare and good group of friends she would always regret having lost. The people she'd known during her marriage had never really been more than acquaintances, a supporting chorus to the choreography of her life as daughter to the chairman of the board. These people were only faces that filled out the background, no one she considered worth the effort of friendship. To a person, they had considered an important discussion one that debated how to best maximize the social season. She couldn't remember any one person who stood out. They had all been the same. And they were all useless.

She had no one left now to turn to for the help she needed.

For a moment, she considered asking Jonathan for help. It seemed only reasonable that after all she'd done for him he could find her someone to help her fight her way through the legal maze her ex-husband had constructed. She could go down to him and tell him how she was about to lose the only thing that meant anything to her in the world, and that he had to help her if only out of gratitude.

Then with a startling clarity she saw the look in his eyes when he'd found out who she was and what she'd done with her life. She knew how he'd react to this new twist to the story, gratitude or not.

It was with a feeling of desperation she hadn't known in two years that Anne finally fell into a tiring, fitful sleep some hours later.

By the next night Anne felt like a zombie. She'd still had to do the heavy work, and had even managed an hour-long trek into the white silence of the woods above the house, restoring some of the internal silence stolen by Jonathan's intrusion into her life.

He had been another matter altogether. Hovering precariously on crutches, Jonathan had, with her help, begun to make his way more comfortably around the rooms of the small house. In between treks, he spent his time in the chair by the window. He communicated a minimal amount, much to Anne's relief, but the time in the room with him further solidified the conclusions she had begun to form about him the night before.

Jonathan spoke little, but when he did he was again politely distant but distant, exerting the majority of his energy on recovering his mobility. He worked hard, never giving himself a break. In his silence, Anne saw the quiet, sweating determination of a man driven. Then, every once in a while, he would throw off a few biting retorts, as if making up for an oversight of some kind.

It probably would have been easier for Anne to handle just the sarcasm. That way she could have decided that her observations about a more vulnerable side to this man were nothing more than the product of wishful thinking. But she couldn't deny his courage in those moments when he tested his own will the way no city-pampered, egocentric executive would have. She knew that those times somehow connected with the brilliant smile he'd saved for Cassie. He was bitter only with Anne.

She was still worrying as she got ready for bed, her exhausted mind ricocheting from the dilemma of Jonathan to the impending confrontation with Tom.

No word had come from Cassie, and there was no letup in the snow. Anne couldn't last much longer. As hard as she tried, the terror returned, especially in the dark, when the dread grew exacerbated by the crowded night shadows. Anne knew that sleep would again be a long time coming.

When she first heard it, she thought it was her own dream. The sounds were garbled and frantic, rising and falling as if heard through a faulty speaker. Names, cries for help, more names. One name. A name she'd heard before, that teased at her memory. Anne's eyes shot open into the dark, a strange chill of prescience filling her.

Silence.

Only the soft ticking of her alarm clock broke the thickness of the early-morning hours. Even the wind had died, leaving her in a frightening void, unable to remember exactly what had awakened her.

Then, faintly she heard it again. A voice strange yet immediately recognizable, floated ghostlike from downstairs.

"Charlie... It's Charlie... He's got me...."

She held her breath, waiting, suddenly cold. The voice was haunted, belonging to a place of nightmares and pain, and she didn't want to approach it.

"Carson...get down...you've gotta... No, move back!" His voice rose to a cry, urgent and frightened. Anne tumbled out of bed. Grabbing her robe she headed for the stairs. She was afraid he'd be thrashing around and would hurt himself, the instinct of action propelling her before the plan of action had a chance to crystallize.

Anne flipped on a small light in the short hallway and stepped to the door, the light falling at an angle across the small bed. The bedclothes were snarled, and the spread was bunched tightly in Jonathan's hands. A fine sheen of perspiration reflected on his face.

"I can't get out . . . can't get out of his line here. . . ." He was struggling, fighting to get free of something. Anne could see him sweating and shaking, his hands opening and closing spasmodically around the blankets. She stood motionless in the doorway, mesmerized by a stranger's dream. She knew she should go and stop it before he hurt himself, and shouldn't let him go through the terror of whatever hell awaited him in his sleep, but his strange words held her rooted to the spot. She couldn't imagine what could possibly have such a terrible grip on his subconscious. The man Jonathan Harris seemed to be would have no room for nightmares.

His next words seared straight through her.

"Eddie, I can't get to you. . . . I'm . . . I'm hit . . . ah, God . . . Corpsman . . ."

He was grabbing at his side, where Anne had found the scars, and writhing in the bed whimpering. "Corpsman, let him . . . No, I'll . . . I can . . . Eddie."

Vietnam.

Anne's hand found her gaping mouth. Oh, dear God, she thought, her stomach knotting up and unbidden tears clouding her vision as she watched Jonathan flounder in his private hell. He'd been in Nam. The Charlie he'd rambled on about wasn't a specific person as she'd assumed. It had been the Vietcong.

She couldn't take her eyes from him, couldn't move to help him. What she saw left her confused and shaken. She wanted to back out the door and escape the pain that echoed in this room. She had enough of her own to consider courting his.

He was quiet a moment, and Anne saw his hand reach out to something, as if to touch it. He made a small blind stroking motion, the way a mother might touch the face of a child.

"Eddie," he whispered. "I'm sorry, Eddie...I...I tried...."

She didn't even realize that she'd moved until she found herself beside his bed. He still writhed, the sounds in his throat rising from an anguish that cut through Anne like a hot knife. She didn't feel the tears on her cheeks as she moved to gather him into her arms.

For a few long moments all Anne could do was hold him to her, rocking him and stroking his wet, tangled hair, her murmurs meant to comfort them both. He held onto her like a lifeline, his choked sobs released with the comfort of her touch. His hands found the rich fall of her hair and wound into it. Anne eased into his touch, bringing him closer.

She never saw his eyes open, and didn't realize that he'd turned his face to hers. When she felt his lips find hers, she responded out of instinct, out of the turmoil she'd brought to this room and the anguish she'd found there. Bending to him, she met his lips with her own and became lost within him.

Anne never had the chance to question what was happening. When Jonathan pulled her down to him, she followed blindly. His embrace was desperate, his hands searching her with almost frantic need. She clung to him, absorbing the fierce possession of his mouth with her own and purging her own pain with the feel of him. Her gown was no barrier to his callused, seeking fingers. He discovered the taut nipples that strained beneath him and consumed them with chafing discovery. Anne heard a small sobbing sound and realized it was her own. Her mind was a maelstrom and her body was on fire. From the moment he'd kissed her there had been no turning away. She felt herself drowning, pulled under by the ferocious pain that had been unleashed by a nightmare and trapped there by her own need to share and salve it. She stroked the planes of his face and the rigid line of his throat, comforting, seeking, the explosion building in both of them driving her beyond reason. Jonathan bruised her mouth with his explorations and savaged her skin with his fire.

His hands trembled when he found her thighs. Anne gasped at their strength. She turned her head to the side, somehow to be free, but Jonathan found her there and brought his mouth down again on hers, harsh with his need. His lips searched her face, her eyes, her forehead, their taste reckless. She arched against him, against the fire that swept her, an agony that was hard to distinguish from the pain. Her own hands sought, roaming along muscle and sinew that stretched in unyielding lines over chest and shoulder, hips and steely thighs.

It was only when his hand forced her thighs apart that she felt any fear. He was desperate with the need for release, for union. She was afraid she'd be hurt. Instinct brought her hands up to him, to find the rock-hard surface of his chest. He was panting against her, his body slick with sweat. She wanted to beg caution and care, but couldn't manage the words. Couldn't even bear to question what fires lit those coalescent eyes. The unbearable heat built in her as his fingers found her and silenced her protest.

Their joining was cataclysmic, as if by uniting they could purge their ghosts. Anne thought she would be crushed by him, engulfed by the white hot light he ignited in her. Her arms came up, her legs circled him, pulling him even closer as he drove into her. His face was buried in her throat, his hands grinding her against him. She arched to meet him. The agony in her belly was unbearable, the sweet torment of his gasping cry, torture. They rocketed faster, their passion soaring beyond need or pain.

Jonathan lifted his head then, his eyes trapping Anne's with their wild, piercing light. She threw her head back to keep those eyes before her, but he took her mouth again, his tongue hot and searching, his breath ragged against her. He brought his hands down to trap her body against his, his pelvis sharp against her soft skin, and thrust into her with a force that made her cry out. What hunger drove her she didn't know but it matched his bruising strength. She brought her hands to his buttocks and forced him back to her again. And the explosion came, rocking them both and tearing gasps from them as they shuddered and clung desperately and spent themselves in each other.

The old clock in the living room struck three, and Anne could hear the wind outside rise a little. In this room the stillness slowly returned, and peace crept back from the dim, shadowed corners where a terrifying dream had chased it. She felt Jonathan's breathing ease, felt his hold on her relax toward sleep. Her own body refused her the release.

Her life in this house had changed tonight. Jonathan had brought out something in her that she had long hidden away. She had been compelled by more than compassion to go to him, by more than empathy for a lonely, hurt person caught in the throes of terror. She had been drawn to him because his pain had seared through her in a way that had never happened before. And she had stayed, she realized now, because her need to give to Jonathan had been greater than his need to lose himself in her. There was nothing she would not do to keep him from having to face that kind of desolation again.

The clock struck again before Anne turned from the sight of Jonathan's soft, sleeping face toward the door, her steps carrying another burden as great as her own. She had to get out of this cabin before she lost her mind. Had to get away and come back, and then maybe she could understand everything that was going on.

"Anne..."

She turned to see that he was awake, his eyes sleep-clouded and unsure. There was no guile there to confront, and Anne suddenly wished there were.

"I . . . was just going. . . ." she stammered, trying to turn again. "It's pretty late."

"Anne."

His voice was strained. Anne turned again and managed to face him. But they had no more words. Their walls had gone back up, the pain of contact too great. They were already far apart, and she didn't think they'd let each other close again.

Chapter 6

It wasn't until the next afternoon, after more long hours of near-silent work with Jonathan, the tedious, mind-numbing waiting alternating with spurts of fierce work, that Anne finally heard from Cassie.

Cassie's call was the first to make it over the repaired lines. By the time the phone rang Anne was pacing around the living room.

"Annie, are you all right?"

"What did they say, Cass?"

There was a pause, a gathering of tact. "I got a telegram. And a phone call."

"A call?"

"Yeah. Hon, it doesn't sound good."

Anne stared out the front window as Cassie explained. The snow was so brilliant, so peaceful. The pine trees she'd watched grow since childhood strained under the weight of it.

The telegram had been brutally curt. If Anne wished to interfere, she would have to do so when Brad and Tom met the new owners in New York. But there was really nothing she could do. The land was sold and Anne had no say in the matter. The accompanying phone call from Tom had contained a threat, thinly veiled as a bribe: if Anne would come home, all would be well.

"Now I know why you left. Tom has all the charm of a pet cobra."

Anne looked up distractedly. "I can get to New York in time?"

Cassie nodded. "Tomorrow. I have it all set. But who are you going to get in New York to help?"

"I don't know. I'll find someone. I still know some people in New York." Couturiers and maître d's, she thought.

"Honey, you'd better get somebody really good. I've heard hardball players flex their muscles before, and your ex-husband made all the right noises."

Anne couldn't answer.

"Annie? Honey, are you okay? Do you want me to come up?"

"Uh, no." Anne wondered if she should tell Cassie about what had happened during the night but decided not to. She still wasn't at all sure herself about what had happened. She just knew that she could hardly bear to be near Jonathan anymore, especially when both of them were held so rigidly by their uncomfortable silence. Anne knew that whatever it was she had discovered in herself when she'd been in his arms was interfering with her ability to handle Tom's threat to her with composure and common sense. She was afraid that she was beginning to lose control.

The sound of Cassie's voice brought her abruptly back from her thoughts. "It'll be okay, Annie. You'll see."

Anne's eyes burned. The snow was too bright, the future too frightening. "I hope so, Cass. I'll see you tomorrow."

Anne hung up the phone and stood for a long few minutes without being able to move. She stared abjectly out at the scenery she had so come to cherish.

"Do you want to tell me about it now?"

Startled, she jerked around. Jonathan was standing by the hallway arch, his eyes understanding. The very sight of him, so strong and determined, brought the tears back. Anne stood silently before him, her hand on the phone, and shook her head helplessly, completely at a loss.

Before she could gather the composure to speak, he'd hobbled up to her and put his hand out. "Come on. Let's sit down here so you can tell me what's going on."

Still she balked, even as he guided her to the couch. Trust was difficult to give in her world. "You don't need this kind of headache."

"You need to talk," he retorted, easing her into the cushions and then gingerly taking a seat next to her. "And who knows? I might be able to help."

"Why should you help me?"

His smile was rueful. "After last night that's kind of a stupid question."

She gave no quarter. "It would be a stupid question if you hadn't already done several one-eighties already. How do I know you're not looking for another excuse to bare your claws?"

For a moment Jonathan looked down at his hands, as if marshalling his thoughts. When he looked back up, Anne thought she had never seen eyes so empathetic. It was as if he had looked away to allow his defenses to fall a little.

"You only have my word, I guess," he admitted, taking her hand. She felt the strength there and longed to be able to rely on it. It had been so long since she'd been able to share any of her burdens.

"But you're right," he went on. "I have been an ass. There's an explanation for it, but it's too involved. I'm sorry, Anne."

"Well," she conceded, "you do have a point." She managed a grin. "You were an ass."

He grinned back, and Anne found herself wondering how long this truce would last. It was all beginning to hurt too much.

"I'm going to lose my home," she finally said, feeling vulnerable and terrified by it. "I have two weeks to prevent it from happening."

"You'll let me help?"

It was hard to meet his eyes. She kept seeing the savage light in them the night before. "I don't know yet. What do you think you can do?"

He shrugged, wincing as his ribs rubbed uncomfortably. "I don't know. It depends on what's going on. I'm a lawyer."

Anne found herself smiling again, the light in her eyes wary. "Of course you are."

"You don't believe me."

It was her turn to shrug. "Maybe if you had some identification."

"I'm serious, Anne. I am a lawyer. I got my law degree from NYU."

"Corporate law, no doubt."

A brief twinkle touched his eyes. "This time, it might be what the doctor ordered."

She couldn't help but flash a big smile at that. "Are lawyers always so original?"

"I can only think fast on my feet when I'm on my feet. Now, are you going to take me up on my offer?"

She was weakening beneath the bright candor of his handsome eyes, and it made her furious. She knew better than to trust an attractive smile. It had taken her months to begin to trust even Cassie and Jim, months she'd spent alone in the cabin, often without venturing out for days on end. Her faith in others had been shattered because she'd once trusted a man with a handsome smile.

But she'd never seen in Tom the emotion she'd found in Jonathan's eyes. Tom had been pure predator: first, last and always. He would never have had room in his character for the compassion she'd discovered in Jonathan. He didn't have the strength, the courage or the vulnerability. Tom had never reached out to another human being in his life, unless it was to further the career and material fortunes of Tom McCarthy. In one harrowing hour before dawn, Anne had realized that the same couldn't be said about Jonathan.

But could the aftermath of the nightmare make all the difference, when every other time she'd allowed him close he'd hurt her?

Before she knew it, she was telling him the whole story. She spoke of Tom's duplicity, her father's death and the deal she'd made with her husband and brother to set her free of their obsession with the company, and how Brad had now managed to throw away her home on a speculation.

When she looked up at the story's finish, she was surprised to see that Jonathan listened quietly, his eyes analyzing and alert. He'd assumed a professional demeanor, as if he were sitting behind a mahogany desk in a three-piece suit rather than propped stiffly on her living-room couch and clothed in Brad's old pajamas. Although his background was still a mystery, Anne was satisfied that he was a lawyer just as he'd said.

"Do you remember any agreements you might have signed?" he asked.

She had to shrug. "Divorce papers relinquishing alimony and the promise not to contest my father's will. I don't know. At that point in my life I wasn't thinking too clearly."

"That's understandable," he nodded. "Who was your lawyer?"

"Frank Wilson. Wilson, Talmadge, Pierce & Franklin of Boston."

"And you think he was in your husband's pocket?"

"I didn't have to think it. Brad finally told me so. He has the need to gloat."

Jonathan shook his head slowly, absently staring at the far wall as he contemplated what she had said. Finally his attention returned to her, his manner all business. Again, Anne had the passing feeling that she was really sitting in an office. "Could they have done anything illegal?"

"Why do you say that?"

"I don't know," he said with a shrug. "Maybe the over-kill when you finally got in touch with them about this. Something's making them nervous."

Anne offered a dry smile. "You don't think my ex-husband wants me back because he can't live without me?"

Jonathan was polite enough not to answer.

Because he had no more questions, Anne knew she had to find out. The effort alone brought the fear back; an iron band tightened around her chest and closed her throat.

"Am I going to lose it?" she asked, her voice sounding very small.

Jonathan turned to her, his eyes troubled. "I don't know, Anne. You might. But you're a strong woman. Even if you do..."

Anne straightened abruptly, her eyes glittering with unshed tears. "You don't understand. This," she said, opening her arms to take in her surroundings, "is all I have. It's all I have left to remind me that I once had a family and was happy. It's the only place where there's anything left of my mother and father. I may get a new house, but I'd have no past. No memories to keep what I went through with Tom and Brad in its place." To keep what she was beginning to feel for Jonathan in its place. Her sense of stability was floundering and only the permanency of the cabin kept her upright sometimes. "This is my anchor, my sanity. Without it I would have lost my mind."

Holding her hand even more tightly, Jonathan captured her eyes with his own, offering her his strength and support, an understanding she knew to be genuine. He nodded to her and brought his other hand to her cheek.

"Then we'll have to fight like hell, won't we?"

Anne managed a small smile, fighting for some composure. "Sounds like a good game plan to me."

He gave her another nod and a smile, the winter light from the window clean and bright against him. Anne took a deep breath and surrendered her trust.

"All right then," he decided. "Let me make a call to someone I know in New York. I can give him the basics now, and you can fill in the details when you get there. He's the best you can get."

"My husband and brother don't own him?"

Jonathan's face lit with an almost piratical smile, teeth gleaming unnaturally. "That," he assured her with finality, "I can guarantee."

She finally nodded back, unaccustomed to the feeling of relief that struggled to take shape in her. "In that case, I'll get dinner while you call."

As she headed into the kitchen, she heard Jonathan dial. "Judson Fredericks, please. Tell him it's Jonathan Harris."

Jonathan finally allowed Anne to steer him to bed when she told him she wasn't staying up any longer to baby-sit him. She saw the weariness escape into his eyes as he let her cover him. He had paled a little, the lines along his mouth etched more deeply. She wanted so much to tell him to ease up on himself, to acknowledge his pain and let her help as he'd helped her. But she knew that this was a place severely guarded in him. He had to let her in first.

Anne stood next to his bed, caught between the image of the man who'd woken up in her house and the one who had offered to help save it.

"Jonathan, thank you," she said quietly. "I have to admit that until you gave me the name of your friend, I didn't know what I was going to do."

He smiled up at her, reaching over to take her hand. "Like I said, it's my way of saying I'm sorry. Besides..." His voice faded as he sought words that didn't seem familiar. "I had to thank you, too." His eyes searched hers. Something deliberate was happening and she wasn't sure she was ready yet.

"It's been a long time since someone's been that... unselfish." The struggle grew on his features, revealing the need for protection, the yearning for communication.

Anne sat gently on the edge of the bed, her hand still in his. She held his eyes just as surely. "I have nightmares, too," she said gently. "Would you like to talk about it?"

Jonathan had to look away. The ghosts were there, so close, and their pain was infecting him anew. Anne felt him stiffen and held her breath.

"You said that there were two times you were helpless to save someone else from being hurt." God, she wanted to hold him again. That dying light in his eyes couldn't possibly hurt more if it were her own. "Was that one of the times?"

For a long moment he remained very still, his eyes looking into hers. Anne waited. She heard the clock again, its rhythm the slow, steady pacing of time. The house muttered around her, and the fire popped in the living room. Her eyes were only on Jonathan as he fought his own battles of trust.

Finally, he nodded. "I was a platoon leader in Nam. Dong Ha. We were searching out VC hideouts when we ran across a whole network of tunnels." Anne felt the pressure build in her as he talked, his cadence as carefully measured as the clock's. "It was an ambush. Out of twenty men, only three of us survived. Ten were blown to hell in the middle of those tunnels." He stopped again, the images so vivid to him that even Anne imagined she could see them. The friends, the kids, the men who'd depended on him dying around him when he couldn't stop it. "We never even saw them. My best friend died right in front of me. He was supposed to be rotated out the next week."

Eddie. Anne felt the tears catch in her throat, a pain of frustration and futility welling in her. Jonathan finally looked up at her, only weariness left in his beautiful eyes, and offered a last shrug. "We never even saw 'em."

"Have you ever gone to see his family?"

"I haven't even been to the Vietnam Memorial." He found something in his hand to study. "I keep telling myself I'll go one of these days. Who knows?" he said with a shrug. "Maybe I will."

"Would it be easier if someone went with you?"

He showed his surprise. That was evidently not a question he'd often been asked. "I don't know. Mind if I think about it?"

"Not at all," she said smiling hesitantly, as surprised as he was that she'd made the offer. "I think I have to do the same."

They allowed each other tentative smiles. Things had changed a lot in a few days.

For a long moment Anne looked down at the handsome, magnetic, lonely man who had exploded into her life like a thunderclap. Unable to express herself in any other way, she bent forward and gently kissed him.

The lips she met were surprisingly tender, the feel of his cheek rough and strong. Instinctively her free hand reached for the curve of his jaw, as if it were a magnetic source of balance. Her fingers found it and tingled with the contact. Her own lips grew pliant, opening to the questioning probe of his tongue.

The brief meeting electrified her. It was as if she had found a wellspring, and the cold, clear waters that surged from it now suffused her body with a giddy effervescence that shocked her. She could hear her breath catch in a sob, deep in her throat, and her eyes closed against the delicious pain of it.

As if it were a natural progression, Jonathan reached up with his own hand and sought the warmth of her breast. Abruptly Anne straightened, his touch still searing her, her nipples stiff against the material of her shirt. Yearning leaped through her like lightning. Looking down at the message in Jonathan's eyes, she knew that she'd come perilously close to losing herself in him.

"You're a beautiful woman, Anne."

The blue of his eyes was suddenly intense, seething. For the first time in two years, Anne remembered what it was to feel beautiful in a man's eyes, to be regarded as desirable rather than capable. She caught her breath, arrested by the feeling, overwhelmingly frightened. For a long moment she could do no more than hold Jonathan's gaze, her hand still lost in his.

"I'm going to have to be able to get out of the mess I'm in before I can deal with new..." She didn't know what to call what was flaring hotly between them. She was afraid it was born of need rather than desire. All she could see was the light chilling once again in his eyes. "We have to be careful, Jonathan. Please understand."

A distance grew between them. Anne stood to a stiff kind of attention. This sudden fear was as powerful as the longing Jonathan had kindled in her. She had been betrayed by her own feelings, and now she knew that she wouldn't be able to untangle herself from this without at best involvement, at worst the kind of pain she loathed. And Anne had a feeling that it had already gone past the point of painless resolution.

She fled to her room without another word, unable to bear anything else Jonathan might admit. He never challenged her, but as the sun finally struggled up the next morning, Anne wasn't the only one who still hadn't fallen asleep.

She left in the morning without ever really talking to him. They passed social amenities as she brought in his breakfast and changed his dressings, but the air was charged and uncomfortable. It wasn't until Mary Dickey—the woman Anne had asked to take care of Jonathan in her absence—

arrived with her two children that Anne finally went in to say goodbye.

When Jonathan caught sight of the preschoolers and considered their combined decibel level with a pained eye, Anne couldn't help but flash him a smug grin. He returned it with one of his own and invited the four-year-old to sit next to him. For a minute, it was as if the night before had never happened.

Anne got on the plane to New York with a sense of unease, unable to keep what had happened out of her mind. In the light of day, it almost seemed a delusion to think that Jonathan really cared for her. She'd probably read too much into the situation.

They had offered each other friendship, understanding and help. He had admitted as much when he'd thanked her for understanding what had happened after the nightmare. Unfortunately, as they became dependent on each other in the isolation of that little cabin, they could easily find themselves in a relationship neither of them wanted or could afford. Their combined emotions were fuses that ignited a pretty powerful powder keg.

Damn it, Anne thought, I'd just made it to the point of equilibrium. Maybe she wasn't ecstatically happy, but she'd been content. After all the years spent in the role of Pete Jackson's daughter and Tom McCarthy's wife she had finally forged the true cast of Anne Jackson, and she liked it. She was happy with herself. Jonathan Harris was a strong-willed, dominant personality, one who considered being in charge of his birthright. Anne wasn't at all sure that he was the kind of man who would encourage a wife to be independent.

He couldn't possibly understand what had gone into the building of Anne's self-determination. Or what it had cost.

She couldn't let him tamper with it and possibly do it irreparable harm. Somehow, she'd have to hold on to her objectivity.

An awfully easy thing to decide in daylight. Especially three hundred miles away from the spell of his eyes.

Chapter 7

Anne had lied about disliking New York. She loved it. She could go there to just sit in one place for days and watch it, soaking in its kinetic energy as if recharging her batteries. Even when she'd lived in Boston, coming to New York had been like an electric shock. The amassed energy of twelve million people trapped within the high, skyscrapered canyons radiated like heat shimmering off streets in summer, charging the atmosphere like a thunderstorm. Her adrenaline shot up just by stepping onto the street.

Now, returning to the city after her isolation in the ageless mountains, Anne felt as if she'd just been thrown into a pool of cold water. She couldn't help smiling to herself as she walked along the crowded streets.

She found herself strolling down Sixth Avenue. The day was brisk, the sky, briefly seen near the break of Central Park, an almost bright blue above the smog. There had been no snow in the city and the streets were clear. Buses, cabs and limos chased along in fox and hound fashion, threatening the crazier pedestrians who stepped onto the street and challenged oncoming traffic like mad toreadors.

Dodging traffic was a game in New York. Anne refrained from trying her hand at it. It had been too long since she had competed, and she was afraid that her timing might be off. Besides, she had an armful of packages to protect.

It would be important to show a good face when she finally met up with Tom and Brad, so she'd stopped off at a few of the designer salons that were scattered along the upper Sixties. The salespeople she'd once known well had greeted her like a ghost returned from the grave. When she'd told them where she'd been the past few years, the reaction had been a universal pause and polite embarrassment for want of something to say.

Typical of these had been Madelyn, a tall, handsome woman who ruled over one of the most prestigious salons with rigid attention to suave style and judicious subservience. She had come to the door personally, hands outstretched as if greeting the proverbial prodigal child.

"Anne, my dear," she'd almost gushed. "We thought . . . well, of course we heard about the divorce. I'm so sorry." Feeling Anne out, she carefully cast for clues to the appropriate direction for the conversation. "We thought you'd simply gone on vacation."

Anne smiled, realizing this was like roller-skating. She'd need to work on her balance a bit more before really hitting the streets, but it was all coming back to her pretty quickly. "No," she admitted with a smile, "I've just moved."

The woman paused again, her eyes careful. "To the coast?" Those three words sounded more like, "We thought better of you." She'd probably never seen the other bank of the Hudson in her life. Anne couldn't wait to see how she'd react to the truth.

"No. I'm living in the mountains."

A nod, the same momentary confusion. "The Catskills?"

"The Appalachians." She let the woman founder only a moment, still holding both of her hands, before saving her. "My father had a retreat there. I needed the...well, the quiet. You understand."

"Of course," Madelyn nodded quickly, now on safe ground as she let Anne's hands go with a squeeze in preparation for getting down to business. "It's most understandable. And you look wonderful. The fresh air, I imagine. You positively glow, my dear."

And so Anne spent the first part of the day in New York readying herself to deal with its people again, getting her rhythm back for the games of the civilized animal. She had to worry about facing not only her brother and husband, but the lawyer Jonathan had recommended to her. After her years of experience she knew only too well how important it would be to make the correct first impression with this man, because she'd have to depend on him. There was truthfully no one else she had to turn to.

In one handshake, she would have to let the lawyer know that she was a woman to respect, not just the former arm ornament of Tom McCarthy. There could be no mistaking her intentions or commitment. And if this lawyer were anything at all like Jonathan, she would have her work cut out for her.

Now, as Anne approached the Café de la Paix on the southeast corner of the park, its striped awning rolled up, she was still smiling. It had been a good day for getting her legs back. She only wished she could have the time to sit by the window and eat a leisurely lunch, watching the human traffic pass along the park. But time was at a premium. She had an appointment to keep.

She settled for a long walk around the fountain at Fifty-Ninth where street musicians played a strange jazz piece for tuba and guitar before she turned into the Plaza Hotel. Anne always stayed there when she was in town, never quite wanting to move away from Central Park, even to the clean geometric lines of some of the newer hotels farther south.

There had even been a townhouse Tom had kept closer to Greenwich Village when he'd found that that was the thing to do, but Anne had always returned to the old-world grandeur along the park where she could enjoy what was to her the only green in the city.

Room service supplied a light lunch while Anne painstakingly dressed and groomed herself for her appointment with Jonathan's friend, sweeping her hair once more up into the simple chignon that Tom had preferred. She wore a two-piece red wool suit with short bolero jacket whose lines fell crisp and clean over her trim figure.

She had carefully chosen her small wardrobe for its simple, classic lines, because these best suited her and her mission. Today, she wore no more ornamentation than alligator pumps and pearl stud earrings. The effect was cool and professional. Anne looked more like a high-powered executive than a rural nurse. There was no doubt in her mind as she stepped into the cab taking her to the lawyer's office that she would need every bit of control she could muster to match the picture she presented. She couldn't get out of her mind the image of Jonathan as he delivered his well-placed barbs born of this city's cannibalism. It was all she could hope that his friend had a little more class than that.

When Anne walked into the office of Judson Fredericks, she was stunned. Walking toward her with an outstretched hand and warm smile was not another Manhattan flash, but a gentleman with the air of a Southern plantation owner. Judson was a handsome, tall, ramrod-straight, old-school lawyer who oozed confidentiality and trustworthiness. His handshake was firm and his smile brimming with the essence of cordiality. He led her into his office and sat her in a comfortable leather chair across from his desk before moving around to seat himself.

The office was decorated in dark paneling and leather, the perfect background to Judson's soft voice, distinguished head of silver hair and deceptively lazy eyes. His attitude toward her was almost openly paternal. It made her want to smile.

The first few minutes of polite observation of formal rules of office etiquette served them both to gain the other's respect. The call from Jonathan provided an easy introduction to business.

"Jonathan said he'd had an accident near your home," Judson said, frowning. "But he refused to illuminate me beyond the usual platitudes. Is he all right?"

"He's fine." Anne smiled. "He injured himself in a fall near where I live, and we were forced to keep him there due to snow and road conditions."

"There isn't any way to get him to a hospital?"

"I live in an isolated area behind the Great Smoky Mountain National Park, and it's a long, hard way to the hospital from there. Especially for a man with a broken leg and a couple of broken ribs."

He nodded, appeased. "Well, I'll certainly take your word for it. But please do tell me if there is anything he needs, and I will be more than happy to make the necessary arrangements." With this, he settled into his chair, as if to signal a change in the direction of the conversation. "In the meantime, let's look into what brings such a beautiful lady to my office. I've been able to begin gathering information on what Jonathan has told me, but I would like to hear the story again in your words."

Anne took a moment to gather her thoughts together, thinking that she already felt she couldn't have brought her problems to a better man.

She told him everything, slowly and in detail, and Judson listened attentively, not even making notes until she had finished. The window behind him suffused the room in soft gray light from the sky high above lower Manhattan. The office itself was silent but for the measured cadence of Anne's words, her manner as carefully composed as her appearance.

The silence, as comfortable as the dark overstuffed furniture, closed in again as Anne finished. Mr. Fredericks finally broke her gaze to contemplate what she'd told him, nodding quietly to himself and tapping on the mahogany desk with manicured fingers.

After a few long moments, he looked up thoughtfully. "Would you like your inheritance back?"

She wondered for a moment if he'd really heard what she'd just said. "I want my land. Nothing more."

"I ask because I'm not sure we can go only that far. You must challenge your brother's right to use that land as collateral for a personal loan. If we go so far as contesting your father's original will. You could end up with more than you bargained for."

She sighed. "All I'm saying, Mr. Fredericks, is that I don't care what they do anymore. I want none of it. I only want my home. But I will do whatever is necessary to keep it."

Again, he considered. Anne kept very still, her hands folded precisely over her bright red skirt. The rich smell of leather and thick carpeting should have soothed but somehow stifled a little.

"I'll have to do some work on it and that will take a little time," Mr. Fredericks finally said, looking back up with studious eyes. "Will you be in New York long?"

"No." She shook her head slightly. "I have to get back. I'll be back next week for the meeting with Amplex Corporation."

"Yes. Fine. And how should I contact you if I need to?"

"I'll leave you an address and a number."

He studied her a moment, considering her features and bearing, her sleek, rich hair, Gucci shoes, the well-manicured nails and faultless bearing. Then he afforded himself a warm smile of wonder. "I, of course, know of your family, Miss Jackson. And I have heard of Peter Jackson's home in the Smokies. But seeing you now, I simply cannot imagine your living there alone."

Anne returned his smile, content that she had made the impression she had sought. "Everyone has his own paradise, Mr. Fredericks. Some day you must allow me to show you mine."

His smile broadened, and again he nodded. "I think it must be a special place. I would consider the invitation a privilege. Hopefully, I'll get the chance to accept."

Anne stood to go, longing to ask about Jonathan's connection with this man, but for some reason hesitated to bring it up. She extended her hand to wish the distinguished lawyer goodbye. When he clasped it with genuine enthusiasm Anne's spirits rose. This man would indeed help her. And again she marveled at the enigma of Jonathan Harris, this man's friend.

The meeting with Judson so encouraged her that she decided to take things a step further and chance facing Tom. There would be nothing to be gained by putting it off, and she thought that he needed to be unsettled a little. It might be good to let him know that Anne wasn't the same person she was when she'd left Boston.

She was quickly surprised by a good portent. When she called to make her accommodations for the visit to Boston before heading home, she found out that both Tom and Brad were in New York on business. She could drop in on them, and without having to overcome the disadvantage of facing them on their home field. She'd have no trouble finding them: she knew exactly where they'd be.

Late in the afternoon Anne stood in her hotel room, readied for the meeting. Turning a careful circle before the mirror, she performed a final inspection. All was perfect. It was as if she'd never left. The vermilion suit highlighted the sun whiteness of her blond hair, the simple style of it offsetting her lithe legs. She had added the diamond-and-sapphire earrings her mother had left her to round out the effect.

Simple and smashing, Tom had always said. Well, he was about to get the full dose of both. Anne hoped that she was still good enough to hide the weakness in her knees and the nest of butterflies that had nested in her stomach. Standing tall and self-assured before the mirror, she smiled. She seemed smooth and cool. She could do it. She hoped.

Anne pulled on the fur jacket that would complete the picture and reached for her purse. A cab was waiting downstairs that would take her to the restaurant where Tom and Brad would be finishing their dinner. When she stepped into the taxi, the wide-eyed admiration of the cabbie was not lost on her. She wished her stomach would settle down a little.

The restaurant was small and elegant. The decor dramatically simple in chrome and burgundy. Anne had known the maître d' for years and found it embarrassingly simple to find out from him that, true to form, Tom and Brad would be dining there before flying back to Boston. She approached the desk precisely at six, knowing how well she had timed her arrival. Louis looked up from his book, his eyes widening in delight.

"Mrs..." he faltered, embarrassed.

Anne quickly saved him from discomfort. "Louis, when are you going to call me Anne?" she said, smiling.

He melted visibly. "It has been too long since we have seen you. Will you be having dinner tonight?"

"After I've taken care of some disagreeable business, Louis. Where are they?"

"The same." He shrugged. "Always the same. Would you like me to take you?"

"No, thank you, Louis," she said, smiling. "I think I'll pop in on my own."

His smile didn't quite match hers, but he nodded her on with some enthusiasm. She walked back into the darkened restaurant, knowing that she wouldn't see them until she was almost upon them. They always ate at the same table in the back, shielded by Plexiglas and muted lighting. A rush of nostalgia threatened her composure as she remembered the times she, too, had been included in the meals here.

Ever since she'd been twelve, when her father had first set up his friend Louis in a business that was now one of the top five restaurants in New York, the Jacksons dined at Chez Louis. Once a week, without fail, they'd be seated at booth fifteen.

"Tom, Brad. I see that you don't break tradition easily."

She stood by the table, praying that she could hold out, wondering what the hell she was doing here. One look at Tom had almost been her downfall. With his blond, well-groomed good looks and smoky-green eyes he couldn't possibly be more handsome or magnetic if he tried. His face was intelligent and controlled, his nose straight, his mouth sensual and his chin perfectly firm. She knew that she was still mesmerized by him and hated herself for it.

In her confusion she almost lost the satisfaction of seeing the shock on their faces. They had just finished dinner. Coffee had been poured and Tom was just about to light up a cigarillo. The match burned out in his fingers.

Abruptly, they stood. Anne smiled with cool eyes.

"What are you doing in New York?" Brad asked sharply.

She eyed him without flinching. "It's nice to see you, too, Brad dear."

It struck her again how truly unremarkable Brad was. He had the kind of face that radiated weakness. His eyes were brown and his lips thin. The only kind thing Anne could say about him was that he had grown a moustache since she'd last seen him, and that it made him seem to blend more easily into a crowd.

Anne had not always disliked Brad. In fact, at one time in their lives, they'd been rather close. That had been when her mother had been alive. Her mother had been able to bring out the best in him. When she had died, so had any spark of decency in Brad. He had become isolated and resentful, developing the facial tics that still plagued him, and blaming his lack of achievement on his father's failure to show him favor. Most of the time Brad was merely annoying, but when he felt he was about to fail he tended to strike out blindly. He hadn't really become insufferable, though, until Tom had joined the business and begun to personally groom him for usurping what Brad had always sarcastically called the "Jackson throne." From that moment, he had never again taken Anne into his confidence. Now, after five years in Tom's shadow, Brad didn't have any recognizable traces of humanity left in him.

She watched him now as he began to sweat and twitch at the sight of her and she could only feel disdain. He didn't have any class.

"Of course it's wonderful to see you," Tom said, an almost imperceptible hesitation in his voice giving away his shock. He had the class in the company. "You're as beautiful as ever, Anne. More beautiful."

"Thank you, Tom. May I join you?"

"Please."

He moved to allow her room. She ignored him and sat next to Brad, knowing that Tom was regaining his balance quickly. She didn't think it wise to push her luck too far.

"What are you doing in New York?" he repeated more conversationally.

Francis, the waiter who'd always taken care of their table, now appeared silently with Anne's coffee and Frangelica. She shot him a dazzling smile, and he bowed a bit lower than was customary. After taking a sip of liqueur, Anne turned back to her family.

"I'm here to see my lawyer," she finally answered evenly, taking note of the quick, surreptitious glance that passed between the two of them and feeling more stable for their need of it. "You?"

"Business."

She nodded absently, sipping at her coffee.

"You haven't been in the city in a while. How did you happen to find a lawyer?" Brad asked, his eye pulling oddly at the words as if he were winking at her.

"Recommendation of a friend. Don't worry, Brad, it's no one you know. And no one you own."

"Anne..." Tom reached for her hand. Anne deftly avoided it, not wanting him to feel the calluses that one manicure couldn't erase. He hesitated only a moment. "Did you get my message?"

"The one about not having any choice about what happened to my home, or the one offering new lodgings?"

"You always have a home in Boston."

"Thank you, Tom. The invitation was eloquent, but I'm going back to Cedar Ridge."

"How long will you be here?"

"I leave tonight."

He frowned handsomely, the perfect modicum of concerned disappointment. "That's too bad. I thought maybe we could spend more time together."

She smiled again, the light in her eyes dry. "See the town? I've seen it, thank you. I really have to be getting back."

"Animals need tending?" Brad's voice was quiet, his insult implicit.

Anne's answering smile, delivered over the rim of the coffee cup, was unruffled at the impotent attack. "I guess I'm a creature of habit, too, Brad. I suppose it's a matter of what one gets used to."

Tom leaned back and lit the cigarillo he'd earlier forgotten. "You know, Anne," he said, his voice soft and dark, the music that had haunted her dreams, "sitting here with you, it seems hard to believe you've been away."

It was time for her to make her exit. She knew where his line was heading and didn't particularly want to be around when it got there. She was still afraid after all this time that she wouldn't be able to walk away from it.

"But I have," she assured him, finishing the last of her coffee and gathering her purse to go. "It's been good to see you two. I'm glad I could get the chance to stop in before my flight left. I'll give Silas and Sarah your love, Brad. My best to Ellie." Ellie was the thin-blooded heiress Brad had managed to marry. Anne turned to Tom. "Anyone I can pass on salutations to for you, Tom?"

His answer was a silent smile that lit his eyes with amusement. Anne was beginning to doubt whether she'd have the nerve to sneak back into the restaurant for their delicious bouillabaisse. Tom and Brad stood with her, Tom taking her by the hands before she could escape. His movements were too smooth to avoid.

"Why don't you come back to the city?" he coaxed, his voice hypnotizing the thoughts of bouillabaisse away. "You belong here."

Anne's answer was cool, even as she wondered whether he could feel the trembling his touch had given birth to. "I'm perfectly happy where I am, thank you. It's been wonderful, but I do have to go."

Retrieving her hands from him, she turned and left. Tom and Brad stood where she'd left them, knowing why she'd come, and, she dearly hoped, more unsettled for her performance. God knew it had taken enough out of her.

Contrary to what she'd said, Anne didn't leave that night. She managed to slip back into the restaurant for some of that promised dinner and the most shameless pampering she'd enjoyed in two years, and then spent a night savoring the luxury of the hotel. Bright and early the next morning she headed home.

It was just about lunchtime when she walked into Thompson's General Store wearing the same suit she'd worn to Chez Louis. She had been coming and going from the mountain for so many years that most of her neighbors had gotten used to the disparity in her appearance. It didn't occur to her that Jim had never seen her like this until she caught the look on his face.

At first it was blank, as if a stranger had walked in. Then it slackened into an openmouthed gape. Jim and Cassie hadn't come to the mountain until Anne's last case of clothing had long since been packed up and given away. They had never seen the transition before or, for that matter, the celebrated city side of Anne Jackson.

For the first time since she'd been coming home from the city, she felt out of place and slightly uncomfortable.

Two hours later she climbed off her horse to find Jonathan comfortably seated in the front porch rocker. By the smile that lit his eyes when he saw her, it seemed that he was glad to see her. She wondered how loud the kids had been.

"Well," she offered with an appraising grin. "I suppose you're pretty proud of yourself."

"It only took me twenty minutes to get out here," he answered nonchalantly. "I was beginning to get stir-crazy."

She could well imagine that it only took him twenty minutes. There was still a fine sheen of perspiration on his forehead from the exertion, but he looked like a kid rounding third for home. His enthusiasm sharpened her pleasure at seeing him.

"A long way from mountain climbing, aren't we?" she said, laughing.

"Annie, you're back." Cassie appeared in the cabin doorway, hands on hips.

Anne faced her with an identical pose. "So, I'm away for two days and the community takes over my patient, huh?"

"We barely got started," she retorted happily. "If it had taken you a couple of more days to get home, we could have had him tending the animals by the time you got back."

Jonathan scowled. "I hardly think so."

Cassie laughed and led everybody back in, Jonathan bringing up the rear. He closed the door as Anne shrugged out of her coat and hat.

"Oh, Annie, your hair," Cass breathed. "I love it."

Anne's hand went instinctively to the tightly coiled chignon, her voice unaccountably embarrassed, her eyes straying to Jonathan's passive face. "Oh. I'd forgotten about it."

"You're going to show me what you got in New York, aren't you?" Cassie demanded, bearing down on her. "I have the feeling that you have wonderful taste when it comes to designer rags.''

Before Anne could move to protest, Cassie had one hand on the suitcase and the other on Anne. Anne had the choice of going up with her to the loft to do some modeling or trying to dupe her way to the kitchen for some tea. She gave up with a heartfelt sigh and followed upstairs as Jonathan settled himself onto the couch.

Fifteen minutes later Cassie stood before her, her reaction a momentary stunned silence. "My God. I wouldn't have recognized you."

Anne hadn't realized that when she'd slipped back into the suit, she had also unconsciously slipped into the city veneer that had barely protected her from Tom.

"Oh, stop it," she objected. "You act like Eliza Doolittle just walked in."

"I feel like it," Cassie assured her with an awed shake of the head. "Do you know how... formidable you look?"

Anne stared at her, unsure how to react. Jonathan's voice interrupted.

"Don't I get a show, too?"

His reaction was even more startled than Cassie's. The minute he saw her, the teasing humor in her eyes died hard. It was as if he'd just met her for the first time, and that he didn't like what he saw.

"Not you, too," she protested, not realizing that even her posture was more suited to her clothes than her surroundings, and the sophistication of it more alien than the sight of Jonathan's three-piece suit.

"Impressive," he said, his voice barely warm.

Anne was confused. "It keeps me from being taken advantage of," she answered, trying to keep the tone of her voice light, but failing.

"Seems a bit superfluous" was all he would say, a distant look in his eyes.

"I'm changing," she decided, turning impulsively on her heel. "This outfit is definitely not the dress of the day."

Before anyone could voice protest, she slipped out of the designer suit and pulled her hair down from the sleek hairstyle into the braids that more suited the surroundings.

As she put the suit away, Anne realized that she had enjoyed donning fashionable clothes again, dusting off the old social skills and seeing how well they'd held up. It disturbed her a little.

She had come to consider that part of her life without merit, had begun to resent its waste. In the end, all she'd been given, been privilege to, had come down around her like a house of cards. It had taken a divorce and her father's death to come to grips with all the years of her life when material luxuries had been only a substitute for a father's attention and a husband's love.

Maybe, she decided, there was some truth to the adage that absence made the heart grow fonder. Or maybe she had just been able to face the old life on different terms. Her terms. For the first time in her life, she had been the one in control.

It was a true pleasure to remember the confusion she'd unleashed by pouncing unannounced on Brad and Tom. It had been only the second time she'd won any sort of victory over them, and this time she'd been in a clear enough frame of mind to enjoy it. But, looking at the clean, expensive lines of her new clothes, she wondered if maybe there wasn't more to it than that.

"Better?" she asked a few minutes later as she reappeared in work shirt and jeans.

Cassie cocked her head to one side in appraisal. "I'm not sure if better is the right word, but I think I'm more comfortable with you like this."

Jonathan was more to the point, driving home his message with the brittleness of his eyes. He spoke with as much rancor as awe. "I'd heard the legend of Peter Jackson's little girl, but I'd never had the chance to see you in action. You must have been some rich bitch, lady."

Chapter 8

Anne was more surprised than she should have been by the sudden change of attitude. Cassie was astounded—she seemed to stop breathing for a moment she was so still.

"Don't you want to know how Mr. Fredericks is?" Anne asked instead, her manner measured and even, her control spread thin over her mounting confusion. Why couldn't he just once not swing back to the attack when she least suspected it?

Jonathan's quick smile at her words was amazingly tender, considering his last words. "Judson is always the same," he said quietly. "Quite a gentleman, isn't he?"

"A refreshing change, I must admit," Anne allowed. "I'm amazed that he'd consort with the likes of you. He seems to be such an upstanding sort."

Jonathan laughed. "He doesn't. He's an old family friend. Judson was born and raised in the wilds of Wyoming, too."

"In that case, I feel better. For a while there I was wondering what the catch was."

He raised an eyebrow. "With Judson? Unthinkable."

Anne took a minute to describe the older man to Cassie, who still stood slightly openmouthed at the exchange she'd witnessed. Anne said nothing about that, just glad that Cassie had finally seen that Anne wasn't making up Jonathan's knack for lightning mood changes. Now if someone could explain them to her, she'd feel even better.

"When will I be able to get back to civilization?" Jonathan asked.

Anne raised her own eyebrow. "I thought you relished the rustic atmosphere."

"I didn't think it was much a matter of choice."

"Can you ride a horse?"

His response was in the form of a pained silence.

"Come to me when you can. Or when the snow melts."

"Why can't I go in a cart or something?" he persisted. "Surely, you at least have wagons or something like that up here."

"We do, but we can't get one up or down the mountain right now. And why are you suddenly so antsy? One foray outside does not a recovery make."

"I'm not used to being so passive."

She grinned dryly. "A real take-charge kind of guy, huh?"

"You could say that. It's been a long time since I haven't been in control." In her preoccupation with making a snappy comeback, Anne almost missed the momentary light in Jonathan's eyes that suddenly made her think of other conversations they'd had. And she stopped, suddenly unsure of what to say. The brief glimpses of vulnerability still unnerved her.

"You confuse me almost as much as he does," Cassie said as she and Anne sat in the kitchen a little while later, voices hushed with secrecy. Jonathan still sat with his book not much more than a dining-room table away.

"Me?" Anne countered with a quizzical look.

"I think I would have hit him." Cassie paused a moment in consideration. "As a matter of fact, I almost did."

Anne laughed, sipping at her coffee and wishing that she could have stolen Louis's pot. Maybe next time she was in New York. "I'm glad you saw it. Now at least you know that I haven't been making it all up to dump a load of misplaced revenge on an innocent bystander."

"But you took it so well." Cassie looked up furtively as her voice got a little too loud. Jonathan didn't react.

Anne shrugged, her attention still purposefully on the hot coffee that was warming the travel chills from her. "I'm getting used to it." A lie, but more immediately acceptable than the truth of what that little confrontation was still doing to her stomach. "He seems to defuse a bit easily if you change the subject."

Cassie shook her head in frustration. "I still can't figure why he would pick on you. He's been nothing but a gentleman with me."

Anne refrained from shooting Cassie a look of surprise. She, after all, had proposed the schoolboy theory in the first place. Anne had seen a part of Jonathan that she thought very few people had been permitted to see. And now Jonathan didn't know how to react to her anymore. Maybe he considered her to have some kind of unpalatable hold over him.

Formidable, Cassie had called her. Why would that have made such an impact on him?

"Uh, I don't know," she finally answered, careful to keep her voice as quiet as Cassie's. "Maybe I threaten him somehow. Maybe he has a wife somewhere he hates who looks like me."

"Well, I have to say that you both have the same dueling styles, that's for sure."

Anne looked over at her friend, recognizing the accuracy of her statement. Maybe she hadn't gotten as far away from the city as she'd thought.

For a few moments they sat in silence, eyes contemplative, the aroma of wood smoke and coffee comfortably filling the kitchen. Then Cassie spoke up again.

"How do your chances look for keeping the Ridge?"

"I honestly don't know," she admitted. "But it was certainly worth the trip just to throw Tom and Brad off balance. I saw them, you know."

Cassie's eyes widened appreciably. "You seem awfully
calm about it."

"Sure, now that I'm far enough away. I have to admit,
though, I sure confounded them with my footwork."

Cassie was still wide-eyed, studying Anne's face as she
talked. "Annie, I'm really proud of you. I've never seen you
this rational when you talked about those two before."

Anne smiled happily. "Maybe I'm finally getting my feet
under me."

"You've done something, honey."

"Hey, I'm being ignored again! I can smell the coffee out
here."

Cassie and Anne exchanged meaningful looks at the
sound of Jonathan's voice.

"Ya know," Cassie said, "I think the saying for this occasion is that little boys don't grow up; their toys just get
more expensive."

Jonathan ate dinner in the kitchen, but Anne begged off
on the excuse that she was tired from traveling. Again, their
dialogue was exceedingly polite and carefully distant, as if
afraid to accidentally wander too near a weak point in their
armor. Anne knew darn well that she should have walked in
and demanded an explanation for his previous name-calling,
but she didn't have the courage. He just might tell her. She
only wanted to get herself to bed and her patient one day
closer to being able to leave her to her silence and peace.

She was all too aware, as she stepped carefully around the
stranger who sat in her living room, that as much as she'd
breached his wall of security, he had done the same with her.
He had drawn out emotions more intense than she'd al-

lowed to surface in a long time. He had moved her. He had made her want to reach out to him, and she couldn't afford to do that. Tom had been reminder enough for any one of the risks involved, and the scene today had only served to emphasize that little lesson in life.

Yet she found herself watching him surreptitiously. There was something about the way the firelight softened his face, the way he ran his fingers through his hair as if to force it into some semblance of order as he pored through a thick volume of Flaubert. His features had lost some of their sharpness since he'd been there, until it seemed that they belonged to someone else who was comfortable in a rural setting.

Anne could imagine him on horseback now, or set in rhythmic motion as he chopped firewood, muscles straining against flannel and denim. She found herself fantasizing about Jonathan, Silas and the rest of the men in the community as they worked together in companionable humor to raise a new church or barn.

Flipping off the kitchen light, she deliberately set those mental pictures aside with the work she'd finished and walked into the living room to face the real Jonathan Harris. He looked up at her with weary question.

"Unless you're planning to spend the night out here, I'd suggest we start heading in," she suggested. "I'm ready for bed."

He simply nodded, closing the book and putting it on the table. Anne reached for the crutches, but he took them from her hands.

"Thanks, I'll get there by myself," he said a bit stiffly. "It's about time I started getting around on my own."

Anne said nothing as she watched him struggle to his feet. He was purposefully pushing her away. Anne, the nurse, was frustrated, knowing damn well that he was working himself too hard again. She could see it in the tight set of his jaw and the creases in his forehead. She was certain that Cassie had helped him earlier, probably with liberal doses of adventure and humor. Now, though, he fought in determined silence as if the whole thing were a grim battle to be faced alone.

Anne, the woman, realized that it angered her. Why was it that she got the feeling that she was such a threat to him? And why on earth did it make her feel so damn ambivalent?

She hated that feeling, always balancing on a razor's edge, wanting more and wanting less at the same time. She thought that she'd been finished with that kind of torment two years ago. After facing what her life had become the last time she'd gotten herself into a relationship with a man very much like the one she faced, she certainly didn't think she should have any trouble about handling her attraction to Jonathan. But she did, and it kept getting worse.

Not five minutes later as she followed him into his room, she discovered just how much worse.

He was trying to maneuver the corner, his progress slowing. Anne said nothing. She merely walked alongside him, watching the effort that once again brought a shine of sweat to his face and carved cruel lines on either side of his mouth. She was angry that he should put himself through this. She was also awed by the store of willpower he seemed to be able to call upon. No one she'd ever known would have put himself through this. At least not without the benefit of a generous amount of painkillers or alcohol. Jonathan had had neither since he'd arrived.

Anne found herself shaking her head, watching the broad back that strained against her brother's old pajama shirt and noting the signs that Jonathan was wearing out. Without warning, he lost his balance.

He had been trying to turn the corner to his room when he caught a crutch against the door frame, throwing him forward. He toppled quickly. Anne wasn't really as alert as she should have been, but her instincts were accurate. Her reaction saved them both from going down.

Jonathan fell to his right as he tried to catch hold of the wall, but his bad leg gave way. Without thinking, Anne clasped her arms around his waist. He gasped at the pressure against his injured ribs. Anne managed to get around and lean back against the wall, her face pressed into his chest as he fought to regain control of the crutches.

"Take your time," she told him, her voice muffled. "I'm not going anywhere." Except down, she thought as she braced her knees against his and fought to keep them both upright. Beneath the flannel shirt Jonathan's heart pounded heavily and his breathing was labored, but he stopped struggling for a minute. Taking some slow breaths, he rested his weight against her.

"We've got to stop meeting like this," he gasped above Anne's head.

Unaccountably, she giggled, adrenaline coursing through her like a heady liquor. "If Silas walked in right now," she managed, "he'd shoot you for trying to molest me."

Or maybe vice versa. She was having more trouble breathing, and it wasn't all exertion. It seemed like every nerve in her was on fire and that her heart was readying for battle. If only his muscles weren't so rock-hard, or his back so lean. Caution, or was it fear, made an attempt to break through the illogical exhilaration but failed. Her early-warning system had been thrown into shutdown.

"Wait...I...have it...." He was moving, straightening very slowly as he once again got the crutches securely under his arm. Anne straightened with him, giving him added support as he went.

"Should I pull the chair over here," she asked up to him, "or do you think you can make it the rest of the way without doing that again? I only have the energy reserves for one rescue a day."

He still leaned against her, wedging her against the door frame so that she couldn't move. "Maybe we could...just stand here for a...couple of...minutes so I can...get my breath." He caught her in his gaze, and Anne knew that she wasn't the only one having more trouble breathing than she should. A chill shot her spine like fire, another warning that she couldn't seem to heed.

"I'm not going anywhere until you do," she answered, her voice sounding breathless. She still had her arms around him and didn't seem to realize it, as if it were a natural thing. His eyes, looking down at her from the shadow-strewn hallway, glowed uncannily as if lit by a pale blue flame. The hottest fire is blue, Anne thought absently. She could feel the heat of his eyes as if it penetrated every pore. She wanted to reach up and test it, to run her fingers by that fire and challenge it, because it seemed to grow hotter even as they stood in silence.

Anne wanted to say something, to break the spell that seemed to be weaving its way around the two of them. She wanted to suddenly pull away, but knew that she wouldn't. And there in the depths of Jonathan's eyes she saw the same conflict: he was weakening just as surely as she.

They needed this; even against their wills wanted it. Physically they needed it as if it were only to obey laws of attraction. Emotionally, neither could think of one logical reason to be attracted, one sane excuse that would explain the fact that they were so inexorably drawn to each other. Anne couldn't be certain of the reasons for Jonathan's distrust of and disdain for her. She had to assume it had something to do with the person she was, or maybe it was from his fear of dependency. She certainly knew why she loathed the idea of attraction to Jonathan, but right now that didn't seem to make any difference.

"I think I should be out getting the animals down for the night," she whispered, still unable to take her eyes from his.

He didn't move. "If you leave, I'll fall over."

Anne was having even more trouble getting her thoughts straight. "Maybe I should let you."

Jonathan didn't smile or reply. He bent to her, where her upturned face waited helplessly, and caught her between his hand and his lips. Without thinking, Anne closed her eyes

against the thrill his touch unleashed in her. Her lips softened against his assault, her arms tightening instinctively
around him. This is insane, she thought even as she pulled
him against her to steady his balance. Nobody in her right
mind would be caught in an unwieldy situation like this. She
felt the hammering of his heart against hers and thought no
more.

He forced her lips open gently, his own softer than Anne
could have ever imagined. With the hand he maneuvered
away from a crutch he explored her back, sliding it purposefully up beneath her shirt to test the softness of her
skin. Anne recognized the feel of his fingers against her
spine like a brand. Arching against him, she sought the heat
he seemed to radiate. She met his tongue with her own and
searched the depths of his mouth, the soft warmth of his
lips. She'd read that women melted when aroused by the
man they loved, but she'd never believed such exaggera-
tion. But suddenly she felt as if her skin had become molten, as if she had been poured into place and that Jonathan
could mold her any way he wanted if only he tried. Her
knees were having trouble staying locked, even when pressed
against his, and she seemed to fit his contours better than
her own.

His hand found her bra and unsnapped it. She allowed his
hand to progress unheeded around her side to her breast
where it unleashed sparks like fireworks.

It had been a long time since she'd realized what may-
hem a set of fingers could wreak when set loose against the
sensitive skin of her breast. Not since Tom had she even
anticipated the feel of a man's hand against the soft swell-
ing, or ached for a slightly roughened thumb to chafe her
nipples to exhilarating stiffness. Anne pressed against his
hand, against the hypnotic strength of his touch. She
straightened a little more so that his lips could find her neck
and send her to gasping. At the same time she felt him
against her, his arousal powerful.

She didn't want this moment to pass, didn't want to forfeit the headiness of his touch, the exhilaration of his nearness. But suddenly she saw the impasse and saw what she'd been ignoring. The fear she'd so far eluded suffused her with its chill until Jonathan's caresses froze her. Anne wished more than anything right then that she were the kind of person who could give in to her needs and wants without thought to repercussions. A handsome man held her in his arms, a man she was drawn to, and she wished she could let him make love to her.

She suddenly felt as if she were smothering.

"I don't know...about you," she gasped even as Jonathan's hands found another sensitive area, "but I'm beginning to lose my balance. We can't stay here indefinitely."

"Any suggestions?" he mumbled into her throat. He didn't seem to notice yet that her posture had stiffened.

"There are any number of obvious ones," she answered, her head against his heaving chest, her eyes squeezed shut against what she had to say. "But I'm afraid I can't think of one that would work right now."

He straightened at that, his eyes trapping hers mercilessly. "What's that supposed to mean?"

Anne took a deep breath to steady her racing pulse. "It means that maybe we shouldn't start something we can't finish."

"I'm not that much of a cripple," he said with a rakish grin.

She faced him with more purpose now, drawing herself up in defense of the lightning even his soft voice was unleashing in her. "But maybe I am. I'm not the type of person who can enjoy this particular recreation so erratically."

"Erratically?"

Both of them were still breathing quickly as if they'd just completed a race. Or were about to begin one.

"Maybe a better word is arbitrarily," she retorted with more force, even though the constriction in her chest threatened to suffocate her. She was too close to him to protect herself properly. She'd never been able to win with Tom, and she was suddenly very afraid that she couldn't win against this man who depended on her to even make it around the house. "It seems to me that you're the one who just finished calling me a rich bitch. That's not exactly my idea of sweet nothings."

"You were a rich bitch."

Anne was nonplussed enough to almost knock him over. "And that's all you have to say about it?"

"Anne," he said in his best conciliatory manner, the set of his shoulders softening, "we want each other. Isn't that all that matters?"

She shook her head. "No. That's not all that matters. I don't consider making love a passing sport." Her eyes flashed now and the intoxication of his touch died. "Do you?"

"No—Yes." He shook his head impatiently, easing his hold on her. "Oh, I don't know. I don't understand myself. I just know that no matter how I feel about you, you have the ability to drive me crazy. And I can't exactly take any cold showers." When his smile appeared, it was self-deprecating. "At least not without help."

His abrupt honesty threw her off again. This man who looked and spoke so much like Tom McCarthy, who showed flashes of the same bloodthirsty instincts, still had the knack of completely contradicting his image by almost grudgingly allowing his defenses to lag enough to be recognized as just that. Tom had never had defenses. He had been predatory to his toes.

Anne felt as if she were going to explode. She was literally and figuratively against the wall. Maybe if Jonathan had come along a few months later in her life she could have handled him with more aplomb. She could have dealt objectively with his confusing, compelling personality and been able to make a decision with the presence of mind she'd so desperately sought when she'd returned to the mountains.

First Class Romance

Delivered to your door by

Find romance at your door with 4 FREE NOVELS from...

Silhouette Intimate Moments®

Catherine Coulter's AFTERSHOCKS. When Dr. Elliot Mallory met Georgina, everything seemed so right. Yet, she was just beginning her career, and a life with him would cheat her out of so many things. Elliot was determined to let her go, but Georgina had a way of lingering in his heart.

Diana Holdsworth's SHINING MOMENT. Derek Langley had been smuggled out of Russia as a small child. Now, with the help of an acting troupe, and its lovely leading lady, Kate, he had a chance to go back and rescue his father. And when he fell in love with Kate, he knew he might never be able to tell her.

Nora Roberts' DUAL IMAGE. Actress Ariel Kirkwood wanted desperately to play the scheming wife in Booth De Witt's new play. As Ariel the actress, she awoke the ghosts of Booth's past. As Ariel the woman, she awoke Booth's long-repressed emotions...and tempted him to love again.

Barbara Faith's ISLANDS IN TURQUOISE. When Marisa Perret saved Michael Novak's life during a raging storm, it gave her a chance to save her own life, too. Yet, she felt she had to return to a husband who did not love her. Which is worse? A love with no future, or a future with no love?

OPEN YOUR MAILBOX to these exciting, love-filled, full-length novels. They are yours *absolutely FREE along with your Folding Umbrella and Mystery Gift.*

AT-HOME DELIVERY. After you receive your 4 FREE books, we'll send you 4 more Silhouette Intimate Moments novels each and every month to examine FREE for fifteen days. If you decide to keep them, pay just $9.00 (a $10.00 value)—with no additional charges for home delivery. If not completely satisfied, just drop us a note and we'll cancel your subscription, no questions asked. **EXTRA BONUS:** You'll also receive the Silhouette Books Newsletter FREE with every book shipment. Every issue is filled with interviews, news about upcoming books, recipes from your favorite authors, and more.

But he hadn't waited to fall into her life, and Anne wasn't sure she wouldn't crumble beneath the pressure of his blue eyes and offhand sarcasm. She didn't yet know how to demand honesty from him. She didn't know whether to expect a commitment. She didn't know that she ever wanted one again.

"I can't, Jonathan...." Anne was beginning to have trouble breathing again. She knew what happening: she was hyperventilating. Some detached voice deep inside her commented dryly on hysterical females, but she couldn't seem to pay any attention. She knew that she had to get away, maybe out to the cool, clean air and moon-painted snow. She couldn't even bring herself to explain to Jonathan the reason she suddenly looked like a rabbit caught in the headlights of an oncoming car. She couldn't seem to pull the whirling memories and pain into a semblance of order to paint the picture necessary to make him understand. She had to escape.

"You're just going to walk away?" he asked quietly, not understanding.

"I have to." Anne felt tears threaten and was unnerved by the unfamiliar pain of them. "I have to go out and get the animals settled for the night. Can you get the rest of the way with some help?"

Her abrupt change sealed her words. Jonathan straightened, supported by the crutches so that Anne could let go.

"I told you before. I'll get there on my own."

When he turned away from her, Anne saw the frost in his eyes and realized that instead of feeling relief at the resolution of the dilemma, she felt worse.

Chapter 9

Anne and Jonathan seemed to have little to say to each other for the next few days. He was making enough physical progress to have free reign of the house. His attitude, however, had regressed. Anne knew what had caused this, but couldn't bring herself to bring it to issue with him.

She'd rejected him, had once again seemed to him in complete control of a situation that he couldn't master. She still didn't know for sure how he felt about her, but she did know now that the tensions in the little cabin had escalated sharply because of that moment of mutual weakness.

He was certainly chafing more and more at being restricted, even though it was his own injuries and not Anne imposing the restrictions. Even so, she was the one who received the weight of his impatience, his silences even more electric than his brief verbalizations. Meals were served and eaten in almost total silence. The only time Jonathan really talked to her was when she asked about his progress. He still experienced quite a lot of pain when he stretched his limits, but that wasn't something he would admit to. It seemed to make no difference that Anne couldn't help but see.

What troubled Anne was the fact that his present attitude bothered her so much. She didn't want his animosity. She wanted to tell him that she hadn't ever felt so alive as when she'd been in his arms, that she was awed by his courage and strength. More than anything, she wanted to go to him when she saw pain suddenly crease his face and invade his eyes. She wanted to hold him the way she had the night of his horrible dream, soothing away the strain, easing the frustration.

More than once she caught herself just short of reaching out to help. Each time the look in Jonathan's eyes had frozen her. Seeing that same struggle in his eyes, she wondered if he was having as much trouble sleeping as she. She wanted to have a chance to talk out the misconceptions they'd built up about each other and understand their limitations. But neither of them seemed to be able to allow the proper doors to open. Neither was able to bend and meet the other halfway. Until the day Mary Lou Sullins' baby was born.

Mary Lou's oldest girl, Emily, arrived on horseback at four in the morning to get Anne. Emily was sixteen and going to be married before the year was out, but she'd decided to wait to help her mother with the baby who would be born six months after the death of Will, Mary Lou's husband. Mary Lou was not in good health herself. She was too worn by her other seven children, Will's long illness and their crushing poverty to bear this baby easily.

It wasn't until well past midnight that Anne found herself back before her fire, a cup of coffee in her tired, aching hands. Staring into the fire, she thought of the people she helped. They were people like the Sullinses who had the babies they couldn't afford, who had more misery than should have been their share and who plodded on day after day just to survive. She thought of the baby, the joy she always felt at the new life she held, and how quickly it had been quenched when she saw the vacant look with which his mother greeted him. He deserved so much, and he would only get poverty and hunger and maybe later the chance to kill himself in a coal mine like his father or scrabble at the dirt they called a farm.

Anne turned to stare absently out the window and watched the fitful moonlight glitter on new-fallen snow like a shower of mystical sparks. She never felt the new tears that traced her cheeks.

"Hey! What's the news from the front?"

Anne lurched to her feet. Unaccountably irritated by the flippant tone of Jonathan's voice, she stalked to his room. He looked as if he'd just awakened, the night-light softening his features and sending up an unwanted aching in Anne's chest.

The sight of her stopped him short. "What's wrong?" he asked suddenly. "Is the baby all right?"

She deflated, dragged down by the bone weariness that had taken hold. "The baby's fine," she told him from where she stood in the doorway, resenting the wealth in this room, hers as much as his. "I guess that means that he has a one in three chance of making it past childhood. His father's dead, his mother's dirt-poor with eight kids and no skills. I had to send them a goat so that the baby would have milk. Other than that, he's fine."

Jonathan's eyes seemed to melt with her words until he was left with an uncomfortable silence to fill. "Have you eaten dinner?"

"No, I'm not hungry."

Before Anne's exhausted brain could comprehend what he was doing, Jonathan swung his feet over the side of the bed and grabbed for his crutches.

"What are you doing?" she demanded.

He grinned. "Fixing you some dinner. Come on."

She watched him hobble out and still stood where she was watching the empty door.

"Get out here or I come in to get you!"

An unwanted grin tugged at her lips and she shrugged, finally following him out the door.

By the time Jonathan served up a meal of leftovers and too-strong coffee in the bright, warm kitchen, Anne had recovered some of her energy, but not much of her spirit. Mary Lou's situation gnawed at her, for it was representative of all the people she helped care for. The disparity between this world and the one she'd left only a few days ago was simply too great, too ludicrous to comprehend. And Jonathan Bradshaw Harris was the very epitome of that disparity.

They had been eating for a few minutes in companionable silence when Jonathan suddenly stopped to consider her with a very appraising eye.

"Why you?"

Anne looked up to face him. "Why me what?"

He motioned with his hands as if to take in everything around him. "Why are you the one to minister to all this? Pioneer nurse and all that."

"What would you suggest I do, start a Junior League?"

"You have to admit that it's a long way from Beacon Hill."

"Yes," she answered definitely. "It is. What's wrong with that?"

"Don't the two hats get a little heavy after a while?"

Within the span of his words Anne's listlessness disappeared, and her eyes flashed with warning. "I don't think I have any difficulty. Neither do the people I live with here. Why should you?"

His face crinkled as if he had witnessed an advertisement for a two-headed man. "The toast of Boston society setting bones and delivering babies?"

"I'm a certified midwife and an emergency room nurse practitioner. Money, after all, does come in handy for some things."

His eyes widened noticeably. "When did you accomplish all of that?"

Her eyes widened correspondingly in mock innocence. "Why, in between cocktail parties, of course."

He grinned without offense and then cocked his head to the side to consider her anew before speaking again.

"Paying the price for daddy's money?"

Anne took her time with the question. It wasn't that it surprised her particularly. She'd asked it often herself and had not always come up with a comfortable answer. She needed to make sure that she could give Jonathan the truth.

"No. I like it here. I have neighbors I can count on and something to do that's worthwhile, and that's more than I've had before. It's my home now."

"You enjoy it, don't you?"

Anne had the feeling that he wasn't referring to her work. "Enjoy what?"

"Belonging in two worlds. Famous socialite and rural nurse. It's real Walter Mitty stuff. You can indulge your expensive whims and then do penance in the mountains."

Color flared briefly high on her cheeks and she straightened, expecting to see the smug smile appear any minute. "Look around you," she snapped. "This is where I live. Do you see any designer touches? How about some calling cards from the jet set? There's not even a box from Bloomingdale's. I haven't been off this mountain two years!"

"The outrage seems sincere," he retorted evenly. "But I don't think you saw the gleam in your eyes when you slipped into those New York rags. If you won't be offended by the comparison, it reminded me of the stories of fire horses and the smell of smoke."

"Do you really think I'm going to be stupid enough to tell you that New York isn't stimulating?"

"You said you hated it."

"I lied. I can't abide smug, self-satisfied people who live their lives by a set of preconceived ideas."

"Me."

"I didn't say that. I merely admitted that I lied."

His eyes opened up a little, the sky there a little wider and warmer with honest amazement. "You really do like it here."

Anne was equally amazed. "Do you like Wyoming?"

Jonathan was fractionally taken aback. Then he shrugged, a bit too complacently. "I was born there."

"That's not what I asked." Suddenly, somehow, she was on the attack.

Again, he shrugged. "It's sometimes nice to see after I've been in New York too long."

"And you enjoy it, don't you?"

He stared, unsettled by her reversal. "Enjoy Wyoming? Sure. There's a sky in Wyoming."

"I'm talking about the double life you undoubtedly lead," she insisted relentlessly. "Maybe you're not a rural nurse, but I bet you're more the adventurer type, the sporting man. 'This executive names mountain climbing and conservation among his hobbies.' Which do you prefer?"

His smile was enigmatic. "There's no contest."

"That's no answer."

"What if I told you I prefer New York? Would you be disappointed?"

Her answering smile was just as cryptic. "I'd have a hunch that you weren't being entirely truthful."

An eyebrow went up. "Why?"

"Let's call it intuition." She leaned back in her chair a little and accused him with a small wave of the hand. "I think that you're an awful lot like me. We're able to exist comfortably in two completely different worlds, and that's hard to understand, isn't it? After living in some place like Wyoming, how do you come to grips with the other life of all the plastic, polished people you deal with? How do you rationalize living in a place where fashion is dictated by the outlandish and the rest of life is dictated by fashion? After having grown up with a moral system that taught the value of basic living, can you really define your life by who you were seen with at the Russian Tea Room or which table you get at Maxim's?''

"And if I do?''

"Then you wouldn't have said anything about Wyoming's sky, or being in New York too long. A true New Yorker would rather not bother with what's above the buildings. It's what's inside them that's attractive.''

Now he caught the fire. They sat across from each other, their eyes bright with the contest. "You mean the power plays, the deals. Having lunch with half a dozen well-connected people and changing the course of history. The stock market jumping at your bidding. Politicians currying your favor because of the power you wield." He paused in friendly challenge, the adrenaline of battle warming the light on his features. "What's wrong with that?''

"You forget yourself," she answered evenly. "I may have been born here, but I was raised in Boston and nurtured in the very arms of JCL. I cut my teeth on power plays, Jonathan. It's wise to remember while you're up there lunching with the powerful that in that world the old are quickly cannibalized by the young. Don't anticipate a very long life.''

"I expect to be around for a while yet. Why do you mind so much?''

Anne shrugged. "Maybe because I wonder how, after growing up in Wyoming, you could be so attracted to the kind of life I threw away." She stared hard at him, allowing an admission that she'd hardly made to herself. "The kind of life I guess I'm still attracted to. The same way you can't really abide by my decision to give up the bright lights for life in the hills. Even though you're as attracted to them both as I am. We're both social chameleons, I guess.''

"Is this what comes of all that time alone to think?''

She had to grin. "Yes. Tell me about Wyoming.''

Her sudden change of tack threw him off balance again. "Wyoming? What about it?''

She shrugged. "I've never been there. What's it like?''

"Have you been west at all?"

Anne thought a moment. "Does Chicago count?"

His facial reaction alone was enough to tell her. "Hardly."

"Well, then, tell me so I'll want to go. Does your family live there?"

"Chicago? No, they live in Wyoming."

She proffered a dry grimace. "Is that what you call a sense of humor?" The easing of relations was not lost on her. The constant strain of waiting for the next barb had begun to disappear with their comfortable banter. Anne looked at the handsome crow's feet that gave Jonathan's smile such character and decided that she was glad. She was very glad.

"I'm not at my best here," he was saying.

"That's good to know. I was afraid you were surly all the time."

Another raised eyebrow. This time his eyes were mischievous. "Wyoming is called big sky country, you know."

"So I've heard."

"It also has the Rockies and the Tetons. Mountains."

"Yes."

"I'm from around Jackson Hole. My family first settled there in the 1870s. Indian wars and all."

"Fascinating. Why, that's real *Roots* stuff."

"You wanted to know."

"Do you mountain climb?"

Jonathan winced. "Yes. So don't tell anyone I know how I got here."

At that she waved a finger at him. "Now that's something I would like to know. How did you get here?"

He looked deliberately confused. "You brought me."

Anne scowled. "I'm talking about how you came to do your swan dive off the Great Smokies in a five-hundred-dollar suit. That's the greatest story the locals have had since a training bomber mistook the lights on the ridge for a control tower and tried to land on Wallace Simson's front yard. And that was in 1945.''

It was his turn to scowl. "I'd just finished some business with the TVA and was sort of in the neighborhood. I'd never been to the Smokies. Thought I'd take a look."

She nodded passively. "If that's just taking a look, I'd hate to see you after a climb."

His answering smile was almost brittle. "I'd had a few drinks. I'd made quite a successful deal at lunch. I'm afraid my judgment was a little off."

"Well, there's something you can certainly pass along to your friends. Don't drink and climb in the cold. It almost cost you some fingers."

"I'd only intended to look. It seems that the back of the park falls off a lot more sharply than I'd thought."

"But that's five miles off the road," she protested.

He shrugged. "In Wyoming that's no more than a couple of blocks."

"Why did you leave?"

This time he was ready for her. "I had other places to go, other things to do."

She nodded absently. "Is the rest of your family like you?"

"No, they're much more like Judson, whom I spoke with today, by the way."

Anne's head went up.

Jonathan's grin broadened. "He wanted to know if I was remaining on my very best behavior for the very lovely lady who saved my life." He tilted his head a little, taking a sip of coffee. "You seem to have made a conquest."

Anne had to smile. "Judson has very good taste."

Jonathan's expression never changed. "I know."

When Anne came in to say a final good-night before going upstairs, Jonathan motioned for her to sit a moment. She settled herself onto the edge of the bed and let him take her hand. His eyes had softened like the light before dawn.

"I think I should apologize," he started out. His fingers were tracing slow patterns against the palm of Anne's hand as he talked. She noticed how quiet the late night was, how intimate. And how warm Jonathan's touch was. "It seems that I've been behaving like a six-year-old again. I realized it when I saw the look on your face after you came back from delivering the baby." He took a breath that sounded more like a sigh. "There are some things that you're right about. New York makes a person very selfish. It's been a long time since I've known anything else."

"I don't think you're exactly a lost cause," Anne challenged with a gentle smile.

A fleeting brightness lit his eyes. "I can handle you much better when I make you mad. All this tolerance makes me nervous."

"All right," she said nonchalantly, the smile still lightening the gray of her eyes. "Have it your way. You were a jerk. Again. You were such a jerk this time that even Cassie began to lose faith in you, and Cassie would try to save the soul of Hitler."

"Better. Thank you."

"Can I ask a question?"

"Sure."

Anne considered the work-roughened texture of his hands and saw him again setting that ax into motion. "What did I do this time to warrant all the venom?"

Jonathan looked uncomfortable, as if he'd just been caught. "You surprised me. Every time I think I have a peg on you, you're not anything like what I thought." The sun neared the surface of his eyes. "I can't seem to keep up with who you really are."

"Now isn't that a coincidence? I seem to be having the same problem. Just goes to show you the worth of those preconceived ideas."

For the briefest of moments his eyes glinted oddly, as if she'd tripped over a secret of some kind. But just as quickly they softened again. An almost grudging empathy sur-

faced. "You know what? Your problem is that for a socialite, you care too much."

Anne saw the gentling of his smile and returned it to him.
"Not at all," she disagreed evenly. "I'm only here to make
the money to keep myself in designer clothes."

They sat together in silence for a few more minutes, the
comfortable sounds of the house enveloping them, and then
Anne stood to leave. Later as she lay in the darkness, alone
in the big double bed, she finally admitted to herself how
much she had missed the company of a man: the familiar
warmth of him beside her as she slept, the quiet support of
shared silence. She'd never realized how cold and quiet the
cabin had been until it had once again been filled with
companionship.

The snow continued to fall for the next three days until it
became difficult to get down the mountain even on horseback. Poor Andy labored his way up and down as Anne
made the few necessary trips out to settle her patients before she made her next visit to New York. On the Thursday
before she left she tried to make rounds, leaving the cabin
and its delicious bread-scented warmth well before dawn to
haul a grievously protesting Andy out into the black cold.

The entire community knew about her plight, which
didn't surprise her in the least. Everyone was pitching in to
free her for the business in New York. The little Red Cross
group was going to keep tabs on her patients, and the four
families who lived closest to the house would take turns
checking in on Jonathan.

By the time Anne once again approached the cabin it was
the wee hours of Friday and she was cold and cramped. The
ride back up had taken six hours beneath the brittle stars
and waning moon. The scene was bewitching, a fairy tale in
snow and shadows, the air clear with ringing silence. Only
the occasional trill of a night bird broke in on her secluded
world. Somewhere near Preacher's Seat a bobcat darted out

in front of Andy, but the big bay just snorted and plodded on, anxious to be back in his barn.

It made Anne wonder as she proceeded up the sleeping mountain how she could so enjoy the pulsating racket of the New York nights where the noise and action weren't even stilled by the hush of dawn. But she did. She could easily thrive on both, living a completely schizophrenic life if given half the chance. She'd relished her time working the emergency room at Mass General, where organized chaos reigned and shouting was the only audible form of communication. But she cherished just as much her life on horseback in the primitive backwoods of the mountains. If only there were a way to combine the two painlessly.

Admitting that, Anne realized without qualification that she was really glad Jonathan Bradshaw Harris had fallen from her cliff. No matter the confusion and tension he'd created for her, his unspoken similarities had given credibility to the puzzling contrasts in her own life. The more she knew him, the more she felt their special kinship.

Much to her amazement, she found him awake when she got home. She saw his light on as she stamped her feet back into circulation on the way to the kitchen.

"Anne? Is that you?"

"In all my glory!" she called back, pulling off her gloves to put water on for tea. She was exhausted, shivering and uncomfortably aware of the pins and needles spreading through fingers and toes as the circulation made a first attempt to return after the long cold ride.

"Why are you so late?"

She couldn't help but laugh. "The last person who asked me that question in that particular tone of voice was my father," she retorted. "And if memory serves me, I was seventeen years old at the time. Want some tea?"

"Sure."

While the water was heating, Anne climbed the stairs to change into her flannel nightgown and robe, pulling heavy knee socks on to soothe her chilly feet. The rush of warmth the heavy clothes brought suddenly reminded her of the night she'd helped rescue Jonathan. It wasn't that long ago, and yet it seemed that he'd been in her house for months.

Anne absently unwound her braid as she thought of that time and how much things had since changed in her little house. She didn't see the soft glow reach her eyes or realize that she'd begun to smile. With her hair brushed out into soft waves that fell over her shoulders, she looked like a different woman than the one who had sat up with Jonathan that first night.

"Is this the woman who took New York by storm?" Jonathan demanded when Anne walked in with the tea. The lines of his face had softened, the weathered lines around his eyes crinkling comfortably with his smile. He was sitting up with another book in his lap, but his hair was sleep-tousled, and he rubbed at his eyes like a little boy.

"This is the woman who took Elder's Crossing by storm," she answered as she set the tray down.

"You look exhausted."

Sitting heavily in her chair, she offered him his mug. "You still have an admirable grasp of the obvious. I've probably ridden thirty miles, visited ten households, drunk gallons of tea and two cups of moonshine, bounced innumerable babies, argued with old ladies and been proposed to—again—by a seventy-nine-year-old widower. It has been a full day." Unconsciously, she rubbed at her frozen feet. There was a huge blister on her heel that hadn't been there yesterday. She'd need to get new boots.

"Give me your feet," Jonathan said abruptly.

She stared at him. "Pardon?"

"Give me your feet. I'll massage them for you."

She didn't move, not sure how to react.

He grinned smugly at her. "Afraid I'll try to take advantage of you? You already set down the ground rules there. Besides, feet aren't my fetish. They hurt, don't they?"

"They're killing me."

"Then don't argue. Hand 'em over. I happen to be a great masseur."

She did and was immediately glad. Having her feet off the floor was pleasure enough, but when he started to slowly work out the kinks, one foot at a time between his solid, capable hands, she thought she'd died and gone to heaven.

Jonathan kneaded the muscles slowly and carefully, almost, but not quite, hurting. Energy surged into Anne's overworked legs, making her want to stretch them. She even forgot the teacup she held in her lap. It felt so good to lean back, close her eyes and enjoy Jonathan's ministrations.

"You act like nobody's ever done this for you before," he observed.

"If they did, I can't remember when."

"Society nobility and never had a massage?" His words remained light and teasing rather than sarcastic.

She thought about it for a minute without bothering to open her eyes. "I don't think so. I can't remember ever having had time. Don't forget, I had a dual identity to support."

"In that case, you'll be happy to know that I also give world famous back rubs."

Anne opened her eyes in time to see him pat a spot next to himself on the bed.

"You should be asleep."

"I'm not the one who's been taking the light of medicine to the backwoods for the last twenty-four hours." Giving the bed another pat for encouragement, he grinned. "Go ahead and be passive for a change. You already know that I have great hands."

She studied him through half-open eyes. "You won't take advantage of me?"

He laughed, once again working on her feet. "I can't imagine anyone taking advantage of you."

"My family certainly seems to have done that," she retorted as she gave up and shifted around to the spot he'd indicated, feet now propped on her chair. Jonathan took her mass of hair in one hand and lifted it over one shoulder and out of the way. Then, gently, his finger took hold of her neck. A delicious shiver raced down her back at his light touch.

"If you'll pardon my saying so, I can't imagine how. You hardly seem to be an easy target. Woman of steel and all." His fingers were moving slowly, working the muscles thoroughly up and down her neck, their pressure progressively more intense. Anne found herself relaxing against his hands, the pleasure of the massage as sharp as pain.

"I have not always been the confident, self-fulfilled woman you see before you." She could feel his breath on her neck and it tickled. More shivers. She wiggled her toes inside their wool socks. The pins and needles had been replaced by a kind of sweet fire that made her want to rub them against something. She could understand how a cat felt when its back was scratched. That fire was beginning to spread. "In Boston I was my father's daughter. My big act of rebellion was running off to be a nurse, but that was all right because nursing was an acceptable profession for a female. I didn't want to be a rock star or anything. And I neatly balanced the defiance by marrying Tom."

Jonathan's hands had found her spine. Subconsciously she could name the vertabrae as he passed over them. Up and down, thoracic, cervical, thoracic, lumbar, the movements slow enough to be hypnotic. She found herself stretching again as he found some particularly sore spots and began to work them out. A curious warmth radiated from his fingertips that was starting to wake Anne up again. She opened her eyes to see the hall light reflecting from the tips of her still-wiggling toes.

"Tom was your father's choice?"

"His dream. Genetically perfect for the big business. You'd love him. He's like you only blond."

It took Jonathan a moment to answer, and in that time a new tension had crept into his fingers. They moved a bit faster. "I'd be flattered if I didn't think that you just gave me your greatest insult."

Anne cocked her head at the words, wondering that Jonathan might have picked up on that. "No, I don't think so. I meant that Tom was the best at what he did."

"Sounds to me like he was a fool."

His statement surprised her. She wanted very much to turn around and find the meaning of his words in his eyes. She wasn't at all sure that she had that kind of nerve. Unaccountably she began to feel the same tension that infected Jonathan's movements, like electric wire that danced on the ground after a storm. It was more than physical proximity or the feel of strong hands searching out her weariness like potent salves. It was Jonathan.

"He's many things, but Tom is no fool," she disagreed carefully. "You remember your description of power? That's Tom. My father was the best, and Tom ground him beneath his feet."

"He threw a lot away in the bargain." Jonathan's voice was softer, surprised. Anne found herself holding her breath. He'd made a discovery, one that his touch transmitted. One that Anne already had come to know.

Her skin was beginning to ache with an addictive need for his touch. The wire jumped in her, its raw ends skittering over the deepest recesses of her belly. She knew that she should get bolt upright and get the hell out of this bedroom before she couldn't. She was too tired to resist and that was dangerous. She was much too close to falling in love, and she couldn't afford it.

"I guess that wasn't what he wanted." Her own voice was beginning to sound a little breathless.

"That's why he's a fool."

It was there in his voice. Anne turned her head to it, and his hands stopped, trapping her by the shoulders. It was in his eyes, too. The truth he hadn't been able to commit to before. For the first time Anne saw that Jonathan loved her. It was as if he'd opened a path for her to the depths of his soul, and all she could see there was a reflection of the yearning in her own eyes. She saw the imminent commitment there and was quite suddenly terrified.

She wasn't ready and might never be. Her footing wasn't solid enough on its own yet. Convulsively, she tried to jerk free, but he never moved. His grip remained strong. Anne tried to give voice, but couldn't. It was all she could do to hold his gaze.

"I'm sorry, Anne," Jonathan said very softly, his hands inexorably drawing her to him. "I lied. I'm not going to abide by the rules." His eyes were so close, his attraction smothering her. Anne dragged in a breath as if it were the most difficult thing she had ever done.

"Jonathan, please..."

He trapped the rest of her protest with his lips, gathering in her doubts with the strength and safety of his arms. Don't, she wanted to cry. Don't open that door. It holds back too much pain. I can't afford this. But there was no way out. The current arced between them, the longing to belong, the yearning for each other. It rose as sharply in her as fire and made her gasp at its fury. There was no turning back now, if there had ever been a time to turn back. Jonathan's hold on her was gentle, but Anne couldn't break free. She felt his hands hesitate, holding her at the waist, and she wanted to cry out for them to find her.

Then Jonathan pulled back, the taste of his last kiss still on Anne's lips. For a long moment he looked down at her, all of the questions he needed to ask there in his eyes. Without a word, Anne answered.

Her heart set a new record, trying to jump free of its mooring like the beating of a captive bird's wings against a cage. Her hands were like ice and she couldn't seem to breathe, but when she saw the tender invitation in Jonathan's eyes, she found herself smiling. With a deliberation that she had never known before and would certainly shock her later, she took hold of his hand and placed it against the throbbing of her heart.

"You're sure?" he asked, and she thought she'd never heard such a sweet question before.

"Not at all," she managed. And then she kissed him.

Later she would think that making love on a single bed with a man in a leg splint should have been awkward. But she couldn't remember anything at all that had been awkward. In fact, in that old brass bed that had held her childhood dreams and memories, Jonathan gave her a gift greater than any she could ever have imagined. He gave her himself. He lavished her with such an attentiveness that she would wonder how she had ever made love before.

When she stood to slip out of her nightgown, the soft durable flannel that had seen her through so many solitary winter nights, he took her hand and drew her down next to him, forbidding her the right to deny either of them any small pleasure they could share together. Jonathan unbuttoned her gown as he leaned over her, his eyes devouring hers with their bright flame. At each button he bent to kiss her throat, her chest, following the progress of the buttons with lips that tasted every part of her.

He never removed the gown but only draped it aside, as if to frame her body for him. After a last, lingering kiss that Anne shared in silent wonder, he turned to enjoy the sight of her creamy skin in the soft light. The tiniest of currents brushed across Anne with delicious warmth. She shivered, unable to stay still, yet unable to move. She could feel the heat of Jonathan's eyes wash over her as if they made contact with her. And when he bent to taste her strong body, he chose her stomach, the slightly rounded abdomen that should have held her children. The touch of his lips and the cool teasing of his tongue ignited a new ache there where he searched her hot skin with his hungry mouth, and Anne moaned with its delight.

Jonathan's hands traced the strong muscles of her thighs, the sleek calves that woolen socks hid, even as his mouth explored the ridges of her ribs. Long before his lips reached them, her breasts were taut with anticipation, the nipples waiting for his fingers to find them. He waited, though, torturing her with his deliberate patience. Sitting above her, he waited as she unbuttoned his shirt, mimicking his actions.

Anne slid her hands around his back and pulled him to her, the sensation of his skin against her like a narcotic. The hair on his chest chafed her breasts and nestled against her cheek. She could feel the taut pull of his back, the muscles there like strong rope. But again, just as she began to gather in the comfort of him, he pulled away, taking his turn.

"You're doing this on purpose," she accused, barely recognizing the anguished sound that was her voice.

"Yes, I am," he murmured back. "I want you to know what it feels like to be cherished."

He sought out her breasts then, first with his hands, which explored with maddening caution, and then with his lips. Anne could see him in the half light as he took her breast in his mouth, a gesture of giving and taking that measured a man's admission of vulnerability. When, a moment later he lifted his head to meet her eyes, she took his beautiful face in her hands and drew him down to her again. And there she held him to her, as if this would bind him to her, even as she tasted the new tears that cleansed her.

He took her with a gentle possession that made her cry out. She lay on her back beneath him, trapped by his power, bound by his commitment. Anne had never realized the breadth of her own passion until Jonathan met her mouth with his own and carefully rocked her to a shuddering peak. It was like a dark flower blooming inside, spreading its intoxicating petals so wide that it would not be bound within her. She began to move against him, wrapping herself around him as if to draw him even closer than he was. His arms encompassed her; his words united them. He vowed to make her whole again and she believed him.

Tears clouded Anne's vision, but she couldn't take her eyes from his face. He smiled at her, his eyes so close that Anne wondered that they didn't singe her. Even as the sweet pain engulfed her and she cried out Jonathan's name as if he could save her, she never lost sight of those eyes. They were the lifeline that had held and guided her. She saw them as they realized her satisfaction and kissed them as Jonathan followed her.

And when Anne and Jonathan were exhausted, their breathing ragged and worn from the gift they had shared, she took his damp, tousled head and lay it against her to rest. There he lay in sleep, nestled against the softness of her breasts, the slow rhythm of his breathing soothing.

For a long while Anne lay staring at the soft play of light against the ceiling, the chill of the late night never touching her. She knew that with the cold of daylight, though, reality would invade the sweet dream set free tonight.

Without realizing it, she gave voice to her dilemma. "What am I going to do when you leave and I'm alone again?"

There was a long silence, punctuated only by the sound of the incessant living room clock.

"What am I going to do?"

Chapter 10

Anne reached Judson Fredericks's office still in a state of anxiety over Jonathan's threat to her fragile independence. When they had awakened that morning each had dealt with the other warily, as if afraid to make too much of what had happened the night before, yet not wanting to treat it too lightly. They had ended up parting without even really talking about it. Now Anne was left with trying to distance herself enough from that crisis to deal successfully with the one Tom and Brad posed.

The office was, as ever, like an oasis of serenity hidden amid the chaos of the city. Judson stood up as she entered and smiled warmly. His sincere compliments pleased her; the dark wood and hushed lighting helped settle her. Anne held out her hand and returned his greeting.

"I've looked forward to seeing you again, Anne," he said graciously, as he guided her once more to the plush green leather chair across from his own. "I hope you don't have plans for dinner tonight. I took the liberty of making reservations in the hopes that you would dine with me."

She smiled at the almost quaint manners Judson displayed. He seemed such an anachronism in this city. He acted more like an old-style southern gentleman than a high-powered New York lawyer. "I would be delighted, Mr. Fredericks."

"Please, you must call me Judson."

Anne nodded her acquiescence and allowed the lawyer to get down to the business at hand. Judson pulled a file toward him and opened it.

"Now, I have been doing some research here," he began, picking up a pair of glasses and carefully adjusting them onto the bridge of his nose with a finger as he studied the papers before him. Perfect, Anne thought with delight. The glasses only made him look more distinguished. "You say you signed the divorce papers and those waiving rights to court approval to the executor's actions in dispensing your father's will, the executor being your brother. Am I correct?"

"I believe so. As I told you before, the time after my father's death was very trying for me. I'm afraid that I trusted my lawyer and signed whatever he told me to."

"Do you remember how many different documents you signed?"

Anne thought a moment, trying her best to pick a few pieces from within the jumbled mess of the weeks that followed her father's death. So much had been shock of betrayal and loss then, it was difficult to remember particulars.

"Four, I think. It all happened three days before I left Boston the last time. If memory serves me correctly, Mr. Martin drove me to the office himself to accommodate me."

"Four," he repeated to himself, again going over the papers in his hand. "You're certain?"

"No, I'm not certain of anything."

Judson nodded slowly in acknowledgment. "Would you have signed power of attorney over to your husband?"

This time Anne's answer was prompt. "Of course not. The last thing I would have wanted at that point was to leave him in control of my life. Besides, what would the need have been? Father left everything in Brad's and Tom's names. Father didn't consider women able enough to control their own money. I waived my chances to contest the will with the stipulation that Tom and Brad let me move back to the cabin without interference.''

Judson was peering at her over his glasses in a curious way. ''Did you read the will personally?''

''I had no desire to. It was read to me, and I found no surprises in it.''

''By your father's lawyer.''

She nodded. ''By Mr. Martin.''

He nodded quietly once again, contemplating the material in his hands. The lines of his face reflected only his concentration on the matter at hand, but the atmosphere in the peaceful office had somehow changed. Anne was beginning to feel a sort of electric charge and unconsciously shifted in her seat.

''There is obviously something of import in all of this,'' she said carefully, not feeling as self-assured as she sounded. Her hands remained frozen in her lap.

Judson looked up and smiled. ''There is. I cannot, however, make any definite conclusion about it until I have a few more documents examined.''

She stared, suddenly understanding. ''There is a power of attorney, isn't there?''

Judson considered his answer a moment before nodding and handing over one of the papers to Anne. She examined it herself. When she again faced the lawyer, it was with eyes only a fraction as chilled as her heart. ''What does this mean?''

''Did you sign it?''

''It certainly looks like it, doesn't it?'' It was as if with the sight of this paper, all of the control she'd so carefully constructed shattered like thin ice. Tom was holding the strings as he had held them all along, and she felt outraged.

"Well, I'll find out for certain. If it is authentic, then your father's will ended up saying just what you thought, and I'm afraid that Tom can do anything he wants with the land."

Her head came up sharply. "Ended up?"

Why did it seem as if the clock was ticking more and more loudly in the unnatural hush? Judson removed his glasses and held them out before him for contemplation before he answered. "I have a copy of your father's will here. It does not read quite as you thought, I'm afraid."

Anne had no answer, unaware that her hands were now clasped together as if to better keep her balance, her knuckles white.

Judson continued. "Your father changed his will toward the end of his life and left the majority of his property and share of stock to you, my dear."

The silence became profound; the street below the window was filled with voiceless animation. Only the clock interrupted with its insistent heartbeat—ticking, ticking. Anne stood and walked to the window to hide her confusion. Forty floors below, an ambulance flashed through traffic, its shrillness lost outside the Plexiglas insulation. The sun lay somewhere behind the skyline, setting the windows afire in an evil blood-glow.

Anne drew a shaky breath. "The cabin?"

"It was left to you. The only direct inheritance your father left Bradley was the house in Boston."

She turned once again, facing the quietly concerned lawyer. "So I signed the power of attorney, just as Brad and Tom had been trying to get father to do before he died, and now they've had the time to legally transfer all benefits of the will to themselves."

Judson didn't have to answer. He waited silently for her to continue.

"What can I do?"

He answered matter-of-factly. "To reclaim the land you want, you must be able to prove that fraud was involved."

"Can I?"

"That remains to be seen. I have already begun to investigate the matter. We have a few avenues open to us."

"I'll have to be frank with you, Judson. I have my mother's inheritance, and most of that I have invested in a clinic to be built near where I live. I don't know how well I can afford your fee." Her smile was rueful as she reflected on the situation. "I'm afraid that's something I never had to consider before. But if I could prove fraud . . ."

"You will, in fact, control JCL. That was that I'm trying to tell you."

"I'm not concerned with the company." She returned to her seat so that Judson wouldn't notice the definite tremble in her knees. "I am concerned with being able to pay your bill. I have the feeling that you've already put quite a bit of work into this. Would you consider a percentage fee?"

"That would be more than generous, Anne," he allowed, "but I think I would rather simply donate my fee to that clinic of yours. At my age I have the luxury of being frivolous if I like."

Anne took his hand in thanks. It seemed to be more than enough for the older man.

"Will we be able to manage it all in so short a time?" she finally asked. "The Board of Directors' meeting is day after tomorrow, and that will be my last chance to contest the sale."

He shook his head slightly. "I have the impression that the meeting will be postponed so that we will end up with more time. But that is another matter entirely, one that I would rather take up over dinner."

Anne offered a tenuous smile. "That sounds like the best idea I've heard since we said hello."

With a return smile that showed a touch of relief, Judson stood to show Anne out. But before he did, he paused with yet another unsettling bit of advice. "Anne, there is one more matter that I feel bears mentioning."

Anne had gotten to her feet when Judson did, and now found that she felt uncomfortable before him. That he had to hesitate a moment to find the proper words to express himself unsettled her even more.

"Have you ever had cause to be...wary...of your husband?" he asked diffidently.

Anne's eyes widened ever so slightly. "Wary? Do you mean other than the fact that you'd have to drag me kicking and screaming into a partnership with him?"

Judson didn't smile at her little joke, which widened her eyes even more. She couldn't imagine a man like Judson Fredericks being forced to use clichés like this.

"It is simply a matter of a number of...well, unusual pieces of correspondence that we have received in the office since we've started to investigate your situation."

"Unusual..." Anne stiffened. "Do you mean threats?" She was furious. The idea that Tom could try to intimidate this kind man who stood before her made her want to walk right over to wherever he was and rearrange his classic features a little. She drew herself up very straight, her eyes like winter ice. "My husband tried to threaten you?"

This time she did get a smile. A quick flash of wry apology. "Only in a very civilized manner, I assure you."

Anne's own smile was brittle. "It would be the only way Tom would operate. He is powerful, Judson. And unscrupulous. If it makes you uncomfortable..."

Before she could finish the thought Judson brushed it aside with a small wave of his hand. "Not in the least, my dear. His rhetoric has only strengthened my own beliefs that this whole situation is at the least more than a little suspect. No, I was more concerned for you."

Anne didn't understand. "Me?"

Again propriety forced him to look around for his words before facing her with them. "You live alone and in an isolated area."

It had been so long since Anne had heard anyone so deliberately tap-dance around a problem that it took her a moment to understand the import of his words. She knew that her eyes once again opened, and that her mouth gaped in incredulous protest, but she couldn't manage an intelligent retort.

"Anne," he said slowly as if the whole subject caused him great pain. "If we are correct in our suspicions that your husband and brother defrauded you out of your rightful inheritance, the scope of their crime is immsense. JCL is one of the most powerful industries on the East Coast. Desperate men have been known to resort to desperate measures."

"Except for one thing," Anne said, smiling wryly. She had no intentions of even entertaining a thought like the one Judson proposed. "Tom would never believe that he could lose the legal fight since he never has before. His fatal flaw, I'm afraid, is that he believes too much in himself and too little in others."

"I would still feel less anxious about the matter if I were assured of your personal safety, my dear."

Anne saw the true concern in those warm brown eyes and wished she could have walked around the desk to give the man a hug. "I'll see to it, just for you, Judson."

For a moment he searched her eyes, only allowing the worry in his own to ease after being assured by her promise. Then he held out his hand. "In that case, Miss Jackson, I believe we have a dinner engagement."

Anne afforded herself the luxury of stopping at the Plaza to change, claiming that the suit she once again wore was strictly business attire. She arrived for dinner in an electric-blue Jack Mulqueen shirtdress that flattered her figure as well as her coloring. Her necklace and earrings were plain gold, her hair pulled up into a heavy sleek braid.

Her appearance on Judson's arm turned heads in the elegant restaurant. She smiled deferentially to him to heighten the illusion as they were seated by the magnificent two-story windows that overlooked the park. Along the walls, matching mirrors illuminated the candlelight ambiance of the lofty white room. Waiters moved silently in black, bending and nodding to the impressive clientele.

"I have to admit that this is something I miss on the mountain," Anne said as she sipped her Manhattan. "There isn't one good French restaurant in the entire town of Elder's Crossing."

Judson chuckled, his office manner relaxing to that of a Southern landowner. Anne was still having trouble placing him in Wyoming. Probably a matter of East Coast prejudices that still tended to crown everyone west of Baltimore with a Stetson.

"This can be just as wearing," he assured her. "In point of fact, I have given much consideration to moving to a small town when I retire. I rather miss it."

"Home to Wyoming?"

He nodded, the silver of his hair gleaming in the candlelight. "Very likely. I have visions of lazy summer days spent along the Snake River with a fishing pole in my hands."

"I can attest to the benefits of that sort of life," she agreed.

"Indeed you can, my dear. Your life seems to agree with you immensely." His appraising eye was gentlemanly and flattering. Anne enjoyed it all the more for the time she'd spent with the taciturn people of the hills who wouldn't consider doling out compliments so easily.

Judson claimed the privilege of ordering for them both, and they settled back to chat about his children and grandchildren, the wife he'd lost two years before and the contrasts between Wyoming and the Appalachians. They did not talk of Jonathan or of the business of the day. Anne knew that that would be served up over coffee.

She enjoyed the meal immensely, from the rack of lamb that arrived pink and succulent with a side of mint jelly to the cherries jubilee that ended the meal in grand style. Judson was the perfect host: attentive, considerate, and well versed in the sophisications of the city. Yet he had never lost the frank honesty life in his native state had instilled in him. He was able to bring Anne up-to-date on the latest in theater, opera and symphony offerings around town and offered to escort her if she were in town long enough. She thought that she would enjoy that very much.

The thought didn't escape her that this was the relationship she'd always longed for with a father who had never had the time to relax away from the demands of his empire, and who hadn't realized his mistake until it had been much too late to do anything.

It was almost eleven before coffee was poured, and Anne was served her Frangelica. Outside her window couples strolled along the street, and a hansom cab clattered into the darkness of the park. Streetlights illuminated the trees as they swayed in a fitful breeze, their limbs skeletal and gray. It made Anne appreciate even more the rich warmth of the restaurant as she sipped at the smooth liqueur.

"Dinner was lovely," she said, smiling at her host. "I'll remember this evening for the rest of the winter as I plod through the snow on my rounds."

"And I will remember it as I spend my winter attending boring meetings with lawyers and CPAs," Judson returned with genuine warmth. "Come spring, I might just visit your little town."

"I'd be delighted." Anne meant it. She'd love to see what happened when she introduced Judson to Silas. She probably wouldn't see either of them for a month as they sought out the area's finer fishing holes together.

"How long do you plan to remain in New York?"

Somehow Anne knew that this was Judson's introduction to business.

"Well, I'll stay for the meeting. I'd love to spend a few days here, but I do still have a patient to attend to."

Judson nodded. "Yes, I did want to ask after him. He sounds as if he's getting along quite well. Is it still impossible to move him?"

"For at least a little while longer. We still have some three feet of snow up there."

"That's quite unusual, isn't it?"

"I believe insurance companies refer to it as an act of God." She grinned. "My horse is about to go out on strike. He's been on rounds three times this week."

"Jonathan wouldn't be able to ride down?"

"Not yet. The nearest rest stop is seven miles down."

He thought a moment. "What about a helicopter?"

Anne shook her head. "I've thought of that, too." She didn't tell him that she had thought of it most frequently when Jonathan had still thought that cynicism was the way to her heart. "The nearest rest stop is also the nearest sizable clearing."

He nodded again as he sipped at his coffee. "I see. Well, at least I know he's in good hands. I have been in contact with his family, and they have been asking after him."

Anne waited to answer until the waiter refilled her coffee and faced away again. "Tell them that he's up and around on crutches, and if he's there much longer I'm going to send him out to milk the cows. And since you have my number, please feel free to give it to them. I have a feeling they make more phone calls than Jonathan."

"Well, he has most definitely been on the phone with me," Judson admitted. "He has insisted on being involved with every step of your case. I have employed several of his suggestions, in fact."

Anne had assumed that Jonathan had been apprised of what was going on, but for some reason she hadn't anticipated this. She'd only seen him on the phone two or three times. But if he knew about the will, he wouldn't discuss that in front of her until something was settled. He obviously had compassion. Why should that still surprise her?

"In any event, my dear," Judson continued, "you must let me know if there is anything I can do to help. Jonathan's parents are old and dear friends of mine, and you have given them an invaluable gift by helping Jonathan as you have."

"I will of course, Judson." She smiled as she decided to finally press the matter. "There is one thing you could do for me now, if you would."

"Of course."

"Well," she said, then hesitated, fingering the delicate lines of her liqueur glass. "As a matter of fact, it's about Jonathan. You've known his family for a long time." He nodded. Anne took a breath to gather enough tact together to continue. "I would ask you to be indiscreet, Judson, and tell me what you know about Jonathan."

Judson allowed himself a small frown of hesitation. "I don't understand."

She grinned wryly. "Since he's been staying with me, he has displayed some curious...oh, contradictions that make it difficult for me to understand him. There have been some incidents that make me think that he's a lot more troubled than he likes to pretend." She gave a small shrug. "I think it's important that I know all I can about him."

"He hasn't said anything himself?"

"No. Only that his family was from Wyoming and his business in New York. I do know that he was in Vietnam." Judson's eyebrow rose. "A nightmare he had one night," she explained, seeing no need to elaborate. "He seems to prefer to play the mysterious stranger."

Judson nodded absently to himself as he studied the hands he'd placed before him on the snow-white table-cloth. "I have not been in real contact with Jonathan for some time," he admitted, looking back up with a sober expression. "My heavens, it's been since before he was in the service: maybe eleven, twelve years ago. He was, I think, a different person then."

Anne recognized the tension his words ignited in her. "How so?"

Judson considered her for a minute as if estimating the risk of further disclosure. Anne thought that he was a very worthy friend.

"Permit me a moment of explanation." At the next table a woman giggled, a shrill, silly sound that seemed to shatter the restrained atmosphere of the room. Judson never noticed. His eyes were at once on Anne and on the past. "Jonathan was born and raised near Jackson, Wyoming. I grew up with John, his father. A fine man. At one time, many years ago, I courted his mother Helen. You would enjoy Helen, I think. She is very much like you. Well, when Jonathan was old enough, he came east for college. He wanted to make a name for himself away from his father's influence, which is, of course, not terribly unusual for an oldest son. Jonathan is the oldest of three.

"Soon after college Jonathan met someone who went into a partnership with him, some type of sales venture, I believe. I never understood the details. I was in Europe on extended holiday when it happened. Evidently a loan was taken out to finance the business. When the venture went under, the partner managed to default, leaving Jonathan holding a rather large loan along with no money and no business. To make matters worse, his father had helped by putting a second mortgage on the ranch and lost it. The family had to move in with Jonathan's brother who lived nearby."

He paused to sip from a refilled cup of coffee. Anne followed suit without really paying attention to what she was doing. A quality of pain had slipped into Judson's voice that presaged the import of a nightmare.

Judson couldn't quite keep his eyes impassive as he continued. "Not long after that, Jonathan enlisted in the marines and put in a request for duty in Vietnam. His mother has always equated the action to a type of suicide note, and it is very possible that she was right. Jonathan shouldered a great amount of guilt for what he'd done to his family. He served two tours of duty and came away with a Silver Star, DSC, Purple Heart, malaria and six months in hospitals for injuries he received."

"No one could prove any wrong on the partner's part?" she asked.

"It seems that the gentleman in question had a certain amount of influence and Jonathan, at the time, had none."

"And he had no other alternatives to take?"

Judson smiled apologetically. "As I said, I was in Europe at the time. I was about the only person Jonathan could have come to for help. In point of fact, when he first called me about taking your case, I was surprised. I have always been afraid that he held my unavailability against me."

Anne shook her head numbly. It was almost impossible to conceive that this had happened to the Jonathan she knew. She understood now, though, what he had meant about being in the same position as her. She couldn't imagine having to face that kind of situation, or having to bear that kind of responsibility. No wonder he dealt so badly with the memories of Vietnam. He'd used his time as his own private purgatory for what he'd done to his parents, and had ended up failing again, at least in his eyes.

"You say you haven't kept in touch with him since then. Do you know what he's been doing?"

He nodded, sipping again at his coffee and then carefully setting the cup down on its fragile saucer. "Jonathan went to law school on the GI Bill. I attended his graduation, but when I saw him then he had changed. When I had known him before, he had been a bright, independent, enthusiastic young lad: very open and honest, and out to conquer the world. When we spoke at the graduation, I could not help but notice that he had taken an almost cynical tack. Hard. He had lost that fine enthusiasm, and was instead...well, driven. That much is easy to see in what he has accomplished since. He has founded and built a rather formidable empire in New York: Bradwell International. They deal in management turnaround. Four years ago he was able to buy back his father's ranch. Since then I expected him to relax a bit. Instead, he has devoted his time even more strenuously to advancing the position and influence of his firm.''

There was much from what Judson said that Anne had to digest. Jonathan's story was not unusual in a city like New York. It was merely another tale of a young man trying to make a name for himself and failing. The values he had brought with him from Wyoming had become engulfed within the alien code of ethics he'd been confronted with, and he'd been overwhelmed.

It didn't surprise Anne, for as she'd told Jonathan, she'd cut her teeth early on that sort of thing. She'd seen better men than him fail. She'd seen her own father, who'd invented the rules, fall a lot harder. It at least helped her understand Jonathan's time in Vietnam and its repercussions. She could better appreciate his attitude and the contradictions that so baffled her. The cynicism, the slick act, the sudden glimpses of compassion. Anne represented everything that he'd once battled against in vain. This was the story behind the first time he'd been helpless to save someone he'd loved from being hurt.

And whether or not he admitted it, Jonathan was still fighting between those two sets of disparate rules. Anne was afraid that he would finally convince himself that in New York the honesty and integrity he'd brought with him from Wyoming had no place.

She could well imagine that he didn't see Judson that often, either. The older man had somehow survived with his scruples intact. That would certainly be salt in a raw wound.

Anne wished that there were some way she could make Jonathan see that he had to keep fighting. The longer he stayed with her, the more she saw the boy from Wyoming in him. It had been that side of him that had attracted her to him in the first place. She was afraid that if Jonathan went back to New York without something to reaffirm his faith in the gentler side of himself, it would finally die out, leaving him in the end no more than another Tom McCarthy.

Anne was beginning to realize how important it was to her that that didn't happen.

For a moment she allowed herself to consider the memory of Jonathan as he'd slept in her arms, his face so relaxed and almost young again. But the picture brought with it pain, a sharp regret for what he'd hidden so carefully behind those brittle blue eyes. She found that she had to force it away again.

"Thank you for telling me, Judson. It does help me understand."

"Happy to do it, my dear. I only hope that spending some time with you might help him somehow."

She couldn't help but grin. "Well, if nothing else, it's helped re-broaden his horizons. Tell me something, just for curiosity's sake. Has anyone told his company where he is? He certainly hasn't."

"Oh, I imagine not. They manage quite well without him, from what I understand, because of the excellent organizational system he set up. He is often away without notice. They've become quite used to it."

"What do you mean he goes away without notice?"

"It seems that it is supposed to be his way to test the efficiency of his people. Sometimes he goes home, from what his mother has written, although more often than not, no one knows quite where he goes. My theory is that he camps alone somewhere near his home. There is much wild country where a man can be by himself with his thoughts."

"I would have thought that he wouldn't have wanted to be caught there," Anne said more to herself.

The waiter appeared silently again, the silver coffeepot in hand, but Judson held up his hand. The man nodded with a small bow of well-bred servitude and melted away.

"As I said," Judson continued, "Jonathan has not confided in me. But the tradition is one his father was fond of employing. The two of them used to camp together when Jonathan was a boy." Carefully folding his white linen napkin by halves, Judson placed it next to his empty coffee up. "Now, my dear, I am afraid that this old man must be getting on his way. But before we go, I wanted to explain a bit more about the meeting with Amplex."

Anne nodded in silence.

"As I said before, I have reason to believe that the meeting will be postponed. It would seem that there is a request that all the board members be present and two or three of them seem to be detained. From what I have been able to ascertain, it may be a matter of weeks." Anne moved to protest, but he held up a hand with a quiet smile. "Think of it this way. The delay is to our advantage. It gives us more time to find a case against your ex-husband and brother."

"I know." Anne sighed, the evening's enjoyment dulled a little. "It's the idea that I'll have to live with this hanging over my head for so long. I never did learn to wait with grace."

So it was that when Judson saw her to the front door of the Plaza, Anne felt deflated and a bit frustrated by the lack of control she had over the whole matter. Somehow it seemed to be getting farther and farther away from her until she was beginning to feel like a pawn.

As she stood in the ascending elevator she slowly rolled her head to relieve the tension the idea of upcoming weeks of uncertainty had given birth to. The more she thought about it, the more she thought that the only thing that would help right now would be a long hot shower.

The idea of the hot, stinging, muscle-relaxing water got her through the walk down to her room and the ritual of undressing once she'd gotten inside. Lights dotted the black park below her room, and the music of traffic battered at her window. Anne's mind could go no farther, though, than the anticipation of a twenty-minute marathon without the hot water running out just as she was getting relaxed.

Only minutes later she stood in the tub savoring the hot water like the strong hold of a lover. Steam rose in lazy clouds around her, fogging the mirror and saturating the small errant tendrils that clung to Anne's neck and forehead. The persistence of the city noise had been silenced by the waterfall of cleansing bliss, and she could almost imagine that she was home enjoying the soul-saving quiet of the mountain.

Finally giving in to temptation, Anne lifted her head to the water and let it drench her hair and flood her face. She would have preferred to stand in a mindless trance, letting the water wash away the tensions that ate at her, but images of Jonathan nudged insistently at her. His hands, the stern lines of his face that so belied his wry, offhand humor. His laugh, so sharp and crisp it sounded like limbs snapping in a dry tree. But most of all, when she closed her eyes, his opened, and she felt herself once again mesmerized by the shifting, settling blue that had unnerved, fascinated, infuriated, and finally overcome her. Eyes that could withdraw completely into themselves to protect the kind of secret that had scarred Jonathan as permanently as the shrapnel that had opened his side, they had also reached out to her without hesitation. She had been seduced by the life-giving fire in his eyes long before she had succumbed to the magic of his hands.

She had never known any man like him before. The comparisons were certainly there to make, because he bore enough of a resemblance to them all. But he alone went beyond resemblance, not only to the men she'd known as Anne Jackson McCarthy, but the ones she'd met as Annie Jackson.

It was fascinating to her. Almost without exception, the men she had known in the city had been typical to the environment with their Hart, Schaffner & Marx mentalities and upwardly mobile outlooks. Only some of the medical personnel she had met had been unique, but she had been firmly restricted from socializing with them. On the mountain where men fashioned their lives around survival, their energies were used on farming and families and sometimes pool down at the hall in Elder's Crossing. Only Jim and a few of the other new homesteaders stood out as ever having known another way of thought.

Jonathan, though, was a real dichotomy. He straddled the two worlds like a man balancing on a knife-edge. As much as he presently loathed to admit it, he was a child of the mountain, raised on the Wyoming version. But he'd also managed to come back after his initial disaster and conquer the city.

It was no wonder to her that he had to disappear to repair his gyroscope from time to time. No matter how badly the city had burned the part of him that had been forged in Wyoming, he still considered it worthwhile to some extent or he wouldn't continue grappling with it.

How Anne would have liked to see him take what he had been taught in his own mountains and make it work in the city. Judson had proved that it would work. Anne would have tried it if things had turned out differently. If only Jonathan could match the drive the city had given him with the scruples his father had taught him, he could make a difference. A real difference. And the Jonathan whom Anne was falling in love with wouldn't have to be lost.

With a weary sigh, Anne stepped out of the tub and dried off. How she wished she were back home before her fire letting the heat from the flames dry her hair, her only problems being those of the people of Elder's Crossing. Her friends. No stranger in her life, no lawyers, no way for a special delivery letter to ever reach her from Boston. She thought that maybe when she got home she'd ask Granny Edwards to teach her to quilt. It was such a peaceful pastime.

Her robe hung on the closet door. She reached for it and caught her reflection in the mirror. For the first time in what seemed like so very long, she actually found it interesting, something she could be pleased with. She could still feel Jonathan's touch kindling life in what had become merely a tool, and remembered how it was to view herself for more than just her work capacity.

She had to admit that where she once nudged at plump, with full curves that Tom sometimes frowned upon a little, she had grown lean with the work she'd done. Her hips were small, her waist smaller, her breasts still high and firm. The times she'd stolen away to enjoy the secluded peace of the sun had left her skin with a rich glow. Ah, the benefits of the outdoor life, she could hear Jonathan say with a smug smile.

Unaccountably, the thought made her feel a bit breathless. She donned her robe and belted it, bending to sweep her hair up into a towel. Straightening, she reached out and opened the door to the other room.

"Well, Anne, I see you're also still a slave to tradition."

Anne stopped short, a cry caught in her throat. Her first thought was to run.

Tom smiled lazily at her from where he lounged on the bed.

Chapter 11

What are you doing here?" Anne hissed.

"Why, I came to see my lovely wife," Tom answered smoothly. "By the way, Anne, you are more lovely than ever. Did I tell you that?"

He stood slowly, languorously, his words and movements making Anne uncomfortably aware of her nakedness beneath the short flannel robe. "You finally lost that weight, didn't you, pet?"

She instinctively took a step back, her composure threatened. "How did you get in?"

Tom's smile broadened with self-satisfaction. "It was painfully easy. I simply told the very pretty young lady at the desk that I was your husband and that I had managed to get to town to surprise you. She was most accommodating." He moved closer, his eyes roving her body in frank admiration. "I suppose that I must admit that there must be something to that backwoods life of yours after all," he admitted smoothly, still approaching without hesitation. Anne knew that she was breathing more quickly, his pres-

ence crowding her. "You may have calluses on your hands,
pet, but your body is finally the way I always wanted it. I'm
glad you came back to me."

Two bright pink spots flared high on Anne's cheeks and
she stopped retreating. "You think I came back here because I couldn't live without you?" she asked with a smile
that didn't touch her eyes.

"You'll always love me, Anne," he purred, his eyes boring through her. "You'll always need me."

With shattering clarity, Anne suddenly saw through him,
to the very core of what drove him. And she finally admitted that his lust for power governed him even with her. She'd
always thought that he had at least wanted her, if not loved
her. It was more likely the truth that he'd enjoyed her, like
a game. Like any game he played in his life. It was only fun
as long as he had the control, the power. How it must have
infuriated him when she'd walked out.

"Why did you really come here tonight, Tom?" she
asked, her voice suddenly chilly. He stopped, an eyebrow
arching in mock surprise. The action suddenly reminded
Anne of Jonathan, and it was all she could do to keep from
shivering. Jonathan wasn't like this man; he wasn't amoral.
And yet, if something weren't done soon, he might be. He
and Tom could be carbon copies all the way to the sneer.

"You want me to be honest?" Tom retorted, his hypnotizing eyes darkening as if he were giving serious consideration to the question. He walked closer, standing so that
Anne had to look up into his eyes. A sly psychological move
of dominance, but it was effective. He was so close, the faint
smell of his cologne overpowering. "I came to take you
back, Anne. You belong with me. You always have. I want
to take care of you. To give you a real home. I was wrong
before to have let you leave. I didn't realize just how much
you meant to me." He laid a hand on her shoulder, gently
stroking in rhythm to his words. "Anne, together we could
have it all."

Anne steeled herself against the electric shock of Tom's touch, the smothering sensation Jonathan's hands had re-awakened after so long.

It didn't come.

Tom caressed her arm slowly, watching his hand as it moved, something that had once set Anne off like dry kindling. But nothing happened. She watched with disbelief, waiting for something to change, for the inevitable to happen. She wanted to cry, to sing and laugh. Her knees remained rigid and her heart cold. She was finally free of Tom McCarthy.

The exhilaration was heady enough to make her smile. Tom saw the change and returned the smile he mistook for excitement, a slow seductive gaze touching the green of his eyes.

Anne's eyes hardened. "If you don't back out of this room right now, I'll start screaming rape at the top of my lungs and not stop until the entire hotel staff and the New York press corps are up here." His grip tightened on her arm, the warmth in his eyes dying. Anne looked down at his hand and then up to those cruel, hypnotic eyes she'd loved as much as she'd hated. Their power had disappeared; the glint in them was no more than selfish. "And then I'll slap an assault and battery charge on you. I'll have bruises on my arm inside an hour. Do you really want to chance it?"

For the first time since she'd known him, Tom was at a complete loss. He seemed to freeze where he was, his expression concealing any emotion he might have been battling.

"Anne, you can't be serious." His voice was strained with the effort. "I can take you back to the places you deserve to be."

Anne eyed him steadily, her feet planted a bit more solidly beneath her. The act of paralyzing him had released her. She had won; she had finally beaten his game. No matter what happened now, she had her freedom from the Anne

Jackson that Boston had molded and Tom and her father had controlled as their right. She was free of them all.

"I said leave, now, Tom. Don't make me ruin your reputation."

His mouth curled into a sneer at her words. "You can't make me believe that you don't want me." Grabbing her roughly to him, he kissed her, his mouth harsh and brutal, his hands punishing. Anne stood still and waited, wanting to laugh and hit him at the same time.

He raised his head, not letting go of her, his eyes smoky with rage.

"More bruises, Tom," she said evenly. "If I were you, I'd quit while I was only a little behind."

For a moment she thought he was going to strike her. She'd never seen him so angry that he couldn't speak. The fact that she didn't flinch from him seemed to taunt him even more. He held her for a long moment, his fingers vise-like, his mouth a bitter slash of scorn.

"Don't congratulate yourself too soon, pet," he hissed. "You just made a bigger mistake than you'll ever know."

And then he was gone, slamming the door hard behind him.

For a minute Anne could only stand where she was, staring after the closed door as if she'd seen an apparition. She hugged her arms tightly around her and massaged her sore shoulders with gentle fingers. She'd been right. There would be bruises: ugly, appropriate reminders of Tom's visit. She took slow, deep breaths, in through her nose, out through her mouth to ease the trembling that had set in once the fear had died.

Then slowly, inexorably a smile dawned. Rising from the corners of her mouth, it swept along the laughter lines that dimpled her cheeks to the gray eyes that sparkled with a new light of triumph. Anne had a sudden urge to call Cassie and tell her that the ghosts had been dispelled, the crutches thrown away. Mixing metaphors, she thought absurdly, not really caring. She had just stood toe-to-toe with her personal devil and overcome him. Tom McCarthy would never again intrude into her life as an unwanted obsession. She had proven to herself that she didn't need that kind of man anymore. She didn't have to fear his power or allure ever again.

Anne smiled even more broadly at the thought that he'd offered to take care of her. Once that would have been a powerful temptation. Once, maybe, before she'd been forced to go against everything she'd been taught since childhood and had learned to take care of herself.

It had always been a foregone conclusion that she should be taken care of all her life, like an objet d'art or a helpless animal. If she'd held onto that logic, she would have remained Tom's property. She would, indeed, have given in to him tonight and gone back to the prison that had once been her home.

Knowing no other hands than Tom's, she would have succumbed to them. But as if to seal the transformation that had taken place, Jonathan had reawakened her self-awareness as a woman when he'd taken her into his arms and made love to her. He had not only made her feel wanted, but treasured in a way Tom had never thought of.

There was a special exhilaration in rediscovering something you thought you'd lost for good. Within a period of weeks, Anne had stumbled back over not only her self-esteem but the wonder of how it felt to be reflected beautifully in a man's eyes. It was too bad it was so late. She suddenly wanted to call Jonathan, too. She wanted to thank him, to tell him that no matter what, she could never be able to return in kind the precious gift he'd given her.

Anne dressed for bed and dried her hair, listening with new contentment to the discordant city pass far below her. Until tonight she hadn't really realized it, but she was a free woman, able to go wherever she wanted or do what she pleased. She could count on not only her own worth and pride, but on the fact that she was worth the love of a good man. And waiting for her like a lifeline to her strength, a symbol of her resurrection, was her home, tucked comfortably away within the mountains and her memory. It seemed that as long as she had that symbol of her past and future, she could do anything.

As long as she had it.

A brief surge of fear flared and then waned as she remembered again the victory she had just savored. The impossible did happen. She would get her home back and from there be able to make the new beginning she very much wanted.

Settling into the big, comfortable bed, Anne wondered in passing whether Tom had really meant to threaten her when he left or whether he'd just badly lost his composure. Even so, it was a relief to know that she would be escaping the city tomorrow to the safety of her cabin. Judson might have just been correct when he told her that Tom might resort to desperate measures, and Anne knew better than most what kind of influence he could manage to wield in this city.

As she fell asleep the thought occurred to her that as much as she wanted to get back to the cabin, she anticipated seeing Jonathan again even more. It didn't occur to her to feel her customary caution.

The next afternoon Judson did, indeed, tell her that the meeting had been postponed and that she would be notified of its new date in due time. Amplex Corporation sent its regrets in hopes that it hadn't inconvenienced Miss Jackson too much. Miss Jackson scowled at the statement and told Judson that she would be back home doing some real work should they feel the need to get in touch with her. And then she made the arrangements to do just that.

Jim was in the store when she pulled in. He still had some difficulty getting used to her in city attire, and was shaking his head when she walked up to him.

"Oh, stop it," she said, laughing. "In five minutes I'll be back in my jeans and you won't be impressed anymore."

She walked on through to the house, where she always changed before making the trip up on Andy.

"Why are you here, Annie?" Amanda demanded in her shrill four-year-old voice. "My mommy's at your house. With David." David was her six-year-old brother who never had much of a reputation for being able to sit still for more than two minutes at a time. Anne couldn't help but grin. Jonathan would probably be having the time of his life, considering how well he seemed to get along with small children. At least she could be sure he'd be glad to see her.

For at least the first third of the journey up the mountain Anne found herself puzzled by an odd tightness in her chest, a sense of unaccustomed urgency. Her ride home had always been her favorite time to meditate. Andy preferred a slower attack on the steep path, and Anne usually enjoyed the pace he set. It gave her the time to watch the wildlife and consider the way of the world. She would think about the people she'd come to know, the grannies who held the power of folklore in these mountains and maybe the serpentine family ties that seemed to bind the hollows she crossed. The road home was Anne's chance to unwind, to catch the first shattering of ice as the creek began to thaw or watch the spiraling flight of a hawk as it dipped and soared in among the shadows of afternoon.

After flying in from a place like New York she knew that she needed the time to unwind even more than usual. Instead she found herself nudging at Andy's flanks, urging him on at a steady pace. For the first time in memory, the cabin seemed to be too far away. When she actually caught herself toying with the idea of getting a real road up to the cabin, she began to wonder what was wrong with her.

It wasn't until she topped the ridge that it actually dawned on her. She'd never hurried to the cabin before because she'd never had someone like Jonathan waiting for her. She reigned Andy in just beyond a long stand of birch and sat staring sightlessly out over the soft gray-and-white folds of winter land that stretched away from her in never-ending succession.

Jonathan. Could he make that much of a difference? Could he be the reason that her chest felt constricted by an iron band and why she had to take deep breaths to ease the alien sense of fluttering in her? Safely encased in their gloves, her hands had begun to perspire. She had never experienced this kind of delicious dread before. But then she'd never been the person she was at this minute.

She had only been gone two days, and already she felt as if a different person were approaching the cabin. When she'd left, she'd done so as a cripple, emotionally hobbled by the manipulations of the man who'd stolen her trust. She'd made love to Jonathan out of desperation, certain that she could never profit from falling in love with him. It wasn't just that she hadn't trusted Jonathan—something she could hardly consider after the example set for her by Tom—it was that she truly didn't believe that she deserved to be loved. She'd really half believed what Tom had taught her.

She returned now having taken the cure. Tom had lost his decisive power to haunt, and Anne had found hers to take charge. The scene with him the night before had illustrated that without qualification. And that, she thought, was the first step to rediscovering the conviction that she had a right to be loved.

So she was back to the question of the moment. Was Jonathan that man? Or was he nothing more than a combination of attraction, infatuation and loneliness? Was love what bound them, or was it need, something that would vanish once the snow melted and they weren't isolated and dependent on each other anymore?

Anne allowed herself a moment to consider what the cabin would be like once Jonathan left and she found at least her own answer. Once he did go, the company of memories and familiar routine would no longer be enough to fill her life. He had changed that life and had changed her.

With a wry smile she realized that she was hungry for the sight of those eyes that had once so frustrated her. The multifaceted personality delighted her where it had once only confused her. Her discovery of that specially guarded place in him had set her tumbling from the safe niche her prejudices had so carefully carved. She'd been drawn to Jonathan as if the fuel that fed him could also revitalize her. If she weren't in love with him, she decided with an odd giggle, she should at the very least tap into him as a source of natural energy.

Anne took a deep breath, filling her lungs with brisk air to try and calm the growing clamor in her. It had been so much easier when everything was hopeless and finite. She had a chance for happiness now but the uncertainty of it unnerved her. What if she were in love with Jonathan? What guarantee was there that she'd be any luckier than before? What in the end did she know about Jonathan Bradshaw Harris? She knew that he had money, a tragic past to overcome and a knack for awkward tenderness that made her want to cry. She knew that he'd made love to her with a fire and sensitivity that had brought her back to life.

Yet he had just as surely lashed out at her more than once without real explanation. It was as if every time he got too close to her, some part of him revolted, rejecting her with a venom that was frightening. She could guess all she wanted about the reasons for it, and the conclusions she had reached all seemed to be sensible. But it was possible that she was wrong; there was a deeper, darker place in him that she hadn't found. Perhaps there lay the animosity that tended to flare unexpectedly. If that were true, if there was more to Jonathan's conflicting persona than even Judson knew, Anne was afraid that she would never find it in time to save her from repeating her mistakes.

Andy turned to eye her, impatiently stamping in the wet snow. His breath rose in swift clouds that dissipated quickly.

Anne patted at him absently for a moment as she gathered
the courage to go on. She hated uncertainty. For the last two
years she'd patterned her entire life-style to avoid it. Yet here
she sat in the throes of indecision, certain that she wanted
nothing less than the conflict that awaited her when she got
home, and yet knowing that she had no other choice but to
go on anyway. She took another careful breath, wishing she
could think of a more effective way to calm down and
amazed that she needed one. Then she nudged Andy in the
flanks and turned him for home.

When she reached the front porch, Anne found herself
hesitating with her hand on the door. She made an unconscious point of stamping the snow from her boots with just
a bit more noise than usual, as if in giving the people inside
some warning of her arrival she could better set the stage. A
small frigid breeze found her neck and provoked a chill
Anne couldn't seem to stop.

Just as she'd anticipated, she found Jonathan seated
comfortably in the wing-back next to the fireplace. In the
instant before he looked up to greet her, Anne struggled to
control her own reaction. The sight of his bent, tousled head
sent her heart skidding unnaturally and set her hands to
trembling. Instead of feeling more secure for the time spent
away from him, she felt as if her balance were suddenly in
great peril. Getting away from him hadn't accomplished in
the least what she'd hoped. The independence she'd gained
the night before was in imminent danger of crumbling before the anticipation of his sharp blue gaze. Any objectivity she'd prayed for in handling this scene seemed to have
been left in that quiet office in New York. Her future would
rest on Jonathan's response to seeing her.

The hard lines of his face shifted oddly as he raised his
face. Momentarily they softened with an almost painful
pleasure, then froze with restraint. After what seemed like
hours, he allowed her a genial smile of welcome.

"Well, if it isn't Miss Fifth Avenue." He dropped his
book in his lap, his eyes bright with measured amiability.

Probably mirrors of what he saw in her own eyes, Anne thought. She could envision them both facing each other with strained civility, waiting for a clue from the other before proceeding. She'd been steeling herself against Jonathan's acceptance or rejection, the indications he would deliver about the fate of their future. Now here he sat waiting for the same from her.

"You're going through that library pretty fast." She smiled back a bit uncomfortably. "There's no other room to work your way up to, ya know."

An eyebrow arched minimally. "Isn't there?"

"Annie, what are you doing back so soon?"

Anne started at the sound of Cassie's voice, her eyes leaving Jonathan a brittle warning of discretion before turning to greet her friend. Cassie stood in the kitchen doorway with David like a shadow behind her. Cassie missed very little and couldn't have possibly missed the static atmosphere of the room, but she refrained from allowing herself comment.

"You keep coming home early," she protested with an easy grin. "How are Jonathan and I ever going to get any time alone?"

"Take him home with you," Anne retorted more easily as she began to discard her over clothes. "I'll keep David up here with me. I'd get more cooperation and less back talk."

Cassie laughed as she walked in, drying her hands on a towel. "Jonathan, you've been insulted. If I were you I'd demand satisfaction."

"Crutches at ten paces," he said dryly.

"I'm afraid it's going to have to be something else," Anne told him. "I only have one pair." It was already easier to talk. It was always that way when Cassie was there with them to buffer what they said to each other. If only she didn't have to leave.

"Well, if you're looking for something you have plenty of, throw muffins at each other," the tall brunette offered. "You have enough in there to fight off a batallion." She

stood behind Jonathan with a hand on his shoulder. Anne
envied her her natural ease.

"No," she obliged. "I'd end up eating the ammuni-
tion."

"What are you doing home so early?" Cassie asked.
"You told us not to expect you for another few days."

"I'll explain over some hot tea," Anne answered, hanging up her coat. "It's kind of a good-news bad-news story."

Cassie turned, almost bumping into David and preceded
Anne into the kitchen.

"Don't I get to find out?" Jonathan demanded.

Anne patted him on the head in mock patronization.
"Maybe when you're a little older." Then, blithely ignoring his unhappy reaction, she walked into the unusually
spotless kitchen and took a seat across from Cassie. Tea was
already poured and steaming from the earthenware mugs.

"David," Cassie said, her arm around the little boy's
waist, "why don't you go on in and talk to Jonathan?"

"Aw, Mom," he whined, scrunching up his face, obviously afraid that he'd miss something interesting.

"Don't 'aw, Mom' me, go on," she answered evenly with
a small push to the backside. David went, the look in his
face leaving no doubt as to his opinion on the matter. Anne
sipped at her tea to hide her smile.

"Are you sure that Jonathan wants to talk to David?" she
asked under her breath.

Cassie grinned. "I think you'd be surprised. Jonathan has
been teaching David to play chess all morning. David thinks
that he's the neatest thing since Spiderman."

Anne's eyebrows went up. "The same Jonathan who took
one look at Mary's brood and almost made it down the
mountain under his own power?"

"The same. He has almost as much patience as Jim. I
think that if he learns to control that nasty streak of his,
he'd make someone a good father...if he hasn't already, that
is."

Anne shook her head. "That's part of my New York report. I found out all about him from Judson." She went on to give Cassie a detailed accounting of her trip.

Much later, they walked into the living room together to find David carefully replacing the chess pieces in their case. "I almost won today," he beamed up at his mother. "Jonathan says I'm good."

"Deadly," Jonathan agreed with an impressed nod. Anne walked over to help David, staying carefully away from Jonathan as if she could more easily remain objective at a distance.

The tension in the room leaped the minute she walked in. She and Jonathan didn't even have to look at each other. The unspoken emotions that had been building between them begged for release, and neither could do it in front of company. Anne wasn't even sure that she had the nerve to confront that kind of conflict once Cassie and David had gone. Again she was assailed by the urge to ask them to stay, until she had the chance to straighten out the turmoil that had erupted in the last few days.

Anne looked up from her little task to see Cassie regarding her evenly. It was as if she'd been reading Anne's thoughts and had come to her own conclusion.

"Come on, David," she said, smiling quietly. "We have to get home in time to help Daddy deliver the mail."

"Thanks for keeping me company," Jonathan said to the little boy, his voice a little tight. "When I get better we'll have to go hiking together. I bet you know the best trails around here."

"Okay." David beamed, making a great show of shaking hands like a man. Anne once again caught that flash of gentleness in Jonathan's eyes as he participated in the ritual, a quick softening at the corners of his face. She physically restrained herself from reaching out to it, as if the warmth in his expression could be soaked up through her fingertips. The tension was mounting in her chest. She could hear it reflected in her own voice as she said her goodbyes to David and accepted his overenthusiastic bear hug.

Cassie delivered her own farewells outside where she could bestow Anne with a smile that at once called up the trust of friendship and offered an almost maternal concern. Her eyes twinkled with their familiar humor.

"Are you going to be safe if I leave?" Cassie asked. Anne had told her about the messages Judson had been receiving from Tom.

Anne's smile was her thanks for her friend's empathy. "I told you. Tom's far away."

Cassie's smile broadened, her teeth gleaming against her olive skin. "Maybe I should have asked Jonathan that question instead."

"That's entirely possible," Anne conceded, trying her best to match Cassie's studied ease. For the first time since she'd made the momentous decision to leave Tom, she knew the paralysis of indecision. She was actually terrified to walk back into the cabin to face Jonathan's judgment. Smiling anyway, Anne gave Cassie an extra hug for her unstated support. She watched in silence as Cassie and David turned their horses away from her and proceeded down the path. Then with a sigh she opened the door to face Jonathan's measured gaze.

"I think," she said with enough force to surprise herself, "that you and I need to talk."

Chapter 12

Jonathan allowed one eyebrow to rise in dry caricature. "Is this going to be one of those little domestic chats I've heard so much about?"

Anne's first impulse was to slap him. She came very close, stalking up without a word to where he sat and even opening her mouth to deliver a correspondingly biting retort. But suddenly, she saw the tension on Jonathan's face was as brittle as hers. He was as shaken as she was by the sudden shift in their relationship. And just as surprised.

She realized with some astonishment that she'd begun to soften. "Would you like some tea while we talk?"

His eyebrow lifted even higher for a brief moment before returning her rueful smile. "Unless there's something more potent. I have a feeling I'm going to need strength."

"Just a keen wit," Anne retorted evenly. "And yes, I have the perfect thing. My Aunt Adelaide used to sweeten her tea with it."

Jonathan pulled a very expressive face, but kept his silence as Anne walked by to the kitchen.

A few minutes later she returned to set the tea things on the coffee table. Curling her feet beneath her, she settled onto the couch next to Jonathan's chair. Her heart was still in her throat. She noticed that her hand shook as she poured the tea and handed Jonathan his blue earthenware mug. She also noticed that his hand was a little damp as he accepted.

"I have sugar if you'd like," she offered, "but usually Aunt Adelaide's tonic is enough."

Jonathan nodded absently and took a solid drink out of the steaming mug. He swallowed convulsively and then coughed. With tears in his eyes, he turned on Anne, his breath still coming in dramatic little gasps. "What the hell was that?" He had hold of ribs that seemed to protest all the activity.

"Tonic," Anne answered evenly, sipping her own tea very carefully. The well-remembered fire of the Jackson all-purpose elixir bit at her throat with a vengeance.

"Tonic, hell," he accused, still wiping at the tears in his eyes. "That's moonshine!"

She considered the accusation quietly, finding it hard to refrain from grinning. "Oh, I guess you could call it that, too."

The next drink Jonathan took was more modest. Even so, he still found it necessary to pause after swallowing, eyes closed, breathing suspended for a moment. "Did you make this, too?"

Anne did grin then, knowing that the two of them would at least start the renegotiation of their relationship on equal footing. "No. This particular jar was payment from a lady I helped with the pleurisy."

"She should have taken this. She never would have known she was sick."

Anne savored the wood smoke flavor of the liquid in her cup. "She did. And you're right, it worked wonderfully. You see, there are some benefits to the backwoods after all."

Jonathan took another taste of his quickly disappearing tea and nodded. "I'll certainly drink to that."

"I think you are."

They both spent the next few minutes in careful consideration of the jet fuel that spiced their mugs. The fire snapped before them, and the clock marked the passing of the silence with soft staccato.

Anne listened to the rhythm of accumulating time with growing unease. There could be no more putting off the talk they badly needed. She couldn't bear to spend another night in the house with Jonathan and not come to a resolution of some kind for the strained emotions that leaped between them. She studied the solid lines of her mug without ever seeing them as she feverishly turned over opening gambits in her mind and equally quickly discarded them. She was so afraid of what she'd find in Jonathan's eyes that she refused to look up at him at all. Suddenly she felt like a high school freshman searching in desperation for a mature introduction to a summer crush. By the time Jonathan did speak up, Anne had gotten so wrapped up in a futile attempt to ease into the answers she needed that she didn't even hear him.

"Anne."

She sat like a statue, the only betrayal of her tension a vein that stood out against her temple.

"Annie." Her head snapped up, but Jonathan's smile was solidly noncommittal. "How about a little more tea?"

It took her a few seconds to answer. "Tea or tonic?"

He grinned rakishly. "Sure. Have some yourself."

She did. Only this time she went into the kitchen and poured herself a small snifter of brandy. She spent the time there as she had on the couch, with no better luck. The longer she agonized over her next move, the more foolish and frustrated she felt.

Never in her life had she found herself at such a loss for words. It was as if in the last few weeks she'd been granted a whole new life with a new set of expectations, problems and guidelines. The difficulty was that she wasn't familiar enough with the new guidelines yet to be able to use them effectively in solving the problem. The problems weren't waiting patiently for solutions until she was ready. If only Jonathan could have waited to come into her life until she'd worn her freedom a little longer.

Returning to the living room, Anne reminded herself that if Jonathan hadn't been here already, there would never have been any freedom in the first place. Whatever else happened, she still had to thank him for that.

"Jonathan," she started to say as she walked in, "I wanted to thank you for sending me to Judson...."

The words trailed limply away when she caught sight of Jonathan. He was on the floor, propped on pillows he'd pulled from the couch. Legs stretched easily before him, he patted to the matching nest of pillows he'd built beside him between couch and fireplace.

"What are you doing?" she asked without thinking.

"Making us both comfortable," he said easily, the crinkle of his eyes warm. "Come on down and join me."

Anne cast a suspicious eye even as she moved to set the tray down on the already rearranged coffee table. "You certainly have been busy."

"Profitable use of time and resources is one of my company's hallmarks," he assured her.

Before she did join him, Anne stoked the fire and turned off the lights. Immediately the shadows crept close and danced rhythmically with the firelight over the walls. The night grew comfortable and intimate, its wind only a suggestion.

Anne pulled off shoes and socks and stretched her feet out toward the fire before she took brandy in hand and leaned back next to Jonathan's companionable warmth.

"You must be an idea man," she said. "This was a great one."

He slipped an arm around her and brought her head to his shoulder. "Well, I had a feeling we weren't going to get anything accomplished on the furniture. You looked like you were waiting to go in for oral exams up there."

"That bad?"

"Worse. I was beginning to feel completely at a loss."

"You?" She instinctively snuggled closer, the strength of his arm about her an exhilarating elixir that put the glow of the brandy to shame. She felt them both ease up, as if this were the prefect position for confessing truths: in intimate contact, but safe from the uncomfortable possibility of allowing revelations to be caught in unsuspecting eyes. Anne smiled at Jonathan's uncustomary admission. "I can't imagine you ever being at a complete loss."

His answering laugh was sharp. "Well, it's happened to me more since I've been here than ever before."

Anne took a sip of brandy and thought of how Jonathan's eyes held their own source of heat. His hand was rubbing at her shoulder, an absent gesture of easy familiarity that kindled its own energy. "Has it been so bad?"

For a moment there was only the answer of a patient fire. Then Jonathan nuzzled her hair, his own head now resting against hers. "Terrible."

Without really knowing why, Anne found herself testing their closeness.

"You don't really do that well, do you?"

He looked over. "What?"

"Being at a loss. Not being in control."

She felt him stiffen a little as he turned back to consider the fire again. "No."

Anne nodded to herself, trying her best to remain noncommittal. "You haven't told me yet about the other time you said you were helpless to keep someone you cared for from being hurt. It was before Nam, wasn't it?"

Jonathan's answer was a rigid, profound silence.

"It takes a lot to make a person so...obsessed," she said gently, careful to not push. "That's the only word I can use for how you've pushed yourself to get back on your feet." She shrugged offhandedly and offered a slight smile. "Anybody else would still be demanding breakfast in bed."

Still he didn't answer, didn't move.

She kept on, feeling even more unsettled. "What happened to you in Vietnam was terrible, but I have the feeling that it was the coup de grace. The final straw."

"Why is it so important to you?" he finally asked.

"Because it's important to you. And because it might help me to understand you better," she offered tentatively. "Your mystery-man image has its drawbacks."

When she felt him relax a little, she knew this particular moment of challenge had passed.

"You didn't ask Judson?"

"Of course I did. He told me what a beautiful woman your mother is and how he used to call on her back in Wyoming."

"That's all?"

"That took two hours. I figured that it would take another four weeks to span the next forty years." She supposed it would have been easier to admit her knowledge, but it was important to her that Jonathan volunteer the information about his past on his own. He had to want to share it with her or it would end up being nothing more than emotional blackmail to hold over him.

"It was a long time ago," he said quietly without moving, his voice pensive.

"It's not that long ago when it still bothers you so much," she insisted, then carefully backed off. "Judson worries about you."

Jonathan moved then. Anne knew he was looking down at her. "He worries, does he?"

She nodded, her eyes passive.

"Do you?"

Anne took a slow breath and turned to him, her eyes honest. "I don't want you to end up like my ex-husband. And I'm afraid something's driving you down the same road."

Jonathan considered her a moment in silence. Then, his features settling into a soft smile, he moved back next to her again, his embrace closer.

"In that case, someday soon I'll tell you all about it."

"Why not now?"

He shook his head a little. "Because this is not the time or place. Soon."

She nodded. His reply was both more and less than she'd hoped for. It was a promise of a future in carefully impressive words, but not the revelation she'd hoped for.

"Jonathan?"

"Mmm?" He was sipping at his tea, his good leg drawn up as a prop for his elbow. His fingers were lacing through her hair, their touch alive.

"You're going back to New York, aren't you?"

He stroked her hair for a little while longer. She closed her eyes against the naked hunger such a simple gesture aroused in her.

"Yes, Anne," he finally said. "I'm going back."

Her voice became progressively softer. "Where does that leave us?"

He bent to kiss her forehead, the touch of him yearning and uncertain all of a sudden. "I don't know. I don't suppose we could hope for another blizzard."

She grinned tremulously. "I could push you back off the cliff."

He kissed her again, his lips lingering on her cheek. "I don't think that would be a good idea. I couldn't stand being in a snowbound cabin with you any longer if I couldn't touch you."

"Is this going to end up being a cheap, tawdry affair?" she demanded, trying very much to sound flippant. She only succeeded in sounding frightened.

At that, Jonathan set down his mug and turned to take Anne's face in his hands. His eyes, half in shadow and half filled with firelight, sought her with an almost physical intensity. Anne finally found in them what she'd so long hoped for.

"I don't think I even want to joke about that, Anne," he said softly. Anne saw the clean, hard lines of his face and thought how they lent sincerity to his words. Her heart thudded and tears stung at her eyes. His hands held her face like a wild bird that might shy away. "Would you agree to take it one day at a time?" he asked. "I want to promise you anything you want right now, but I'm not sure I can."

She felt even more unsteady than before. "Your seven children need you?"

He made a face at her. "I know Judson better than to think he would have forgotten to clear up that small detail within five minutes of meeting someone as lovely as you. There is no wife, no children; no one in my life." A grin tugged at the corners of his mouth, softened by his admission. "At least there wasn't anyone until I woke up to find you hovering over me like something out of a Raphael painting. I fell in love with you long before I wanted to."

Anne found herself smiling back, the light brighter in her eyes, a certain determination in her voice. "Isn't that always the way? If you hadn't been so darn stubborn, we could have been enjoying ourselves all along."

His eyebrows shot up again. "Me? I've seen murderers treated with more courtesy by the jury that hung them!"

Anne had no choice but to admit the truth of his charge as she snuggled back into the comfort of his arm. He immediately encircled her with the other. "I guess I was a little prickly. I had a small problem to work out."

"So I heard. A husband who talked like me. What ever became of him?"

Anne grinned again with triumph. "Oh, I gave him his walking papers. Once and for all."

Jonathan moved against her. "You don't say. Well, I'll have to check that out for myself."

Anne looked up to see what he intended and was met by a kiss. At first slow and exploratory, Jonathan's mouth gentle on hers, it began to build of its own accord. Before Anne knew it, she was completely within Jonathan's embrace, his lips crushing hers, his tongue searching hers feverishly. His beard chafed her cheek. His breath tickled her ear. By the time he drew back over a minute later, they were both out of breath.

Jonathan's eyes gleamed with satisfaction. "You know," he said softly as he brushed Anne's hair over her shoulder, "it would certainly be a shame to waste such a good fire."

Anne couldn't refrain from a wicked grin. "What do you have in mind," she said just as suggestively, "a wienie roast?"

Jonathan didn't even blink. "Only if we get too close."

She chuckled, a low throaty sound that Jonathan enjoyed. "But you have a broken leg. Wouldn't that be awfully cumbersome?"

His hand was beginning to drift from her shoulder. Anne could have sworn he'd dipped his fingers in fire. They seared easily through her blouse as he moved to her top button.

"You didn't seem to find my leg cumbersome the other night." Bending down, he kissed the flesh he had exposed by freeing her buttons. Anne was having even more trouble breathing. His fingers had almost reached her waist. Jonathan seemed to find particular pleasure in the soft mounds of Anne's breasts where they swelled above the restraint of her bra.

"The other night I was... in a... rash..." she admitted weakly, her head far back into the pillows where Jonathan's other arm cradled her.

"A rash."

She could tell that he was grinning as he deftly slipped her shirt off and teased her nipples through the filmy material that held them. The suggestion of his touch was almost more than she could bear.

"You think you'd have to be in a rash to make love again?" Rather than remove her bra, he began to undo her belt, his lips leaving blazing trails across her throat. He was taking so long it was torture, teasing her with his touch, the promise of taking her, and then holding back.

"Oh... I think the... idea... shows promise..." she managed. She opened her eyes to see his face etched in firelight, his soft lips and laughing eyes, the small cleft in his chin. Then she reached up to draw him to her.

He waited a moment, his face very close to hers, his breathing rapid. "You let me know when you think you're in a sufficient...rash." His kiss was quick, a temptation. "Okay?"

She caught his head with her hands and pulled him to her for another kiss. A long kiss that left him with no illusions as to her intentions. "Okay."

The firelight bathed them, casting their skin in living bronze as they settled into each other's arms and the luxury of discovering each other. Jonathan slipped Anne out of her jeans, his hands painting her legs with fierce chills. Then Anne helped him out of his clothes, both of them laughing at the difficulty they had getting around his homemade splint and Anne kissing his ribs when he complained that laughing made them hurt. She allowed herself to run her hands over the thick hair on his chest and then trace the scars that stood out oddly in the soft light. This time she tasted his belly, the hard, flat plane so well developed that she could trace every muscle with her tongue.

For a long while, Jonathan refused to remove her bra and panties, as if he loved the temptations of secrets not seen. The scintillation of his fingers against the silk shocked Anne to a sharp aching. Taking her own time in exploring the exhilaration of his sinewy body, she surprised moans from him and set him to gasping when she teased him with her teeth.

She took his buttocks in her hands, so firm and tight, and pulled him against her so that she could enjoy his excitement. Then she pushed him back on the pillows and took great pains to teach him how to kiss, telling him so and laughing with him. Aroused by the soft strength of his mouth, she let her tongue slip in to taste the pleasant roughness of his, the smooth curve of his teeth, the sweet warmth of his lips. It all seemed a revelation. It was as if she'd never tasted a man before, and each new place she found set her to smiling with the delight of discovery.

"Well," he finally asked, his hands teasing her so that she almost cried out, "are you in a rash, do you think?"

She paused as if in consideration. She was on fire and freezing at once, her muscles quivering with the effort of control. "I think so."

He dropped a kiss on her nose and grinned, the spark in his eyes one of tender exhilaration. "About time."

Letting his hands slide carefully down from her throat, he undid the clasp between Anne's breasts. Her bra fell away, though the straps were still on her shoulders. Jonathan didn't bother with them. He bent to her breasts, taking first one in hand and then the other. Anne had never known such gentle attention. Tears reached her eyes as she cradled his head to her, his hair so wildly black against the milky whiteness of her skin. The core of her own arousal coiled like a tensed animal within her, her love for Jonathan an exquisite pain. Yes, she guessed she'd have to take it one day at a time. She could never have asked more in life than the delicious intensity of this moment.

As he eased toward capturing her breasts, first with his tongue, then lips and finally the sharp thrill of his teeth, Jonathan slid her panties down and away. Anne allowed his hands to part her thighs, searching upwards to find her long since accommodating.

"Doesn't...all this...hurt your...ribs?" she found herself demanding, ever the nurse.

Jonathan raised his eyes to hers, his fingers trailing new, even more unbearable fire. "Not really. I guess I must be in a rash, too." He punctuated his grin with another lingering kiss.

Unable to wait even longer, Anne took him in her hand, surprised again by the power of his arousal, and led him to her. From that moment, whatever control they had managed between them vanished. They clung to each other as if terrified of their parting and reached their peak together, shuddering and murmuring, their lips bruised from the hunger of their meeting. Again Anne cried out, wondering that she could be so overwhelmed. She felt her body become electrified, even to her toes, her scalp tingling as if she'd been hit by lightning.

Lightning had never happened quite like this to Anne before. Suddenly she wondered what she'd ever found so provocative about Tom. It occurred to her that he'd treated her exactly as she'd expected to be treated. Tom had been exciting, but had never really known how to give excitement. He had taken a woman rather than cherished her.

For a long while Anne lay silent in Jonathan's arms, her head nestled in the hollow of his shoulder, her old blue-and-white afghan helping to ward the creeping chill from both of them. She would have given anything to never have to move from this spot and not have to face the uncertainty of the future. She knew that Jonathan loved her just as she loved him, but she knew too that wouldn't answer all of their questions. He still didn't seem able to trust her with the responsibility of his troubled past and had refused to address their future. He wanted to return to the city, and she wanted to stay in the mountains. And she wasn't at all sure that either would find cause to change their minds. The impasse seemed too great to overcome, and it frightened her.

"You never did tell me what happened in New York," Jonathan said lazily.

Anne had been absently running her fingers through the hair that trailed from Jonathan's chest down to his navel, a dark line that begged exploration. She moved her head to take in his eyes, sleepy and content in the dying light, and decided that she loved them more than any other of his features. She could watch them forever.

"I told you," she answered. "I exorcised myself of the ghost of one ex-husband."

He shot her a wry look. "You didn't tell me," he corrected. "You showed me. And, may I add, with great conviction."

"And enthusiasm," she added.

"Overwhelming enthusiasm." His kiss of appreciation took a minute longer. "What else happened?"

She shot him a mischievous grin. "You mean you didn't ask Judson?"

Jonathan was all innocence. "Me?"

She nodded. "I figured you'd be on the phone ten minutes after I got out of his office."

"Well," Jonathan demurred with a wry smile, "I tried. The phone's out again."

Anne nodded with a self-satisfied smirk. "Serves you right for not telling me sooner about what Judson told you about the will."

"I did that for a reason," he protested.

She bestowed her own kiss of appreciation. "I know. It would have been torture on me to have been stuck here with only half the information. Thank you."

Jonathan's eyes sparkled darkly in the firelight. "So, what else happened? Besides the exorcism?"

Anne shrugged happily. "Nothing nearly as important as that."

Jonathan made a face at her. "You were saying something about Judson before."

"Oh," she said lightly, "that. I was thanking you for sending me to him. I don't know what I would have done otherwise."

Jonathan nodded, his eyes contemplating the glowing embers. "I'm glad he helped. I wasn't even sure he'd take a recommendation from me. I haven't seen him in a long time."

Anne held her breath, hoping for more. When it didn't come, she stifled a sigh and turned to the fire herself. "Stick around. He's coming for a visit in the spring when the new clinic opens. In fact, I may name it after him. He's donating his fees to it."

Jonathan's voice still had a faraway sound when he answered. "That's Judson all right."

"He seems to think very highly of you."

"Rank prejudice. He's my godfather."

Anne turned to him in surprise. "You never told me that."

Jonathan shrugged. "You never asked."

"I suppose you're going to tell me that you went to law school because of him."

It wasn't until she'd said it that she remembered that Jonathan had gone to law school after Nam. After he'd changed.

He looked down at her, his eyes suddenly unreadable, with a hint of the old animosity flashing through. "No" was all he said, leaving her even more troubled. "No, you can't blame that on Judson."

"Well," she said hurriedly, trying to cover her confusion. "He thinks I can get the cabin back. But then, you know that. You've been helping him, from what I hear."

He shrugged easily. "Judson doesn't have as keen an acquaintance with the devious mind as I do."

Anne couldn't help but grin. "Can't argue with you there."

"Tell me what happened," he said, scowling.

So she told him, leaving out only the now shoddy-sounding threat situation. It might have been that Judson didn't tell him about Tom's boorish behavior, or maybe Jonathan didn't make much of it, because he never questioned her about it.

At the end he nodded quietly, his eyes once again beyond her, and lapsed into silence. Anne couldn't help but wonder where he'd drifted, somewhere far beyond the walls of her small home.

Was he thinking about Judson, she wondered, or the time he'd stood impotently by as his own home was lost? Whatever it was he was remembering, it brought a hard, flat sheen to his eyes. They seemed almost emotionless, as if the memory had long ago lost its power to move him to passion, and left only pictures and sounds behind. She didn't like it, or the fact that he wouldn't share it with her. Well, she thought with new purpose, I can only keep on trying.

"Tell me about Wyoming."

He started. "What?"

"Wyoming," she persisted. "I want you to describe it for me."

"Didn't I?"

She took up a thoughtful pose. "Let's see. You mentioned the Tetons, I believe. The sky and mountain climbing. Is there any more?"

His gaze was at once amused and tender. "Maybe. But if I tell you about Wyoming, does that mean you'll tell me about where you grew up?"

She took in the room with her hand. "I grew up here."

"What was Boston, a field trip?"

She looked into his eyes a moment, realizing that the tables had been turned and not sure that she was any readier than he was for confessions. "Are your memories of Wyoming painful?"

He shook his head.

"My memories of Boston are. I don't feel like digging that all up tonight, if you don't mind."

Jonathan reached down to gently stroke the pain from her eyes. "It's a deal. Tonight's for the good memories. What are yours?"

She didn't hesitate. "My mother. And the mountain."

"Your mother, then. I've seen a bit of the mountain, but you've never talked about your mother."

Anne smiled a bit wistfully. Her mother had lived in the privacy of her memory for a long time now. "No, I guess I haven't."

They ended up talking through two more hours and another pot of tea. Jonathan spoke with reservation at first and then, warming to his topic, opened up with an expansiveness that surprised Anne. He described at length his boyhood home where mule-ear deer would mingle with the horse herds to get at the winter hay; where trout flashed in a thawing spring-fed river that rushed along behind the stone ranch house his great-grandfather had built near the south end of Jackson Hole. He described it in the different seasons with the words and recollections of a small boy's awe, his eyes alight with the pictures.

His father had taken him on pack trains high in the mountains twice a year to fish and camp. This was where his great lessons in life were learned. His father had taught him self-sufficiency, Wyoming style, and how to live off the land. Jonathan even admitted the veracity of Judson's theory that he returned often to challenge the mountain much as he had in his childhood.

Anne lay still, listening intently and encouraging him with cautious questions and observations. She never was able to push him beyond recollections of his boyhood. He never even admitted to an education beyond eighth grade. She didn't mind, though. The places he'd described to her were the ones she had wanted to find, to share with him so that he could rediscover their worth. It was at least a beginning in bringing their seemingly incompatible life-styles closer. By the time he turned to hear her part of the bargain, he looked as if ten years' weight had been lifted from his shoulders.

When Jonathan did exact the price for his admissions, Anne balked. It had been too long a time since she'd talked to anyone but Cassie about herself. It was a chance she suddenly wasn't sure she wanted to take.

Jonathan, with unusual tact and gentleness, drew the story from her. Before she knew it, she was describing her mother, the shy, blond beauty who had preferred her adopted home in the mountains to the strain of the Boston social life into which she'd been born.

Anne wasn't sure if she'd ever really forgiven her mother for dying three days after Anne's ninth birthday. Elizabeth Harrison Jackson had died in the cabin with the Millers and her children in attendance to ease her pain. Silas, so tall in Anne's young memory, had shepherded Anne and Brad in and out as he'd thought necessary, never once leaving the children in the final day of their mother's life. Anne's father had arrived too late.

One of the things Anne held in memory of her mother was the baking days in the cabin. The smell of fresh-baked bread, her gentle singsong laugh and hands as delicate as porcelain.

It took Anne a moment to realize that she'd been silent for quite a few minutes. The picture of her mother dressed for a big benefit, glittering with family diamonds and cleaning Anne's bicycle-scraped knees lingered in her mind. Suddenly she had the urge to walk up to the small graveyard above the house. She hadn't been there in so long.

"I'm sorry," she said, smiling quickly. "I got a bit lost for a moment."

"That's all right," Jonathan assured her, his voice so close that his breath swept her cheek. "I was enjoying the sight of your eyes."

"My eyes?"

He nodded. "I'd always thought that gray was such a cool color. It isn't really."

She smiled up into the endless depths of blue. "Rank prejudice."

He never answered, but bent to gather her back to him, his eyes brimming with his delight in her, his lips more gentle than his touch.

Late in the night as a brittle moon shed its light through the window and time became lost in its own rhythms, Anne and Jonathan made love quietly, their passion saved for another time. As the fire once again ebbed at their feet, they explored and thrilled in each other, offering each other the salve of friendship and tenderness. Celebrating their new intimacy, they brought their bodies together comfortably, softly, their sounds of satisfaction more like the music of night breezes.

Anne slept that night where she was, covered only by Jonathan's arm and her afghan, the cadence of his breathing beside her as soothing as the murmur of the sea. It had been too long since she'd slept peacefully in a man's arms. It seemed as if she'd never slept so contentedly before, happy to enjoy the moment as it greeted her without re-criminations from the past or dread of the future. She re-fused to consider the fact that since she'd stepped back into the cabin her emotions had vascillated more often than a wind sock in a thunderstorm. For these few hours in the cocoon of a warm house, she felt whole and happy and wanted no more than that.

She decided to momentarily ignore the uncertainties of her future: the threat to her home and life-style, the theat-rical doom predicted by a vengeful ex-husband. For the hours she lay protected in Jonathan's arms, she could avoid the doubts she still had about him and concentrate only on the delicious comfort of his embrace. Tonight, she was happier than she could remember. Anne decided to let to-morrow take care of itself.

Chapter 13

Four days later when Silas returned to help with the chores he spent a good deal of the time sniffing and snorting to himself, something that amused Anne to no end. That was Silas's way of expressing paternal concern and disapproval. He was trying to let her know that he'd been a lot happier when Jonathan had been unwanted and confined to the guest room. According to Silas's solidly suspicious mountain upbringing, now that Jonathan was able to spend his day with Anne, there was too much chance for immoral hanky-panky, if not imprudent relationships. Especially now that Anne no longer seemed to object to Jonathan's presence.

It seemed to particularly gall Silas that Jonathan could spend the majority of the lunch hour in the kitchen making Anne laugh. She could actually see the old man's contemplative eye on the crutches that were propped behind Jonathan's chair. Given half a chance, there was no doubt that the old man would walk off with them in an attempt to confine Jonathan to the sickroom where he belonged.

Anne did not think it prudent at the moment to point out to Silas that that was the last room he'd want to confine Jonathan to in an attempt to keep Anne's virtue safe. She also decided with a grin toward his disapproving frown that now was not exactly the time to tell him that her virtue hadn't been safe for a few days.

So distracted was he by the way Jonathan seemed to fit so nicely into Anne's life that it wasn't until he was almost ready to leave for the day that Silas remembered the package he'd brought for her. Bundling into his heavy jacket, he walked out to rummage in his saddlebag. Anne followed to the front porch where it seemed that the cold wasn't as biting as it had been. She watched Silas with arms wrapped around her chest.

"This come for you yesterday, Annie," he was saying as he tugged a fat manila envelope from the cracked leather pouch. "We didn't know as it'd make any difference if it waited a day before I got it up to ya. You haven't really cared much for the last letters ya got."

Anne grinned, hearing Jonathan hobble out behind her. "You're right, Silas. I haven't been too crazy about any of that mess."

Jonathan filled his lungs with air and peered up into the breathtaking blue of the sky that made his eyes look like mirroring lakes. "So, this is what it feels like to be on the outside. I'm going to have to ask the warden to let me out more."

Anne flashed him a withering look. Silas turned to see him standing by her and took a long, meaningful look at the sky himself. "Gonna thaw soon," he said, nodding a bit as if to seal his verdict. "That snow'll be off this mountain in no more than a few days."

"All of it?" Anne asked, taking in the monstrous drifts that obliterated the angles of the barn.

Instead of gauging the snow as Anne had, Silas turned his speculative eye on Jonathan. "Enough." Then he nodded again, just once, and stepped back up onto the porch to hand Anne the envelope.

It was all Anne could do to keep a straight face. She had never seen Silas this upset, at least not since Ef Tate tried to make unpopular advances toward his daughter Rose. Once again Anne recognized the kinship between Silas's family and herself. His clan had been more of a family than her own since her mother and father had died. Now, they were the only family she had.

"Will you be going by Jim's on your way home?"

He nodded in his slow way.

"I may have a reply to this. Come in for a little more tea and let me go through this really quickly. Please?"

Silas could never refuse her anything. Still grumbling, he followed her back into the cabin and once more shed his jacket. The protest did ease considerably when he saw what Anne had set out to sweeten his tea. His wife Sarah, a Bible Baptist, took no hold with drinking. Silas, who attended church with her on Christmas and Easter and the odd revival, had much more liberal views on the subject.

Anne took up the best defensive position right between Jonathan and Silas at the table and tore into the package Judson had sent her. The kitchen fell into silence without her participation in conversation. After the first few minutes the only sounds to be heard were the rustle of paper, the clock in the living room and a tentative clink of china.

From the first line she read, Anne completely lost contact with the other people in the room. Judson wasted no time in telling her that he was delivering an emotional bombshell, and he didn't go far to apologize. Anne must decide, he told her in carefully reserved language, whether she wanted him to proceed further or not, since her legal option had become an all-or-nothing proposition. He had tracked down all of the information to her case and more besides. He had also obtained the proof that she had not, in fact, signed the power of attorney paper. Because of that and the provision of her father's will, everything Tom and

Brad had orchestrated from the time of her father's death had been not only unethical, but illegal. Copies of all documents were enclosed for her elucidation.

The bottom line, Judson wrote succinctly, was that if Anne wanted her house back, she'd have to accept the whole empire. Before she made that kind of decision, he suggested she read the enclosed copy of her father's will. It would, he hoped, help her better assess her position.

Anne picked up the accompanying forms, separating the will out to be read last. Judson had arranged everything chronologically from the power of attorney to the futures deal Brad had made. The documents were all in tortuous legalese, but it didn't take Anne long to recognize the pattern Judson had outlined. By the time Brad had made the mistake that brought the situation to a crisis, he and Tom had acquired complete control of the entire Jackson empire, leaving Anne no more than the family jewelry they knew she would never sell and her mother's small trust that they couldn't break anyway. As she'd told Judson, they'd contrived to create a situation she'd assumed had already existed. Frustrating yes, but no bombshell. They'd already come to these conclusions.

She looked down at the will and didn't notice how profound the silence had become in the bright kitchen, or that Jonathan and Silas watched her with identical expressions. Afraid of what the will would tell her, she picked it up as if it were alive.

It took no more than four paragraphs for Anne to be dealt the blow.

The will had been made before the last time her father had returned to the mountain, at the height of the power struggle. Anne could suddenly see again the gray of his face in those days, the stubborn refusal to disbelieve his son. She remembered his increasing dependence on her, and that he'd almost reached a point of expressing a love for her she'd sought as long as she'd remembered. He'd died still searching for the way to bridge a lifelong gap. And she had been left behind still wondering, as it always was with children of a hard man.

She wondered no more. What he had never been able to say, he'd expressed eloquently in his gift to her.

... to my daughter Anne, the only member left of the Jackson or Harrison families worth the honor of those names and histories, I leave all that is her inheritance, both in fortune and in heritage. I leave her the responsibility of directing both of these in the honorable, far-seeing fashion she so often suggested to me. And in bequeathing my entire estate to her with the exception of the house and furnishings in Boston, which I know she wouldn't want, I have every belief that she will carry out her responsibilities in a way that will justify the pride her family has always had in her.

For long minutes Anne stared at the words, unable to focus on them, unable to move beyond them. Why hadn't he told her? Why couldn't he have, just once before he died, verbally expressed the love that echoed from these stringent pages? She could see now that it had always been there, though expressed only in a manner he could manage. Money and schools and opportunity. It was a tragic thing when the most important words a man can give his child could only be offered in his will.

Without a word to Jonathan or Silas, Anne stood and walked toward the door. She didn't see Jonathan move to follow, or Silas hold him back with a hand on his arm.

"Leave her be," he said, his eyes on her retreating figure. "She has business to attend that you got no part of."

The evening air was softer than it had been in a long time, the sunset less crisp at the edges. Beneath Anne's feet the snow folded into shadows cast in a painter's blue. Anne stumbled along, blind to the beauty around her, her eyes clouded with the tears of futility. The graveyard was only a short pathway up beyond the house, nestled in among pines and the oaks her ancestors had planted. Her parents were buried here together, their headstones as simple as the rest with only names and dates on the slim rounded stones.

Just the sight of their names brought back the pain, all of the different unresolved aches of their leaving. Her mother, so frail, fighting so hard to stay with her children, the apology in her eyes still fresh in Anne's memory. And her father.

It was because of her father that she'd avoided the graveyard so assiduously. It was a hard thing to face someone who caused anger and guilt at the same time. It was harder still when death had removed the chance to explain or be understood. Anne stood at the foot of her father's grave as if she could absorb there the feelings he'd never been able to share face to face. She wanted to understand the man who had written the words of that will.

She stood as the sun disappeared over the next ridge and pulled most of the light with it, until the first of the stars came to life in a peacock sky. She couldn't say for sure that she felt any great relief in the time she spent alone with the memories of her father. A lifetime of ambivalence didn't disappear like shadows with the flick of a light switch. But she did know that she felt different. Now, when she asked the questions she'd asked herself for so long, she found answers. Someday, she thought, they would be enough. She knew at least that the love she had so frantically tried to lavish on her father had been in its own way returned. She hadn't been the fool she'd feared.

When Anne returned to the kitchen, she found Jonathan and Silas where she'd left them. She could tell by the empathy in Jonathan's eyes and the pride in Silas's that they'd read the will. It didn't upset her in the least. She smiled at them with watery eyes and sat down to finish her tea.

"Silas, would you ask Jim to send a telegram for me?"

He nodded, more animation in his eyes than she could ever remember. "Ya goin' for it?"

Her smile widened, and she cocked her head at him in mock disbelief. "Well, what do you think?"

When he answered, his eyes were dead serious. "I think he had a right to be proud of you."

Anne couldn't think of anything to say, but as Silas left, she stood on tiptoe and delivered a hug that had him crimson.

That night Anne slept quietly in Jonathan's arms, savoring his silent understanding and companionship. In the morning she invited him outside to help her with the chores. He followed gladly, precariously balancing himself in the snow, his head on a constant swivel to take in the scenery he'd only viewed from the porch below.

"It's not the Tetons," he said as he worked his way through the door Anne held for him, "but it has its points."

"Why, thanks," Anne retorted dryly. "You've made it all worthwhile."

Due to obvious restrictions, Jonathan took over the less strenuous chores of feeding, milking and grooming. That and, when the mood struck him, kibitzing. His company taught people efficiency, he said, and it was the least he could do to teach Anne some. He also said that Anne's rather ascerbic retort was not unusual for someone who refused to see that they needed professional help. Anne's reply to that was a simple but effectively threatening display of the fertilizer she was in the process of mucking out. Jonathan took the hint and kept his peace.

"When do you think I'll be going down the mountain?" he asked a little later as he sat milking the cow. Bessie swung her head lazily around at the question, munching her hay as if in calm consideration of answering herself.

Anne looked toward the animal's back from where she was cleaning some tack to see what had prompted Jonathan's question. His eyes betrayed nothing as he rocked easily back and forth with his task.

"Silas almost dragged you down yesterday," Anne told him, going back to work.

Jonathan chuckled. "Does he not like me for the same reason you didn't like me?"

"More or less."

"Him and how many others?"

She shrugged noncommittally. "Let's say that the older people in the valley feel compelled to look after me."

"Would they mind if I didn't go back down at the first chance?"

Anne smiled more to herself than to him. That kind of scandal would be consumed with relish and condemned with fervor. She could almost hear the whispers already: "...that fancy gigolo taking advantage of our Annie..." She would have to stock up for all the curious and concerned visitors.

"They would," she finally admitted, "frown on it."

"So I figured. Well then, how much longer do you think I can successfully hide out in Shangri-la?"

Anne looked up at him and saw the genuine regret that was taking shape in his eyes. For a long moment she stood very still, sharing it with him as she saw the consequence of his trip back to civilization. Unable to face new pain, she said quickly, "Oh, a week at best. That's if Silas's thaw doesn't come. But I've never known Silas to be far wrong."

They would now measure their time left in hours, hoarding it like water on a desert. The uncertainty of the future colored the present with bittersweet light. Anne rubbed slowly at the soft, fragrant leather, using the activity as an antidote for the fear.

"Tell me something." Jonathan spoke up after a long silence. Anne turned to him. His eyes, gemlike in the morning light, were laughing, the crow's feet at their corners wrinkling suggestively. "Have you ever made love in the hay?"

Anne stopped what she was doing. "What?"

"You heard me." With a brisk twist of his hand, he indicated the loft, spilling with winter hay. The warm, fragrant hay was suffused with animal scents and age-old illusions.

"Jonathan," she objected instinctively, "I've just finished chores. Cleaning chores."

He would not be deterred. "Your cheeks are glowing and you have bits of straw in your hair."

"And I smell like horse..."

"Anne," he objected gently, a hand out in invitation. "Don't you want to find out what all the notoriety is about?"

Now her eyebrow arched, the enticement of his offer already waking tremors of excitement. "Do you mean that *you've* never made love in a hayloft?"

"No. I mean that I've never made love to you in a hayloft. And right now I want to. Very much." His hand was still out to her, his face still inviting much more than even his words as he got slowly to his feet. Anne only hesitated a moment longer before she walked over and held out hers in kind.

"Tell me one thing and I'll say yes," she said grinning. "How do you plan to get up the ladder?"

By now Jonathan had a tight enough grip on Anne's hand that she knew he wasn't going to let go, no matter the answer. "Very carefully."

He did, too. Balancing on the injured leg, he hoisted himself up with the good one, using his phenomenal set of chest and shoulder muscles.

What had begun in fun ended in earnest. Anne barely had the time to spread out an old blanket over the hay before Jonathan pulled her over next to him and took hold of her with an intensity that startled them both.

"This...is what happens to you," she panted between heady kisses, "in a barn?"

His smile was rakish, his eyes alight with their peculiar fire. "This is what happens to me," he amended, holding her beneath him and burying his face in her throat, "with you."

His impatience infected her as his hands undressed her. In no more than a few minutes she lay naked in the sweet, soft hay as Jonathan got out of his own clothes. Anne couldn't wait though. With an aggressiveness she wouldn't have recognized in herself before, she pushed him to his back and finished the job.

The sight and feel of his strong body beneath her hands set her pulse rocketing. Suddenly she was damp with perspiration. She couldn't seem to hold still, moving against him as if the friction of their bodies could further feed the flame that raged in her. She reveled in the coarseness of his hair against the smooth skin of her thighs, stomach, chest. She rubbed her cheek against him and nipped at the tight skin of his belly. And when she took him in her mouth, full and throbbing with power, she heard him groan with pleasure.

Jonathan could only take so much of that before he pulled her back to him, trapping her beneath him as if afraid she'd escape somehow. His excitement fed hers until it seemed unquenchable. His lips found her neck, the back of it where the small hairs anticipated pain and pleasure, and his tongue teased her unbearably. When she moved to meet his lips with her own, seeking the delicious heat of his mouth, his hands sought out the small, special places of her body that brought her even closer to the precipice.

Anne had never remembered such abandon, such fierce primal release. It was as if between them she and Jonathan had found a uniquely kindred energy source, a passion neither of them had ever really realized. They had also learned, instinctively, how to prolong their pleasure in each other until they were both drenched and gasping, eyes uncannily alike in their intensity. Together they teased and held back, promised release and then withheld, until they could bear it no longer.

"Please," she begged for the first time in her life, her voice shrill and breathless with the intensity of him inside her. "Please...now..."

With her plea, Jonathan took her to him almost brutally, his arms all but crushing her, his mouth ferocious. Captive

ithin what could have been a prison, Anne met her free-
om head on, the brilliance at the pinnacle so overwhelm-
ig that its delight was agony. Unbelievably, when Jonathan
ached the same peak moments later, Anne followed again,
ide-eyed and trembling.

For a long while later they lay exhausted in each other's
rms, too spent to even marvel aloud at what they had
ared. Anne supposed that she dozed for a while once the
elicious fire that had coarsed through her limbs finally
obed to a pleasant glow. She lay for a long time savoring
ie feel of Jonathan against her, the heady aroma of him
nd the slightly scandalous comfort of the hayloft. When
ie should have been inside her house making preparations
r going out on rounds, she curled into the curve of Jona-
an's hip and tested the texture of his chest with lazy fin-
ers. All the while she found herself smiling and thinking
iat this sort of thing could easily become a habit.

"They were right," she finally said.

"Who?" Jonathan's voice sounded sleepy and content.

"Whoever decided that haylofts were so notorious. They
iould be."

He chuckled, his fingers just as lazily exploring the soft-
ss of her breast. "It's something about losing your inhi-
tions," he suggested.

"Inhibitions, hell." Anne grinned back at him. "That's
ot what's usually lost in haylofts. When I'm a parent, my
aughter's not going anywhere near one."

It didn't occur to her until after she'd said it that until
ily a few days ago, she had given up the idea of children
r good. The realization would have been more exciting for
r if it weren't for the fact that she just as quickly under-
ood that she had meant parenthood with Jonathan. She
iew what her chances were there. A little of the light died
her eyes.

Jonathan must have sensed her feelings. "Tell me some-
ing, farm girl," he said, neatly changing the subject.
What do you plan to do if you win the suit?"

She didn't hesitate. "Stay here. Help run the clinic like I'd planned."

He shook his head. "What about the rest of the family holdings? Do you think that if you ignore them they'll go away?"

Anne thought a minute before moving up to her elbow. Leaning over to talk to Jonathan, she let her hair fall in a curtain to his chest. Her eyes were cautious. "I'll find someone to run them."

Jonathan's eyes were patiently amused. He didn't move. "Where did you say you cut your teeth? I suppose you think you can simply have everyone send résumés to the cabin so that you can pick the person to run seven industrial divisions and all the other subsidiaries right here from the mountain."

A new wariness crept into Anne's voice. "Applying for the job in person?"

The hint of a smile brightened. "That's the Anne Jackson I know and love. No, I'm not applying. I'm trying to tell you, my lusty wench, that no matter how you try to avoid it, if you win, which I think you will, you'll have to spend some time in the big city settling your affairs. And that I will also happen to be in that big city."

There was a moment of silence before Anne replied, unable to keep the memory of Jonathan's New York bred personality from her voice. "We've passed the country test. Let's see if we can do it in a corporate boardroom?"

Jonathan reached up and kissed her firmly on the mouth. "You do have a way with a double entendre."

"Still no promises?"

It was Jonathan's turn to pause. "Do you think it would be wise?"

Anne knew what would be wise, but a hayloft was not the place for common sense. She stifled the new uncertainty his words had given rise to and smiled provocatively. Without a word, she began to slowly rock back and forth, her hard

ning nipples grazing against Jonathan's chest, the shower
f her honey-colored hair enclosing them from the world.

Jonathan groaned in mock exasperation. "What do you
hink I am, Superman?"

She grinned down at him, her movements more pro-
ounced. "I was thinking that it takes you such a lot of ex-
rtion to get up and down from the loft, we might as well
make the most of our time up here."

"Much more of this kind of exertion, and I won't be able
o get back down at all."

Anne's eyes lit up with an even more wicked light as she
ooked over to see that Jonathan wasn't nearly as noncha-
nt about her advances as he made himself out to be.
"Another double entendre? If it is, I can't wait."

He groaned at her humor and pulled her back down to
im.

Anne wasn't the least surprised when Cassie showed up
he next day. When she opened the door to find her friend
n the front porch, Anne hugged her warmly.

"Silas came to see you, huh?"

Cassie's grin had frozen into surprise the minute she saw
nne. "My God, Anne," she gasped. "What has hap-
ened to you?"

"What do you mean?"

"You look positively pregnant."

"I beg your pardon." As yet, neither had made the first
ove to go inside.

"I never thought I'd say anything so trite, but you're
onest-to-God glowing!"

"Get inside, Cassie," Anne suggested dryly, moving to
ccommodate her. "You're getting snow-blind."

Cassie walked in, never taking her eyes from Anne as she
ed her coat and hat. "Annie, I mean it. You look won-
erful. No wonder Silas was so indignant."

Anne had to laugh at that. "You should have seen him."

"Oh, don't worry. I got the whole show. He snorted and stomped around the store for a good twenty minutes before he decided that he didn't need to buy anything at all. I've never seen him so upset."

"He thinks that I'm about to repeat my mistakes." The headed as usual toward the kitchen, and Anne stopped a moment to throw another log on the fire.

"Are you?"

"I doubt it. Coffee or tea?"

"Coffee. Where's Jonathan?"

"He's still asleep. He's been pushing himself pretty hard the past few days." Even before she got the words out, Anne was struck by her latest unintentional double entendre and found herself grinning like a high school girl.

Cassie didn't miss a bit of it. She allowed a half smile to touch her eyes. "Before I forget about it, I have a good reason for visiting. A telegram."

Anne reached for the envelope with a scowl. It wasn't until she saw the return address that she relaxed. "Oh good, it's only from Judson."

Anne had hardly begun to read before Cassie saw the relief in her eyes grow to puzzlement. "What's the matter now?" she demanded.

Anne looked up, quickly trying to cover the worry that must have shown through. "Oh, nothing. It seems that we've stirred up a bit of a hornet's nest."

Cassie's eyes became immediately suspicious. "How, and what nest?"

"I'm sure that Silas told you about the papers that he delivered yesterday."

"And your decision to do unto your husband what he's done to you. Yes, and I think that congratulations are in order. What nest?"

Anne used her hand to brush away the concern in Cassie's expression. "Just Brad. He overreacts. Judson says I should be careful around him." Anne saw Cassie's expression sharpen and held out a threatening finger. "Don't you are tell anyone in town," she admonished. "I'll have 'em ll up here sitting on my front doorstep with their shot-uns."

"Maybe that's not such a bad idea."

"Don't be silly. This isn't the Hardy Boys. Judson said at Brad had been 'visibly upset.' That means that Brad's een a jerk. I'm sure he stormed into the office and made a w vague and silly threats, and that Tom had to pull him ack off. Brad never did know how to handle a threatening tuation."

Cassie didn't give up easily. She was leaning forward now. But this is a threatened jail sentence and a loss of every-ing he has, Annie. Maybe you should move in with us ntil this is all resolved."

Anne reached out and took her friend's hand. "Cassie, I rew up with Brad. He's all bark and no bite. Believe me." ut Tom wasn't, she reminded herself uneasily. How reatened would the two of them have to be to do some-ing spiteful like a little trumped-up blackmail or sabo-ge at the clinic? Damn it, she was tired of having to worry bout those two. It was about time she let them know in no ncertain terms that she'd had about enough of their neat ttle squeezes. She wasn't impotent in the face of their at-cks anymore. For not the first time, she realized that she as glad that she'd thrown down the gauntlet.

"You weren't going to let me have any of the coffee ake?"

The two of them started at the sound of Jonathan's voice. ooking up, they found him lounging in the doorway, othed in Brad's old plaid shirt and corduroy pants, utches propped against his sides. Again Anne noticed that s frame strained the material of the clothes.

"I didn't know you were up," Anne greeted him, darting warning glance at Cassie.

"Congratulations, Jonathan," Cassie said blithely. "You ok great."

Anne decided that Cassie had meant that to be signifi
cant and ignored it.

"Thanks," he said warmly. "Getting dressed only too
me forty minutes start to finish this morning." He hobble
in and gently lowered himself to the seat next to Anne. "
it were a competition, I could beat every little old lady i
Miami."

"You do in my book," Cassie retorted offhandedl
"None of them looks that good in their work clothes."

Anne ignored her again. Jonathan laughed, holding h
chest to support irritable ribs.

"Cassie, I'm going to miss you."

Cassie shrugged with a mischievous grin. "Don't go."

Jonathan returned her grin, but with an odd loss f
words.

Chapter 14

Three days later Anne stood at the front window watching the melting snow drip steadily from the eaves. Silas's prediction had come true with particular vigor, almost as if nature itself were conspiring with him against her. Jonathan would be gone in another day.

Anne sighed and rubbed at her eyes with a hand as she tried to hold off tears that had threatened all morning. It wasn't fair. Just when they were becoming really close, when the tentative forays into commitment had begun to gel into something tangible.

Jonathan had begun to find a new ease with the softer side of himself, content in the evenings to do no more than talk in the comfort of a fire lit room or read a good book. He'd lost much of the restless impatience that had marked his early days in Anne's home. More than once she caught him in moments of amused surprise as if he found it hard to recognize himself anymore.

Anne, watching him grow, had discovered a new matching place in herself that flowered within his reach. She was beginning to tap into a reservoir of love that she'd never known existed. Her time with Jonathan only fed a hunger for him that grew instead of diminished. Anne Jackson realized that for the first time since her mother died, she could love someone selflessly and completely.

Now, however, Jonathan would return to the city and the life that had forged and still supported the part of his character she wished she'd never seen. No matter how hard she'd tried in the last few days, she couldn't seem to move past that idea, past the picture of the man he'd been when he'd first arrived on her doorstep. Because of that, she couldn't seem to see her way to anything but an all-or-nothing relationship. New York or West Virginia. Choose, Jonathan.

And she knew what he would choose.

"Annie." Jonathan put a hand on her shoulder.

She jumped, not having heard him, his touch burning with new unquenchable fire.

"You're getting pretty good with those crutches," she said, not turning away from where the sun lit her strained face. "I didn't even hear you."

The night before they had made love in front of the fire again, but their words had had a ring of desperation, their laughter an uncomfortable shrillness. The snow had begun to melt yesterday.

"You weren't paying attention," he said easily. She didn't answer. He stood just behind her, a hand now on either shoulder as he looked out above her head. "Two weeks ago I would have paid any amount of money to see that sight."

Anne sighed wistfully. "Me, too."

Jonathan chuckled. "You mean you were about to throw the toast of New York out in the cold?"

"Right on his ear."

It was a moment before he asked the next question. Anne faced the silence like a penance. "When are you throwing me out?"

She took a long breath, the weight of his hands almost unbearable. "If this thaw keeps up the way it is, Jim and Silas could be up here tomorrow."

Say you won't go, she begged silently, the knot of unshed tears choking her. Change your mind and make a commitment to me, please. I can't let you go and survive.

Jonathan's voice, when it came, was quiet and strained. "Come with me, Annie."

She shook her head, struggling to keep her voice under control. "I don't think so, Jonathan. I don't think I'd like you in New York."

"You're locked in too tightly to those preconceived notions of yours," he argued quietly. "I might surprise you."

Still she didn't turn, but stood very still, her hands shoved deep into her pants pockets. "I'd like to think you would. I just…well, it's hard to get past old disillusionments. I don't know if I could compete with the lure back there anymore. I don't know if I really want to try."

"Then what do you think we should do?"

She could only shake her head. She felt his leaving already, and a great gap widened in her, a void where the life-giving force of his love had laid.

With gentle pressure, he turned her around to face him. She could hardly bear to look up at the sky-blue of his eyes.

"What do you think we should do?" he repeated, never releasing her from her gaze or grip.

"I think you should probably go back as you planned. Then you can give yourself some time in the real world to balance out your time here. Maybe we'll see each other when I'm there on business. Then if you want, you can come back for a while and we can decide what to do."

He drew her even closer until the ache of desire grew indistinguishable from the sharp pain of loss. "What about you?"

"I'll be here." She looked down, control almost impossible within the range of his eyes.

His one hand moved against her cheek, his touch caressing. Barely suppressing a moan for the agony of his touch, she lifted her head away from him, her eyes closing against the tears that began to spill. He followed and kissed her, his mouth searching hers with tender yearning.

"I love you, Annie."

Anne opened her eyes and thought that the morning sun in Jonathan's eyes would blind her. His face shifted and melted beyond her tears, and she saw the pain in its lines. What he had to do was no easier for him than it was for her. She was so afraid that when he walked away from her, he would walk away from himself. If that happened, he would have to forget her or never be able to live with himself. She wanted to tell him that. She wanted to be able to bribe or coerce or beg him to stay. She could only manage a half smile.

"I love you, Jonathan. You've given me back my freedom."

"No," he said with a slow shake of his head. "You did that, Annie. I happened to be around when it happened. That's why I think you'd survive in New York."

It was becoming increasingly difficult for her to answer without giving way to pain-wracked sobs. He wouldn't change his position. No mention yet of his staying. And she couldn't change hers. There were only so many steps she could manage at one time. "I'm not that strong yet, Jonathan. Until I am, I have no business back there with you."

"You're stronger than you think, Annie."

She couldn't answer at all. She could only look up at him, the eloquence of her turmoil glinting in tear-filled eyes. Without another word, Jonathan gathered her into the strong comfort of his arms, his lips finding that hers tasted of bitter salt. In her quiet desperation, Anne threw her arms around him, clinging to him as if he could save her. The kiss deepened as Jonathan eased her lips apart. His hands were around her waist, sure and sustaining, his hard body easing gently against hers. Slowly, inexorably, as his mouth took command of hers, his embrace tightening until the two of them swayed with the power of their need.

Anne felt his hands against her skin, fingers exploring and remembering, their touch igniting her own hunger. An obsession, a sure, sudden knowledge that she had to be next to him right now, to touch him and rouse in him the same unbearable tension he had sparked in her. Right now she needed him more than anyone or anything else in her life. She needed to know that what she'd given him had not been wasted or foolish, and it seemed to her that his most beautiful statement of that had to be made without words.

Jonathan understood as if her thoughts were telepathic. With his arms tight around her, he lifted his head a little and smiled. Anne found no guile there, none of the smugness that had once ruled their relationship. She saw only tenderness, the warmth of his love like the sun in the endless sky of his eyes.

Her tears still fell without restraint, but she smiled tremulously back. "Well," she managed in a throaty, hesitant voice, "it's probably a good thing you are leaving tomorrow. I haven't been able to get a thing done for a week."

"Yes you have, farm girl," he said. "You've made me fall in love with you. And for the first time in fifteen years, you've made me wonder whether I really want to go back to New York."

Jonathan took her to her own bed, the high old four-poster with the goose down mattress that overlooked the sunlight and felt the firelight. In the bed that had been her grandmother's and hers before her, Anne lay next to Jonathan in much the same way her ancestors had, giving and receiving the same timeless gift. Jonathan's eyes smoldered as they ranged the length of her body, their gaze raising goose bumps as surely as if they'd grazed her skin. The strong light from the front window threw him into a soft kind of relief, shadows outlining the taut muscles of his chest and arms and settling into the planes of his face.

Anne thought of the chiaroscuro of the painting masters, the dramatic play of light against dark. It couldn't be any more breathtaking than the pattern of white sunlight against Jonathan's skin. Without thinking she used her fingers as imaginary paintbrushes, stroking the rich, healthy colors into the contours of his body, the rounded edges of his shoulders and arms, the hairy coarseness of his chest. Along to narrow hips and strong, muscled thighs.

Still the tears came, as if contact with him were as painful as it was essential. Jonathan kissed them as they fell, following their traces to her throat and breasts, tasting the saltiness in her hair as she lay. With gentle hands he untangled her braid and fanned her hair out beneath her like a gilt frame. His eyes were tender but his touch hungry, impatient, and it was the contrast that was compelling to Anne.

She drew him to her breasts and begged him to savor them. She felt his fingers flutter against the sensitive skin of her thigh and invited them to explore. When they found her, their touch so light as to send her gasping, she arched against him, aching for union with him.

Jonathan whispered into her hair and nuzzled her ear, his hands driving her to a new, more urgent rhythm. The nerves in Anne's skin jumped to acute life, teased by the soft, curling hair of Jonathan's chest against her taut nipples, enticed by the scratch of an hours-old beard against her cheek and tortured by cool fingers against hot flesh. Unable to remain apart any longer, Anne led him to her, begged his arms to enfold her, his legs imprison to her. He waited long enough to capture her eyes with his own. Then together they moved in a like rhythm to a world beyond the finite one they inhabited. The sun was an explosion within them; the day, for a moment, endless; the future contained within a heartbeat and the gasping cry of release.

After Jonathan had drifted into a contented sleep, Anne lay wide awake within his embrace. She couldn't sleep, couldn't relax into the mindless peace Jonathan had found. Comfortably enclosed within his arms, she was even more painfully aware of the relentless passage of time. By tomorrow night she would once again sleep alone in her big bed. She would reclaim the isolation of her world only to find that it no longer gave her comfort.

When Jonathan left, her home, the haven she'd come to treasure for its secluded severity, would become for the first time a lonely place, a place not so much safe as empty. Another voice had become ingrained into the memories of these wooden walls. Another presence had become incorporated into the essence of what Cedar Ridge was. Only this presence would not easily relegate itself to the past.

Moving quietly so that she wouldn't wake Jonathan, Anne slipped out of his grasp and got dressed. Without any conscious intent, she made her way back down to stand before the big front window to look out on the softening snow.

The sun was rising high, and it glittered metallically. Small rivulets were beginning to cut paths into the white lawn that sloped away from the house toward the road. Soon its brown would be visible, parallel lines of sodden mud that wound down the mountain toward the town. The river would rise with the melting snow, and the trees, so deformed with the weight of the heavy snow, would begin to spring back up at the sky. As she watched, a large mound tumbled off a pine to the left of the porch and thudded to earth, the tree straightening a little. It wouldn't be long.

Anne couldn't exactly decide why she always brooded at this window. It seemed that the serenity of the scene before her helped to settle her so that she could gain a better perspective on the priorities in her life. The world around her home was always the same and always would be. It was stable.

More snow fell, the sound like a body falling. Anne watched it like the approach of a flood.

She tried, one last time, to find the resolve to follow Jonathan to New York. Looking back carefully she assessed her time there, the scant days she'd spent testing the city and corporate waters. She'd done well, she knew that. The old demeanor had slipped on as easily as the new clothes. She knew that if she went back with Jonathan now, she'd probably end up enjoying the games she would resume playing. At least to a certain extent. And she truthfully thought she could live anywhere as long as she was assured of his love.

The dilemma rested not so much in her own reaction to New York but in Jonathan's. She had to know what it would do to him before she could make a commitment. The drug of that world was far more alluring than any chemical known to man, and far more lethal. It had changed Jonathan before the eyes of his friends and family and left scars more unforgettable than those he carried from Vietnam. Anne knew all about that drug. She'd seen firsthand too, what it could do to a person.

Jonathan was going back to see how he would handle the kind of power that moved the nations of the world. It had beaten and claimed him once, altering him so thoroughly that Anne knew his parents must look at him now with the eyes of frightened strangers. She had no more guarantee than they'd had, those who'd loved him so much, that he wouldn't succumb yet again. She had known him for only weeks out of his life, and no matter how much she wanted, she couldn't hope that that time would automatically protect him.

If she went with him as he'd asked, it would only be worse. There she would be, the constant reminder of what she thought he should be, nagging at him with silent, anxious eyes. If he were going to hold onto what he'd gained here he'd do it on his own. If he weren't, her being with him would do no more than make their final parting resentful and bitter.

If she were to lose him, she would much rather it be while they still loved each other. If he had to go, better she saw him turn from her with regret.

Anne was so preoccupied that for a few minutes she lost track of what was before her. She didn't see the visitor approaching until he was through the clearing. Startled, she shifted her concentration to him.

It was a man, but not one of her neighbors. They didn't dress like that. She couldn't see him very well yet, but she wondered whether it might be one of Jonathan's corporate executives come to pay a social visit. He was attired in a manner suspiciously similar to Jonathan's when he'd arrived. Maybe, she thought dryly, it was a kind of corporate uniform for the woods.

She supposed that she should go out to greet him, wondering half-heartedly why anyone would make a trek like that on foot in snow that was still a good foot deep. The man was either very determined but stupid, or just plain stupid. Someone in town would surely have lent him a horse with the directions to her cabin, if only he'd asked.

Anne was about to turn for her coat when something caught her eye. A familiar posture to the visitor's walk. He looked as if he were denying the fact that he was walking up a mountain even as he did it, as if he wouldn't be caught dead here if he didn't have to be. She wanted to laugh.

It was Brad.

No wonder he didn't have a horse. After what had been going on in the last few weeks, no one in his right mind in Elder's Crossing would go out of his way for Bradley Jackson. In fact, she was surprised that Silas wasn't giving him an official escort to make sure he didn't give her any trouble.

Brad was the last person Anne expected to see. After all, the only time he'd been to the cabin in the last five years had been to bury his father. Brad believed that if a limo or air service couldn't get you there, it wasn't worth going. Now, looking at his rather clumsy approach, Anne desperately wished she could get her hands on a camera. Pictures of this would make delicious blackmail material, if for nothing else than to remind him in his worst moments of megalomania what a fool he really was.

She waited until she heard him on the porch before throwing the door open, the grin on her face not so much welcoming as smug. She decided it might be a lot more fun than what she had been doing to gloat over Brad's discomfort instead. When he looked up from stomping his two-hundred-dollar L.L. Bean boots on the porch, he had nothing but malice in his eyes for her, his mouth twitching irritably. Her grin broadened in delight.

"Well, if it isn't the prodigal son," she greeted him. "What brings you so far from the big city?"

He straightened and smiled in return, the light in his eyes brightening oddly. "I'm glad you're here," he told her almost amiably. "It'll save me some time."

"Time for what?"

He motioned to the door. "Can I come in?"

"Why not?" Anne moved in to allow him by. "Coffee, tea? I have some semistale cake, if you like."

He stood inside looking around as if reorienting himself. "I'd almost forgotten how very...rustic this all was." He spoke as if the words had a slightly bad taste to them.

"I kept it just the way you left it," Anne assured him dryly. "I knew some day you'd come back."

He looked over at her with the same attitude of distaste with which he'd considered the cabin.

"I'll take some coffee."

Anne nodded agreeably. "Convention usually dictates that one remove coat and hat before sitting at the table."

"I'm still cold. It was a long walk."

She couldn't help but grin again. "I'll bet it was. What was the matter, all the horses already hired?"

He wasn't amused, but Anne certainly was. She wanted to go and get Jonathan. It would probably do him good to see what the other side of him could resemble. Maybe he hadn't been as bad as Brad—few people were—but he'd certainly worn that look of disdain when first considering life in the boonies. It was lucky for him that she didn't have the heart to wake him just for Brad.

Anne sat across from her brother as he sipped the steaming liquid in his cup and thought about the time she'd spent with him in this house. His memory should have been imbedded in this place like everyone else's. There should have been pictures that popped into her mind when certain things were handled, or aromas sensed. Like the way she could still see her father fishing down at the stream, his back sunburned and hair bleached blond, his pleasure in the silence brightening his stern features. Or her mother's delicate hands as she and Sarah worked over the wedding ring quilt that hung highest on the living-room wall. Sometimes, she even felt a pull of Tom's personality, filling the rooms like heady smoke.

But try as she might, she could not conjure up any kind of special feeling for Brad here. Even as he sat at the table where he'd eaten so many meals and worked so many jigsaw puzzles, he didn't conjure up any sensation that he had once belonged to this place. It was as if he were truly a stranger in his own house. What saddened Anne was that he didn't care in the least.

By the time he finished his cup of coffee, he'd lost much of his original antagonism. The side of his face had calmed to slow fluttering motions along the side of his mouth, and his lips didn't curl back so much in that perennial sneer. Anne knew that it was because he was anticipating the bombshell he obviously planned to drop. He wouldn't have gone to all the trouble of getting to the cabin for a trivial matter, and they both knew it. What pleading he might have done for leniency from his sister, he would have left up to Tom and adept lawyers.

She exchanged monosyllables with him, willing to play his cat-and-mouse game for the time being. She didn't want him to know how frustrated and worried his sudden appearance was beginning to make her, how very much she wanted to ask where Tom was while Brad made the jaunt up the Appalachian Trail.

Judson's carefully worded warning was still too fresh for her to take Brad's casual arrival lightly. He had something unpleasant up his sleeve, something like another legal paper Judson hadn't unearthed that would negate Anne's hold over her own destiny. But if she were going to get Brad's goat, she couldn't allow him to start with any kind of advantage.

"So tell me, Brad," she finally said quite civilly into her coffee cup. "Have you come up here to reacquaint yourself with historic architecture?"

"Just a leisurely stroll in the woods," he retorted.

"Of course," she said with a bright smile. "Well, it's always nice to see you. Oh, I'll tell you what. Since you're here, there are some clothes that you might like to take back with you."

"No, thank you."

Emptying his cup, he set it down before him and allowed Anne a measured gaze almost completely free of tics before a slow, sporadic smile caught at his mouth and made Anne uneasy. His look was anticipatory. He considered her leisurely, then took hold of his coffee cup with a corner of the tablecloth and slowly wiped its surface. Anne couldn't help but stare at the odd behavior. Brad's eyes turned to his work.

"Well, Anne, I'm afraid that I'm too greedy to put this off any longer, even for you. I have a tight schedule, so I don't have the time I'd like to sit and socialize about old times." His eyes sprang on her, their look of expectancy now boiling uncomfortably. Anne recognized the look. He was feeling cornered, and thought he'd found a way out. Brad simply couldn't help gloating. What worried her was that there was very little control in his eyes right now.

"Put off what?"

He smiled again, his one eye blinking absurdly. "Simple, Anne my dear. The solution to my problem. This cabin has become a millstone around my neck, and you're the one who put it there."

She couldn't help but laugh. He'd taken his juvenile attempt at revenge too far. "Brad, honey, how long have you been rehearsing that? Why you sound almost threatening. It must be a line you read in one of father's mysteries. Just what does it mean? You've called in someone new to handle the case?"

Her sarcasm didn't seem to bother him. It had always awakened a storm of facial irritation in the past. Instead, he continued to smile as if relishing some private joke. Anne was becoming hard-pressed to sit still.

"No lawyers, Anne. They seem to have come up empty-handed." He paused to let her carefully digest his words. "Just like Tom did when I sent him."

"You sent Tom?" she laughed. "Be realistic, Brad."

"I sent him."

There was a mad kind of glee in his voice now. Anne watched him, realizing that he was serious. He really thought that he had sent Tom to bribe her. Brad might have had his petty delusions in the past, but Anne had never known him to completely lose his touch with reality.

"Brad," she tried more gently, suddenly very uneasy with the picture that was forming. "What did you come here to say?"

"Say?" he echoed hollowly. "I didn't come here to say anything. That's all finished."

Within the space of his words, something else appeared in his eyes, something Anne had never seen there before. Beneath the avarice, the sarcasm and disdain, a new glow began to flicker: a manic purpose, a look of hungry malevolence.

A real madness.

Anne froze, suddenly very afraid of her brother. He watched her with eyes that seemed to see something else altogether, something she didn't recognize. With uncommon perception, she understood that he was acting out a scenario he had practiced many times. He was living a dream he had created within the walls of isolation he had built long ago.

She could see now the revenge he had plotted and savored through the long, ineffectual years when he had lived on jealousy and resentment. The revenge was to have been carried out against her father. And now, because he was out of his reach, against Anne. Whatever he was about to do, Brad had done a thousand times before in his fantasies. Now he had lost the ability to comprehend the difference.

Anne noticed again that the facial twitches had stopped. Brad was in perfect control. She suddenly realized how far the game had gone when Brad pulled a gun from his coat— a short, ugly little .22. The famous Saturday night special, whose availability was legend and whose bullet did an obscene little dance inside the human chest cavity. And this gun was pointed directly at her.

Chapter 15

Brad, this is absurd," Anne protested without thinking. "What do you think you're doing?"

Brad smiled giddily, his mouth an almost perfect crescent, and leaned comfortably back in his chair. "Actually, I think I should be grateful to you for bringing this whole mess to a head. You can't imagine what a pleasure it will be to put a match to this white elephant." He looked around with a little giggling sound, as if savoring the thought. "Pete Jackson's place. The legacy, the symbol of history and family, everything that he preached ad nauseam but never practiced. 'The tie that binds.'" His lips curled into a sneer and his gaze returned to his sister. "But Bradley didn't belong. He wasn't the bright, the gifted, the beautiful. He was only second best, and old Pete didn't even acknowledge his existence until he made good his threat to usurp the throne. You know, Anne, you never knew what you missed. You were never in the contest for the real world, at least not as far as Pete was concerned. Women didn't have to compete for something that could be theirs. So it was safe to lavish the worldly goods on you as the royal princess. The household pet. Weren't we all surprised when ole Pete decided to get back at Brad by leaving the household pet everything.''

Anne's mouth was dry. Her heart raced painfully. All she could think of doing was trying to run. Every tactic she'd ever used with gun-wielding patients suddenly disappeared and she was afraid she'd lose control. The sense of unreality was increased by the fact that a part of her still refused to believe that it was Brad who sat so nonchalantly before her with a gun in his hand.

"So what are you going to do," she challenged instinctively, still reacting as she always had to him, "shoot me because I was cute and cuddly? Or is it that I'm the only one left to blame?"

His silent, smiling shrug made her want to scream. She didn't know how to talk to him, what to do to defuse him. Looking at him now, she knew with a sinking finality that he was long past reason. He was acting out his cruel fantasy, and try as she might, she couldn't get beyond her feelings of disdain. She wanted to scream at him, to insult him for the stupid way he was handling this. She also realized that she wanted to beg for her life.

"Brad," she said, her voice barely in control. "If it means that much to you, I'll forget the lawsuit. Take the land. Do whatever you want with it."

He shook his head with a smug grin of satisfaction. "Too late. That fine lawyer of yours didn't waste any time before contacting the authorities. I've been checking on it, you know, and I figure that if Tom and I were convicted, maybe we'd serve eighteen months in minimum security. I'd come out of it with the house on Beacon Hill and a comfortable living. But Anne, with you dead, I'd inherit the estate anyway, so I'd walk away from the whole thing in under two years in an even better position than when I went in. And Tom wouldn't have his fingers all over my money anymore." He waved the gun at her, punctuating his enthusiasm.

"Now, here's the fun part. I have an alibi. At six tonight, as usual, Tom and I will be waiting for Louis to seat us at our booth. And I've been seen going into my room earlier today to work on our unfortunate financial setback that could well cost me my ancestral home. Every once in a while my voice has been throwing recorded tantrums just loud enough to be heard and noted." He was enjoying himself immensely, like a small child getting the last piece of cake. Anne was frightened. The gun was once more leveled very steadily at her chest. "You know," he went on blithely, "I can't thank you enough for showing me such a good time today. Being able to see the look on your face right now is worth all the trouble I've gone through. I've been dreaming of something like this for years." He looked around the room with malicious glee. "As for the cabin, well, let's call that a settlement of old debts."

"What an interesting turn of phrase."

The interruption jolted Anne. She whipped around to find Jonathan lounging in the doorway. Even knowing that he gave them no physical advantage, she breathed an instinctive sigh of relief. Jonathan would know what to do. He would help defuse the situation by just being there.

Then she noticed that something was wrong. Jonathan seemed to not even notice that Anne was in the room. He gazed passively at Brad, but the light in his eyes burned eerily. A new, unexplained tension suddenly exploded.

Anne instinctively turned to Brad, maybe for some kind of explanation. The sight of him only added to her confusion.

Brad had turned white. His mouth hung slack as if he'd been hit, and his expression, which had only moments earlier been smugly pleased, caught fire. The left side of his face contorted madly. An evil enmity Anne had never seen before glared in his eyes as he struggled for control.

"What are you doing here?" he hissed.

Jonathan smiled lazily. "Waiting to run into you, it would seem."

There was a moment's silence Anne somehow couldn'
break. It was as if a field of physical malevolence ha
sparked between the two men that no one could interrupt
They were two men Anne didn't know, consumed by some
thing she didn't understand but instinctively feared. Sh
watched each in turn, seeing a similarity in their expres
sions. She wasn't sure which one to be more afraid of.

Brad got slowly to his feet, the gun still steady, still poise
at Anne. His eyes never left Jonathan.

"So it was you all along," Brad finally said with som
wonder. "I should have guessed."

Jonathan shrugged with that strange smile that mad
Anne chill. "You've been outclassed, Bradley."

Brad nodded absently, still pondering something. "Yo
managed to hide yourself well in that dummy corporation
It was, wasn't it?"

Jonathan nodded with a small grin. "I'll take that as
compliment. I went to a lot of trouble."

Suddenly Brad turned on Anne, his malice threatening t
consume her. Still too stunned to comprehend what wa
taking place, she flinched from him.

"And you, little princess. Your part in this was a strok
of genius, especially after the wonderful act you put on tw
years ago. You like your revenge served cold, too, do you?"

Anne was too overwhelmed to react. "What are yo
talking about?" She turned to the stranger in the doorway
"Jonathan, please tell me what's going on. How do yo
know Brad?"

Somehow she'd gotten to her feet, though she didn't kno
how. She faced the two of them as she held the back of th
chair for support, her hands sweaty.

Brad came after her and she started away. He looked fro
her to Jonathan, amazement dawning.

"She doesn't know," he breathed, again facing Jona
than and ignoring her in her small corner. He actuall
smiled at the man in the doorway, shaking his head wit
grudging admiration. "My God, what a masterful game

onathan, you have my respect. It was a brilliant move." He
was really beginning to enjoy himself again, that little gig-
ling sound escaping from him. It was as if he'd just re-
nembered that he was the one with the gun in his hand, and
hat his new victim was far more amusing than the old.

Anne turned on Jonathan again. "What didn't I know?"

Brad wouldn't be denied the pleasure. "Anne, my dear,
ou know that Amplex Corporation Board of Directors
ou've been waiting to hear from? I'd like to introduce
ou." He made a show of indicating Jonathan with a grand
vave of the gun, and then giggled again.

Anne blanched, trying to understand. Reality was fast
eaving her behind. When she turned to Jonathan for ex-
lanation, he merely acquiesced with a passive shrug. She
elt herself go deathly cold. The last of her foundations was
eginning to crumble away beneath her.

"Why?"

Again he shrugged. "A story too long to tell in the time
e seem to have."

She turned on Brad as if expecting help, but he just
rinned. Her helplessness seemed to delight him all the
nore.

"An old score to settle," Jonathan added evenly, his eyes
oncommittal.

His words set off a chain-reaction in Anne. A flurry of
isjointed memories clicked together into place like a slot
nachine: Jonathan's odd trek back into the winter moun-
ains in a custom suit, his animosity, the bits of out-of-the-
vay knowledge he'd collected about the family. His interest
1 Peter Jackson's daughter, Brad Jackson's sister.

Anne realized that she'd stopped breathing. She faced
onathan and tried to discover some of the affection that
ad filled his eyes when he'd looked at her only hours ago
nd found none. His eyes were as cold as treacherous ice, a
ragile covering for dangerous emotions below. His emo-
ions were directed only at Brad. She challenged him to look
t her again, her eyes bright with disbelief.

"Brad? Brad was the man who swindled you?" She kne͏
she'd struck home even before he answered.

His answer was conversational, his voice as unemotiona͏
as the surface of his eyes. "Then Judson did tell you?"

"He told me. And because of what Brad did twelve year
ago, you engineered the futures deal so that he would be sur͏
to lose his family's home, too?"

He didn't offer an answer.

She swung on Brad. "Did you do it on purpose, Brad͏
Did you set out to ruin him?"

"Of course I did," he sneered, his reaction classic. Hi͏
eyes gleamed maliciously as he looked at Jonathan and re͏
membered whatever had set him off twelve years ago. "H͏
was always so perfect, so *right*. So I outclassed him, didn'͏
I, Jonathan? I got him caught between a rock and har͏
place to teach him a little lesson in where the real powe͏
lies."

Jonathan didn't bother to answer Brad either. Ann͏
found that she was shaking her head as if she could den͏
what was happening. She wanted to lash out and didn'͏
know at whom. It was too much to accept. Brad probabl͏
couldn't even remember what incident had been the cata͏
lyst for sending him after Jonathan. Jonathan had spen͏
over a decade in return to exact his own brand of revenge͏
and Anne was the one caught in the middle.

Anger crowded her almost as closely as the terror o͏
Brad's eyes. She lashed out at Jonathan for deceiving he͏
for according her a false security and then callously strip͏
ping it away again. She attacked him because she loved him͏

"Was this all your quaint idea of Biblical justice, or di͏
you think that I had a hand in what Brad did?"

She got no reaction. Jonathan was watching Brad.

"God, this is too good to be true." Brad giggled, his fac͏
jumping erratically. "It seems that I'm about to have m͏
cake and eat it, too."

Jonathan finally gave Anne her answer then, his eyes sti͏
rigidly veiled. "I think Brad plans to make the point moot.͏

Brad laughed, the sound grating. "Indeed I do. But you sure have helped make this a most unforgettable afternoon. It's just too bad that I can't tell Tom how I found Jonathan Harris playing house with my sister, and that she didn't even know that he'd come to steal her precious home." His excitement was peaking as he considered the two people he held at bay.

At that moment Jonathan moved slightly to ease his bad leg. Brad jumped, swinging the gun around at him. "Don't you move, Harris," he shrilled a bit too loudly.

"Don't worry, Bradley," Jonathan answered calmly. Tugging at his pant leg, he revealed his homemade splint. "I'm not in good enough form for heroic gestures today."

"Why, Jonathan," Brad said with new delight. "I think you're keeping something from me. What happened to you?"

"I fell."

"You don't say. That's too bad. Hope it wasn't anything serious."

"I'll recover." Jonathan smiled evenly.

That seemed to appeal to Brad's sense of humor. His laughter was strident and loud. Then, abruptly, he stopped, his attention newly diverted. "Well now, let's see. Jonathan, you do complicate matters a little. I guess I'll have to get Anne to tie you up first. You see, the robbers tied the victims and ransacked the house before they... well, you know. It was too bad that Mr. Harris had suffered his injury and was able to offer no help to his hostess." He giggled again. "Really, Jonathan, you appeal to my sense of poetic justice. But remember, I have the gun. I'll be just as happy to shoot you now as later."

He backed up to the pantry and opened the door, never turning his back on his hostages. "Anne, I assume you still keep the clothesline in the same... ah, here it is. I should thank you for being such a creature of habit." He showed the roll to Jonathan. "It's been in the same place for the last twenty-five years at least. This place always has been a shrine to the fallacy of permanency. And Anne, as the dutiful daughter, has served it quite well, I think. Something like a vestal virgin.'' Still watching Jonathan, Brad flipped the ball of twine at Anne. She caught it instinctively.

When it seemed that Brad was about to head off on another self-serving tangent, Jonathan interrupted with a small, rueful smile. ''I hate to be a bother, but could we continue this when I'm sitting down? I'm wearing a bit thin.''

Brad stared oddly at him, as if his concentration had been broken. Then he smiled. ''All right. I guess the next act takes place in the living room anyway. Please proceed.''

Anne walked over to the door to see that Jonathan's crutches leaned against the wall beyond him. He moved now to reach for them. Edging aside enough to let her through, he slipped them under his arms and leaned heavily over. If Anne hadn't been so close when he turned to follow her, she never would have heard him.

''Can you tie something I can get out of?''

She nodded automatically, just enough, and moved past him.

Jonathan turned to follow, walking very carefully, just as he had the first few days he'd been up. At first Anne was confused. He had been careful all along, putting as little weight on his injured leg as he could. But she knew darn well that he had no reason to be having so much trouble. He was breathing heavily as he lurched a single step at a time across to the couch. When he lowered himself very carefully to a sitting position, a small gasp escaped that sounded very real.

''You're not telling me everything, Jonathan,'' Brad accused with relish. ''How did your accident happen?''

''I ... told you ... I fell.''

Brad shrugged. ''Be that way. All right, Anne. I'd like your best Girl Scout knots. Hands behind his back. And even though I doubt sincerely whether it would make any difference, tie his ankles together. Jonathan, you do look awful. I guess I can assume that more was injured than just your leg."

Anne piped up, beginning to get a glimmer of Jonahan's strategy. "Quite a lot more. He shouldn't be anyplace but bed." Absurdly, she thought of how she sounded like an old English movie.

"Ah." Brad nodded, his eyes wide. "Compassionate to the bitter end, Anne? This is the man who made you the fool of the century, and you still think of his welfare. Good instincts, you nurses. All right, Jonathan, after she ties you up, feel free to lie down." He shook his head with glee. "To think that you went to all that trouble just to surprise me."

"You know…me…any little…revenge…I can…get…." Jonathan still seemed to have trouble breathing, his chest heaving with exertion as he tried to speak. Anne was impressed, even though, as Brad had said, Jonathan had just finished making a fool of her. His quick thinking could still save her life. Even now he was putting on the act of a lifetime as he wiped away nonexistent perspiration from his upper lip with the back of a trembling hand. He even managed somehow to look gray. Anne decided to ask him later how he did it.

"Isn't there some kind of…code," he gasped, his eyes coldly amused, "about taking…advantage of…an…injured man?"

Brad stood by the front door, alternately watching Anne's work and the scene outside. Anne's pastoral landscape. The sun rode straight up in the cold winter sky, glittering brightly off the snow so that the glare from the window cast the house in an uncomfortable gloom. Brad blinked repeatedly as he turned his attention back on them. His expression had frozen into disinterest, his smile faded. "None whatsoever, Jonathan." Anne couldn't see his eyes well, but she thought that the tic was worse.

Jonathan did smile, a chilly and rueful sight. "Funny…I had a feeling that would be…your attitude."

Anne straightened, hoping that Jonathan could manage to get the knots free and wondering what he intended to do once he did. She thought as she watched the tableau before her how dim the big fire in the fireplace appeared in contrast to that of the sun, how its dull red glow seemed almost evil.

Brad moved close enough to give Anne's work a half hearted check and nodded, again motioning to her with the gun. The fact that she flinched again amused him. "Now Anne," he directed, his voice businesslike and distant, "if memory serves me once more, there's a big can of gasoline in the barn. You'll walk there ahead of me to get it."

The band that constricted her breathing tightened. She stared at him, still fighting the belief that he could really carry out his threats. She was still not able to accept the fact that Brad was doing this, enacting a well-planned murder, torturing them like a great, slimy cat with his prey. Jonathan tried to catch her eye and nod, attempting to calm her, but she couldn't even accept his assurance. She didn't, after all, really know him, either. What did he want from her after all this? What had he wanted all along? The ground was falling out from under her, and she had nothing left to grab onto. She couldn't function anymore.

"Anne!"

She started, Brad's voice cutting into her. She looked over at him, at the tic that pulled again at his eye as if he were winking at a lewd joke, at the absurdly small gun that he wielded so ungracefully, and at the inappropriate walking boots he'd bought new to make the trek up here. It was at that moment that somewhere deep within her mounting terror a black rage was born.

This was all wrong. There had to be something she could do to stop him. He was lost up here in these mountains. His arena was the inside of a corporate office. This was her home, her world. Brad couldn't walk into it from his world of climate control and lawyer-spawned courage and expect to overcome her with such a silly little gun. He was on her turf, and it should have been to her advantage.

She caught Jonathan's eye and found reassurance in his calm gaze. They'd make it. Together they would be able to outwit Brad. She'd have to fight the bitterness of Jonathan's betrayal long enough to manage it, work with him until they were free and then rip his lungs out. He'd help to save himself if nothing else, and he was as comfortable in this world as she. They just had to get Brad to stumble.

She had to keep her head. Oh, God, if only she could keep the picture of Jonathan's eyes at bay long enough. She had to forget the soft blue of a mountain stream.

"I'm going, Brad," she said evenly, trying to hide from him the deep breath she had to take to steady herself. As she walked by him, the tic pulled again, more spastically. Maybe he wasn't as controlled as he seemed. Unless Anne were even more wrong than she'd been so far, he probably hadn't even had the courage to pull the official strings of Jonathan's ruin those long years ago. How could he possibly be expected to retain the temerity it took to do something this awesome face-to-face? She didn't want to think of the real power that obsessions gave to the delusional person. She didn't think she could survive the idea that Brad was invincible.

Anne walked ahead of him into the brittle afternoon air, the clean touch of it helping to settle her a little. Brad said nothing as they traversed the way to the barn, but the gun never wavered far from the center of her back, the feel of it a very unpleasant reminder.

Stepping into the barn calmed her even more. Andy whinnied over to her and Bessie stamped in her stall. The smells were familiar and warm, the sounds muffled. Somewhere in the back, melting snow dripped steadily from the rafters. Wanting to give Jonathan as much time as possible, she stopped as if to orient herself to the dark building.

"Don't play games, Anne," Brad warned irritably. "The gas is in the old tack room. At least that's where Pete used to keep it, and I can't imagine you defiling the sacred memory by moving it.''

''I had my canning equipment in there this year. I moved the gasoline.'' She paused as if in thought. ''The question is where...''

Brad shoved the gun into the small of her back, his patience wearing. ''I'd rather not shoot you here, but that's always an option, Anne. Does that help you remember?''

''Oddly enough, it does.'' She led the way to the back of the barn.

Only five minutes later, unable to stall any longer, Anne started back, the half-full ten-gallon can heavy in her hands. Brad had checked it when she had pulled it out, evidently convinced that she'd also kept a gas can of water handy on the off chance that anybody would come up and force her to set fire to her house. His tic was becoming worse with the passing minutes and now pulled sporadically at his mouth. He'd begun to finger the gun like worry beads, which didn't encourage Anne at all. It was still pointed straight at her back.

She opened the door to the cabin and had to once again adjust her eyes to the gloom. At first all she could see was the fire to her right, still burning steadily and making the air close. Then, she was able to make out the furniture. it wasn't until Brad stepped in behind her that she realized that Jonathan was gone. It took no more to galvanize her. Almost without hesitation she dropped to the floor, the gas can landing upright in front of her.

''What the hell are you...?''

Then Brad saw, too. His eyes shot open as he began to swing around. He never got started. A poker whistled out of the darkness and caught him on the left shoulder. He cried out and fired, the sound deafeningly close. Anne rolled away from it without giving another thought to the can by the fire. She saw Jonathan lunge from behind the door. Brad saw him and screamed, the sound a mix of fury and fear.

From where she'd taken cover Anne watched the struggle, the two men's shadows against the throbbing glow of the fire. For a moment they were one silhouette, indistinguishable. Then Jonathan moved. Getting a hand on the gun, he tried to force it away from Brad. The two of them fought for it in silence. Jonathan still had the poker in his other hand. He brought it up to strike and lost his leverage on the gun. Anne could see it, small and deadly, caught high between the two of them and glinting dully in the light. The shadows still wavered in sweating silence, the only sounds now oddly the melting snow and the crackle of the fire. She watched impotently, unable to move or even breathe for the fear. Jonathan couldn't take this much longer.

Suddenly Brad lunged hard. The two men crashed against the wall, sending the hall tree over in a clatter. Jonathan lost grip on the poker and gave a sharp cry as he hit the wall on his weak side, his bad leg buckling beneath him. He never let go of the gun. Sweat glistened on his face as he brought the other hand up and pried at Brad's grip, trying to slam the gun against the wall to loosen it. Jonathan was losing his balance. His right leg was almost useless, and Brad was trying to aim for it in an attempt to cripple him. Frantically, Anne looked around for help.

The poker lay exposed by the door. Quickly, she scuttled out from where she'd taken refuge by the chair and scooted over to get it. She could help Jonathan with it. He was rapidly wearing out. She could hear the rasping of his breath as he struggled.

She got hold of the poker as Brad shot an elbow at Jonathan and caught him at the ribs. Jonathan gasped; his hold loosened. Brad began to edge the gun down toward him. They didn't see her. Crouched behind them, Anne had just enough time to warn him.

"Jonathan!"

She made her move. Swinging with everything she had, she caught Brad flat against the kidney. He screamed and reeled around, pulling the gun with him. Anne dove away in an effort to put the couch between them. He fired seconds later. The bullet thudded into the couch inches from Anne's head. Already flattened, Anne peered out to see the astonishment in Brad's eyes.

"Damn it!" Jonathan lurched away from the wall to keep Brad from getting to Anne. He caught him against the couch. The gun rose between them again, glinting oddly like a sacrificial offering. Jonathan pushed and pushed more, bending Brad back at the waist. Anne was so close to them now that she could almost smell Brad's terror, and Jonathan's rage. She brought the poker up again, moved just beyond Brad's field of vision and stood waiting.

Jonathan's eyes were fire, their only color the terrible glow of blood and fury. He had a hand around Brad's throat and began to squeeze. Anne could hear the gurgling noises as Brad fought for air. The gun wavered between outstretched hands, slimy with sweat. Jonathan was gasping almost as loudly as Brad.

Brad kicked hard and Jonathan jerked upright, his mouth contorted in soundless agony. Anne raised the poker above her head.

Brad got ahold of the gun. He slammed it against the side of Jonathan's head. Then he swung it point-blank at Anne.

She froze.

Jonathan staggered, unbelievably still on his feet, trying to clear his head. Blood streamed down his face, glittering blackly in the light.

"Brad..." Anne saw him pulling at the trigger and couldn't move. She couldn't move. Brad's breath came in sobs. His hands shook and his face contorted cruelly, but he pulled steadily, almost casually at the trigger, ignoring Jonathan as if he didn't exist. He was enjoying the realization of his fantasies, feeding on the blank terror in Anne's eyes. A split second that filled an eternity.

"Anne!" Jonathan lunged. His football tackle caught Brad at the waist and sent him over backwards. The gun clattered hard against the chimney as Brad fell back over the couch, his body buckling oddly at the waist. He slammed to the floor, knocking into the gas can.

Anne screamed. Jonathan seized Anne at the knees and pushed her over. They hit the floor together behind the couch just as the can fell into the fireplace and exploded. The blast deafened her, knocking the wind out of her. She lay stunned and disoriented. With a rush, flames shot straight up, their brilliance consuming the chimney. Anne could only lie and watch, detached. Through the sudden roaring that filled her ears she thought she heard a long, terrified shrieking and wondered who it was. Then she saw the roaring flames, leaping along the walls and dancing patterns across the ceiling. She couldn't breathe.

"Anne, get out!"

Jonathan was pushing at her, yelling in her ear. She could only see one of his beautiful eyes. The other was caked shut. His eyebrows were gone. He was coughing and choking, his face washed in sweat and blood.

"The window! Come on!"

He jerked her up and she turned to look. The shock stunned her anew. The whole cabin was engulfed, the fire already devouring the loft and staircase and turning the furniture into kindling. She doubted they could get to the door. Even the hall tree, wedged at an angle against the wall, blazed, her down jacket melting into bright liquid. The quilts, generations of Jackson heritage, were already almost gone.

Jonathan had her by the arm, his hand a vise. She couldn't move and couldn't keep trying. There was nothing left, nothing to fight for. It was coming down around her, like another house of cards. Her beautiful bed, the one her great-grandfather had made, was burning. Lost.

"Annie, come on!" Jonathan screamed at her, his face almost hideous in the blood-red light of the flames. "We have to get out now!"

"No..." She pulled at him, trying to get free, but she was too numb, too overwhelmed to move. She wanted to curl back into a ball and give in. She couldn't do any more.

Jonathan never hesitated. Grabbing her around the waist, he pulled her back down and literally dragged her across the floor. "Keep your head down."

Thick black smoke blocked out the brilliant sunlight. It looked like a halo, a far-off streetlight in the fog. Anne kept her eyes on it as the terror woke in her. She was coughing, tears streaming down her face as she stumbled along next to Jonathan. Cinders, bits of wood and quilt fell around them. The heat was terrible. Anne could hear Jonathan's coughing, sobbing breath and wondered how he thought they could get out of this furnace alive.

Halfway across the floor, Anne had to rip through Jonathan's shirt to get a flaming piece of upholstery from his back. He never felt it. He never stopped moving, head down, his leg dragging painfully behind him, his arm tight around Anne.

Anne followed him blindly, looking up only to try to find the window again. It was getting harder to see. Harder to breathe. God, they weren't going to get out. She could hardly move. Where was the window? Had they gone the wrong way? The room couldn't be this far to get across.

Then the smoke shifted, just enough. There it was, a few feet ahead. Jonathan stopped, his back heaving with the exertion of just breathing.

"A little farther!" he screamed above the din of the fire that sought them. She nodded, sobbing now with the effort to breathe. He moved on and found the chair, still miraculously whole. Next to it was the floor lamp.

Pushing Anne's head down to the safety of the floor, he grabbed the lamp and swung it through the window. Cold air rushed in with the shattering of glass and the fire exploded over their heads. Anne felt the heat across her neck like a scald. She brought her head up, terrified.

"Jonathan?!"

He was out, reaching back in for her. She climbed, the light of the sun hurting her eyes. She wondered why. Nothing was more brilliant than the orange of the fire. She took Jonathan's hand, and he pulled her through the broken glass. Good old jeans. They kept her from getting cut.

Anne tumbled out onto the snow-packed ground, landing next to Jonathan. She couldn't get a breath. It seemed enough to stop there and heave in great draughts of air, but Jonathan pulled at her again. She looked up to see that his face was black and wondered offhandedly if hers was too.

They made it to the door of the barn and fell, gasping and choking to the cold dirt floor. Anne thought her ears were still muffled. She couldn't hear anything but her own labored breathing and a dull roaring sound. She shook her head, trying to clear it. Then she heard the slow dripping of the snow back at the far side of the barn. She realized that nothing was wrong with her ears. The world outside was quiet. She looked up to see that it was a beautiful, crystal winter afternoon, the white light almost surreal. Even the brushing of the wind was silenced. There was only the dull rush of the flames as they consumed the cabin.

She looked over at Jonathan as he leaned against the other side of the doorway, his legs outstretched. His breathing was harsh and loud, and he wiped at the sweat on his face with a trembling hand. Immediately, Anne slid over to him.

"Can you breathe?" she demanded. He nodded, not very convincing. "How is your leg?"

"Fine...broke a...couple of...ribs...again, I...think."

He was clutching at his side and leaning to favor it. She tried to get his shirt up so that she could better check him, but her hands shook so badly she couldn't work very well.

Jonathan shook his head at her, not enough breath for words. She took the hint and let what was left of his shirt go. Jonathan managed a grin and carefully lifted an arm in invitation. Hesitating only a second, Anne accepted his offer and stayed within the comfort of his embrace.

"Do you . . . believe I never . . . wanted to hurt you?"

"We have plenty of time to discuss that," she said. "Concentrate on breathing right now."

"Whatever happens," he insisted, still breathing with short, painful gasps, "you won't ever . . . lose Cedar Ridge . . . I promise."

Anne looked over at the inferno that had once been her home and realized with some surprise that she forgave him. "You saved my life," she said quietly. "The rest, I think, is gravy."

"I . . . wanted you to . . . know."

Anne turned to him, to see the genuine regret in his eyes, the pain of a man who saw the woman he loved suffer, and she found a smile for him. "I know."

Farther inside the barn Andy stomped and whinnied, the smell of the smoke unsettling him. Jonathan turned at the noise.

"Do you think we . . . should try and get down to . . . town?"

Anne shook her head. "No. I have the feeling that the town will be coming to us." The roof of the cabin gave way with a long crash that demanded their attention. A wide column of thick black smoke lifted straight up into the sky. "They'd never pass up an opportunity like this to tell me how much I need a real road up here."

She watched the destruction a while longer, her mind still too stunned to sort it all out.

"Anne?"

She turned to him with a crumbling, watery grin. "All of my Nancy Drews are gone. I had the . . . whole collection . . . for . . . when . . ."

It was a long time before her sobbing subsided. And an hour later as the sun impaled itself on the western trees, twenty riders crashed into the clearing at a dead run to find Anne and Jonathan sitting together at the side of the barn door watching the last of the fire as it licked the charred ruins of the cabin.

* * *

Anne stood in the cabin doorway and watched the new spring sun warm the top leaves of the trees, the first light refreshing and clear. It had been her first night home since the fire. Since that time she had been living the life of a Gypsy, traveling to Boston to settle family and business affairs, New York to consult with Judson and then back to Elder's Crossing to oversee the clinic construction and her practice.

It had only been a week since she'd closed the door for the last time on the house in Boston. She had dreaded that especially, anticipating the pain and remorse of selling it. She had, after all, spent much of her life there. But when it was over, she'd stood in the echoing marble foyer to look around at the sterile surroundings and felt only the emptiness of the place. She had left nothing behind.

It had been while she had been on that final trip to Boston, flying out as the last of the snow had given way to crocuses on the mountains, that the cabin had been finished. A completely new modern structure, with a lot of glass, whose design had been decided the day she'd buried Brad next to the father he'd so envied and hated. It had been at that moment that she'd realized with inescapable finality that her family was gone. All her childhood memories and dreams had been put to rest beneath white headstones and black ashes. It was time now to move on to a new life, symbolized by the radically new structure on her ancient mountain.

Anne turned from the door and walked back through the house that still had a loft and a high wall for the quilts her friends had already begun to collect for her.

She'd made it into the shiny white kitchen where she was pouring herself coffee from a new pot when she heard the sound of a vehicle approaching. A smile of anticipation lit her features. Pouring a second cup, she slipped out of her thick robe to reveal a pale pink lace-and-silk teddy. Then, picking up the cups, she walked to the front door, golden hair swinging gently down her back.

"You up already?"

"I'm a farm girl." She grinned lazily, leaning against the open door and waiting for him to turn to her.

When he did, Jonathan dropped the box he'd been lifting with a flat thud. "Good God, woman," he gasped, "you're not supposed to shock a man like that." His eyes didn't seem to mind so much. Anne couldn't get enough of the sight of him, so tall and handsome and whole. He had not dealt well with the hospital, nor it with him.

"And you're not supposed to run out on a woman the day after she's married."

"Important mail," he assured her, bending to pick the box back up. "Special delivery."

Anne scowled a little. "I was afraid you'd run back off to New York."

"Not for six more months." He stomped up onto the porch and nudged her backside. "That was the deal. And may I say," he leered, depositing a quick kiss on eager lips, "I can't wait to see what it's like to ravage the chief executive officer and chairman of the board of Jackson Corporations Limited."

"You ravaged her last night," Anne reminded him, settling onto the couch and putting the coffee cups on the glass-and-wood coffee table.

Jonathan set the box down before her and grinned. "No. Last night I ravaged the finest rural nurse in West Virginia. Open the box."

"What is it?" She studied it before going to the masking tape.

"Your wedding present."

Anne eyed him suspiciously. "The pearls were my wedding present."

"Open it."

When she reached into the packing a few minutes later, Anne drew out a book—a small book, no more than one hundred and ninety pages. Then came another. The rest were packed lovingly beneath, some new, some originals, all familiar and treasured.

Anne looked up at Jonathan, tears in her smiling eyes. "How did you . . . ?"

Jonathan's eyes were bright and happy, the pain at their depths long since exorcised. "You once said something about collecting Nancy Drews for our daughter to read."

She put the books down and eased herself into Jonathan's arms. "Did I tell you that I love you?"

Jonathan kissed her with a gentleness that brought more tears. "Seems to me you did."

She grinned suggestively and stretched against him, the silk whispering against denim and flannel. "Did I show you?"

"Yes." He kissed her again. "But I think it would be okay if you showed me again."

She did.

Silhouette Brings You:

Silhouette Christmas Stories

Four delightful, romantic stories celebrating the holiday season, written by four of your favorite Silhouette authors.

Nora Roberts—*Home for Christmas*
Debbie Macomber—*Let It Snow*
Tracy Sinclair—*Under the Mistletoe*
Maura Seger—*Starbright*

Each of these great authors has combined the wonder of falling in love with the magic of Christmas to bring you four unforgettable stories to touch your heart.

Indulge yourself during the holiday season...or give this book to a special friend for a heartwarming Christmas gift.

Available November 1986

XMAS-1

FOUR UNIQUE SERIES
FOR EVERY WOMAN YOU ARE . . .

Silhouette Romance

Heartwarming romances that will make you
laugh and cry as they bring you all the wonder
and magic of falling in love.

Silhouette Special Edition

Expanded romances written with emotion and
heightened romantic tension to ensure
powerful stories. A rare blend of passion and
dramatic realism.

Silhouette Desire

Believable, sensuous, compelling—and
above all, romantic—these stories deliver
the promise of love, the guarantee
of satisfaction.

Silhouette Intimate Moments

Love stories that entice; longer, more
sensuous romances filled with adventure,
suspense, glamour and melodrama.

Silhouette Romances
not available in retail outlets in Canada